Mistletoe from
PURPLE SAGE

Also by Barbara Burnett Smith

Celebration in Purple Sage
Dust Devils of the Purple Sage
Writers of the Purple Sage

Mistletoe from
⇥ PURPLE SAGE ⇤

Barbara Burnett Smith

ST. MARTIN'S PRESS
NEW YORK

MISTLETOE FROM PURPLE SAGE. Copyright © 1997 by Barbara Burnett Smith.
All rights reserved. Printed in the United States of America. No part of this
book may be used or reproduced in any manner whatsoever without written
permission except in the case of brief quotations embodied in critical articles
or reviews. For information, address St. Martin's Press, 175 Fifth Avenue, New
York, N.Y. 10010.

Library of Congress Cataloging-in-Publication Data

Smith, Barbara Burnett.
     Mistletoe from Purple Sage   /   Barbara Burnett Smith.—1st ed.
         p.   cm.
    ISBN 0-312-16930-2
    I. Title.
    PS3569.M483M57   1997
    813'.54—dc21   97-15665
                                               CIP

First Edition: November 1997

10 9 8 7 6 5 4 3 2 1

To my wonderful sister, Carol,
who is really my "forever friend."
With much love.

❧ ACKNOWLEDGMENTS ❦

I'd like to offer special thanks to Tyler Smith and Mitchell May, because some of Christopher's best lines were really theirs.

I'd also like to thank Mickie Bellah, of Mickie Bellah Advertising, and Danny and Kate Reed, of Danny Reed Advertising. In the past they kept me from starving, and showed me enough of agency life so that I could create Rose Sterling Advertising. Oh, and their agencies do far better work, and much more timely, than Rose Sterling!

Two of the great sayings in this book I snitched from friends Dee Willis and Sharon Watkins. Additionally I received invaluable information from Delphine Chavez, the sabom-nim" of the Fighting Dragon's dojo. My thanks to all three.

I'm also grateful to my friends and readers who always improve my manuscripts: Debbie Meyer, Chuck Meyer, Susan Rogers Cooper, Susan Wade, Caroline Young Petrequin, and my adorable husband, Gary.

Mistletoe from
PURPLE SAGE

✤ CHAPTER 1 ✤

ON THE day before Thanksgiving I decided that what I wanted for Christmas was a little holiday chaos. Now that my son, Jeremy, was sixteen, Christmas would be a quiet event with the three of us, Jeremy, Matt, and me, sipping eggnog by the fire while Christmas carols played softly in the background. Very civilized.

When Jeremy was little, and I was a single parent, we'd celebrated with my sister or brother's family in a house too small for rambunctious kids, barking dogs, and frenzied parents. At the time it was frazzling, but now I missed those days.

Oh, I still had my annual holiday insanity of shopping and wrapping, mailing and baking, but that all ended a few days before Christmas. Then there was nothing but peace and gentle serenity, which I was dreading.

As I turned in to the ranch, and headed toward our two-story house, I remembered my mother's age-old admonition: Be careful what you wish for because you just might get it. But what could be so bad about a chaotic Christmas?

I parked in front of the house, honking the horn twice. No one appeared. My adorable new husband, Matt, had told me that morning he was spending the day in town with the CPA going over year-end tax-planning and investment strategies, something I'm delighted I don't have to think about. Apparently he hadn't made it back yet, and Jeremy had gone to a friend's house in Purple Sage to work on some project. That meant the house was all but silent as I unloaded the groceries and Christmas wrapping paper and such.

1

It took four trips, but eventually everything was deposited on the breakfast table except for one roll of green yarn that had found a comfortable home on the floor. I left it there, deciding I needed something to perk me up before I tackled the job of putting everything away. Heavy drugs were my first choice, but I didn't think the two Midol in my purse were going to be sufficient. Some ice tea was next on my list, and as I crossed the kitchen to get it, I noticed the light blinking on the answering machine. It was probably Jeremy saying he was ready to leave and would I come get him. I punched the button to find out.

While the message tape rewound, I pulled open the refrigerator. The tape began to play and I heard a female voice with a slight New York accent. I hadn't heard that voice often in my life, but I knew exactly who it was. The refrigerated air swirled around me as I listened, hardly breathing.

"Jolie, hi, this is Fran Espinoza at Guidry-Long Literary," she began. As if I didn't know my own agent. "Listen, kid, we got an offer on your book. I have to tell you right off it's not a very good offer, but with first books they rarely are. It's a good house, though, and a good editor. It'll get your foot in the door. So it's what time?" The voice paused. "Oh, hell, who knew it was that late? Listen, I'll be out of the office until Monday, but I'll call you then with details. Have a nice Thanksgiving." A click and a beep, and she was gone.

I closed the refrigerator door.

"I'm an author," I whispered to my kitchen. I was almost afraid to say the words out loud. "An author! Me." The blood slammed through my heart so fast I could feel it leaving stretch marks.

I grabbed up the phone and started to call Matt, but remembered that he wasn't reachable.

My hand shook as I replaced the receiver. I could hardly believe it. I had sold a book! I was an author. This was a big occasion. A momentous moment. An ecstatic event!

I let out an exuberant warhoop that echoed through the empty house.

✢ CHAPTER 2 ✢

THAT PHONE call went to my head like frothy champagne.
Weeks later I would be in the grocery store, trying to decide between 2 percent and nonfat milk, when an uncontrollable grin
would sneak onto my face. My mind would fill with visions of
myself autographing books for an ever-increasing line of fans. I
would begin to consider what dress I would wear for the Edgars
or the Agathas, and end up drifting off on a cloud of fantasy.

Unfortunately, later at home I would come out of my altered
state to discover that I had purchased both kinds of milk, as well
as cream and half-and-half, but had forgotten the rest of the
things on my grocery list. It was playing hell with my budget, and
our eating habits. Besides, people were starting to talk.

That phone call did more than affect my daydreams, though.
It also did something to my self-image. I had always seen myself
as a writer simply because I wrote. In the past I had written advertising copy, news stories, and books. Even if I never got published, I could legitimately claim to be a writer. However, now
that I had made a sale, I belonged in the much more elusive cat-
egory known as author. I had leapt up the food chain; gone from
gopher to gazelle; tripped the light fantastic into a fantasy world
where I was special, invincible, and solidly okay. Even without my
makeup on.

That's a heady experience, and probably the reason I said I
would "love" to attend the twenty-fifth anniversary party for
Rose Sterling Advertising. It was being held in conjunction with
Chester Sterling's sixty-eighth birthday.

Rose Sterling was the Austin advertising agency where I worked before I married Matt. Chester Sterling and his wife, Rose, had founded it, although Rose had passed away a few years later. It was Chester who hired me away from another agency and kept me gainfully employed for almost nine years. I think he's a wonderful man, but for me to even consider attending that party was another sign of my temporary madness.

Unfortunately, before I recognized the idiocy of accepting, I had told Matt about the event. He immediately set up a trip to Austin around the party. He scheduled meetings with several companies he was involved with, and arranged for us to stay with his sister, Prissy, and her husband, where we would celebrate Christmas.

And it all would have been fine if it hadn't been for the Rose Sterling party, because that's where I would have to face the man I'd had an affair with some five years before. He had been, and still was, a married man, and although he'd been separated from his wife at the time, I still feel guilty.

In this day and age most people wouldn't think twice about what I'd done, but there is something for me that escalates the sin. Michael and I had begun our affair right there in the office, and as I later learned, despite our discretion, Audry had known what was going on the whole time. On those days when I came in looking like hell from staying up all night with Michael, no matter what excuse I made, she knew where I'd really been, and worse, where he had been. When we said we were going out to visit a client, she knew the truth of why we were leaving the office. And when she discovered us alone in the coffee room, supposedly discussing business, she knew that wasn't all that was being said. It must have hurt terribly, and if Saint Peter turns me away from the pearly gates, I'm sure he will mention Michael Sherabian's name.

There is another problem, as well: I've always worried about Matt learning the whole truth about my now all-too-close past. Matt and I began dating just two months after Michael went back to his wife. Ours wasn't a rebound romance; I've always believed I just happened to meet the right man at an awkward time. Because of that I never told Matt about Michael and me. At first it was too close and too intimate a detail to share. As my relationship with Matt progressed, it became a flaw I kept hidden for fear it would alter his opinion of me. Eventually it was too late to talk about it.

Of course, there was a part of me that was looking forward to the party. All of us at Rose Sterling had spent nine hours a day together; we'd labored to hit deadlines, suffered through personal crises, and generally functioned as an extended family for one another. I'd hardly talked to them in the four years since I'd moved to Purple Sage, and I missed them.

And so I found myself drinking tea at Matt's sister's house on the Sunday a week before Christmas.

With the party a mere eight hours away, even the smell of her Christmas tree and the sounds of Bing Crosby crooning "White Christmas" weren't bringing my mood to anywhere near the festive level.

"Your party tonight sounds like such fun," Prissy was saying. "You know, I've met Chester Sterling. Back when I was working for the Literacy Council. Such a nice man. He must have been wonderful to work for."

"Yes, Chester was, is, very nice," I said, hoping my smile looked normal.

"And he had a wonderful way of making everyone feel welcome. He reminded me of a big, ginger-colored bear. Always hugging people and thanking them, even though he was doing the advertising as a contribution. So charming." She smiled at me and I could see the family resemblance between her and Matt. Both have dark eyes and lashes, although Prissy swears that Matt's eyelashes are twice as thick and curly as hers. The eyes are striking in contrast to their lighter hair. Matt's is soft brown until he spends time in the sun, while Prissy's is artfully streaked to a much paler shade.

"Oh," Prissy added with an impish grin, "and Chester's son-in-law is to die for. Did you know him, Jolie?"

"Me? Uh. Yes. I did." I focused on Matt and smiled.

"Michael Sherabian is even better-looking than you, Matthew!"

Matt laughed. "So now I know why you give so much time to charity. Has nothing to do with the worthy cause."

"Some days it does, some days it doesn't," she said, cocking her head and flashing a mischievous smile.

"Maybe you and Ross could go with us to the party tonight," I said, thinking I had found a buffer between me and my fears. "I'd be happy to call—"

"No, no," she said. "It was at least a year ago. Probably neither of them would even remember me."

"You certainly remembered them," Matt said with a younger-brother grin. "Actually you remembered, what was his name? Michael?"

"I can't help it, Matt," Prissy said. "He was incredibly good-looking and charming. I'm serious, this man walked into the room and four women had hot flashes. Two others hyperventilated." Prissy turned to me. "Jolie, if I'd been you, with Michael around, I don't know that I'd have bothered with Matt. Or was Michael married back then?"

I reached for a cookie and said, "He was married to Chester's daughter. Audry. That's how he got started at the agency. And actually, he spent a lot of time at our Atlanta office."

"I hope Audry wasn't so foolish as to let him go off by himself."

"Oh, uh, part of the time, I think so. Then they both moved there." That was almost immediately after they got back together. Four days after the last time I spoke privately with Michael, which meant there had been no closure on our relationship. It still seemed as if there were things that needed to be said.

The kettle on the stove began to whistle and Prissy stood up. "How about a warm-up on your tea, Jolie?"

"Yes, please." I held out my delicate china cup, which she put back down on my saucer.

"I'll bring the pot," she said as she moved toward the kitchen.

6

"Oh, and help yourself to some more cookies," she called from the other room.

In the center of the table was a Waterford platter piled with exquisitely decorated Christmas cookies that Prissy had made. "They're almost too pretty to eat," I said, then looked down and realized I had unconsciously broken all the edges off the one sitting in front of me. Like pulling petals off a flower.

Luckily Matt's attention was elsewhere. "I'd take another cup of coffee," he said, rising and following Prissy.

That left me alone and I took a long shaky breath. I had survived one conversation about Michael, but the party was still to come. I hate having things hanging over my head, especially something like this that needs some communication.

In anticipation of the party I actually had tried to bring it up with Matt a couple of times. On each occasion we were interrupted—Jeremy, the phone, Bart, the foreman of our ranch. After several tries, I decided we could discuss it on the drive down, but then we'd ended up coming on different days, so we each brought our own car. I had begun to think that I shouldn't say anything; that this was one of those old secrets better left buried. Didn't Dear Abby advocate that? It was certainly easier to deal with, at least in some ways.

"By the way, Jolie," Pris called from the kitchen, "how do you like the remodeling we did? The architect calls that the great room."

"And it wasn't just wishful thinking," I said, looking around the room that was off the breakfast nook where I was sitting. "It really is great." In both dimension and decoration—the floors were pale hardwood, and the ceiling tall and arched. To my right was a rounded fireplace, and at the front of the room a bay window that looked out onto their elegant yard.

In the curve of the window was a Christmas tree that stood at least fifteen feet high. It was lightly dusted with artificial snow and decorated with twenty-five years of Christmas memories, collected since the time when she and Ross had married. She had shown me a tiny bear ornament that their daughter, Stephanie, had made in first grade. It was faded after all these years, but held an honored spot on the tree.

"We got the last of the furniture in and the tree up this past weekend. I think it turned out rather well," Prissy said as she returned with a china teapot covered in roses, and poured tea into my cup. "Careful, it's hot."

"Thanks."

As she sat down she glanced toward the front door; her gaze lingered and grew more intense.

"Something about the foyer isn't right?" I asked. While I couldn't see the whole area, which was as large as some bedrooms, I thought it was as impeccable as the rest of the house. There were stemlike flutes of glass that formed a chandelier, and two carved niches in the white adobe that held tall baroque candleholders from some exotic spot. Artsy things, as Jeremy called them.

"Oh, no, the foyer's fine," Prissy said. "I was just remembering—never mind." She shook her head. "Christmas surprises, you know. We have several."

"Really?"

For a moment she looked undecided, then she forced a smile. "Yes. We have one for you, too, and it's arriving later."

"A surprise for me?"

"I can't say another word. I promised." She looked up at Matt, who was returning from the kitchen bearing a brilliantly glazed blue pottery mug.

"I'll give you a hint—" Matt began.

"Enough, Matthew!" Prissy cut him off quickly and firmly. "Santa Claus is coming and that's all we're saying. Is that understood?"

"A little stressed, are we, Prissy?" he asked, half teasing, but I heard some concern in his voice, too. "I was only going to give Jolie a hint."

"Yes, I'm stressed. It's Christmas, for God's sake, and with guests—" She stopped. "Damn, now see what you did, Matt? I didn't mean you two. I love having you here."

8

"But company always brings a little stress," I said. Except that in the past, Prissy had thrived on entertaining. Two years before she'd had eight guests staying with her, had given a Christmas party for two hundred, and had her house on the Holiday Parade of Homes for a charity that required her to serve tea every afternoon. She'd handled it all without a flutter of nerves, so what was different now?

Matt touched my hand. "Maybe I'll just run on and leave you to deal with my sister." He turned to her. "I'm assuming I can get downtown in half an hour. Is that still realistic?"

"You can get there, and probably get parked," Prissy said, "if you don't hit any traffic. You have a meeting this afternoon?"

"I'm meeting Trey at the Hyatt. We're going over the financials of Austin Edge."

Trey Atwood was the mayor pro tem of Purple Sage, as well as Matt's best friend. Both men spend a portion of their time out of town, keeping tabs on the companies they have investments in. Austin is the perfect spot for high-tech business, and Matt loves delving into a company's inner workings to decide if it will eventually be a success.

"Isn't that one of the new incubator computer companies?" Prissy asked. "Are they involved in software or hardware?"

"Software," Matt said. "I can't believe you know the difference. Aren't you the one who told me computers were a passing fancy?"

She waved away his words. "That was before I saw what all they can do. Besides, computer software companies are a very good investment right now. Ross thinks it's like the new frontier." Ross being her husband, Ross Linden, the management consultant who can steer companies toward success. "He says there's a lot of money to be made because everyone is into computing. Even *I'm* on the Internet."

Matt looked suitably impressed. "My sister the techie."

"That's exactly right. We have three computers in this house, four phone lines, and enough cord to rewire Louisiana and half of Alabama. I now speak computer. It's better than my French."

9

"Want to be my technical advisor?"

"You can't afford me," Prissy said before turning to me. "Now, Jolie, what do you want to do this afternoon? Anything special?"

I wanted to adopt a new identity and live in an anonymous post office box, but it didn't seem feasible.

"I'd like to get a birthday present for Chester," I said. Chester had always protested when people spent money on him, but in truth, he loved little gifts that showed the giver knew him well. I had scoured the stores in Purple Sage and had come away with a Purple Sage mug. Chester collects mugs and this one was hand-thrown, so it wasn't a bad start. I had also picked some mistletoe to add to the decoration on his package. He would like both, but I wanted something to go with them.

"Didn't you say you had a mug already?" Prissy asked. "Does he drink coffee or tea?"

"Tea."

"We could go to my favorite little tea shop and create a blend just for him," she said, sipping from her own cup. "Most tea drinkers would love something like that." Her eyes closed appreciatively while she sniffed the steam rising from the fragrant brew.

Earlier she'd told me all about her tea blending, and how we were drinking a special combination of mango and peach, with just a hint of lime.

"This is nice," I said.

She opened her eyes. "We'll do something exotic, or whatever you think he'd like. And I can help you package it. Did I tell you I took a calligraphy class? I can add a label with the ingredients."

Martha Stewart could take lessons from Prissy Linden. Probably had. "Sounds perfect."

"My favorite thing for stress—retail therapy!" she said, jumping up. "That's 'shopping' to the layman. We don't want to get caught in the Christmas shopping traffic; it seems to be worse than rush hour." She glanced at her watch. "And, Matt, you should be going, too. What time is the party tonight?"

"Seven," I said.

"You probably won't want to arrive until seven-thirty; still, you'll have to leave by seven. And if you figure an hour to get ready, and an hour to eat dinner—oh, or are they having dinner?"

"A buffet, I think."

"Well, I'll just serve soup and bread here at the house. That shouldn't fill you up. I froze some homemade soup last week; I think you'll like it." She was clearing off the table, sweeping my crumbs into her hand. "What that means, Matt, is that you'll need to be back here by five. Can you do that?"

He nodded as he picked up our cups. "I certainly can, Julie. You are Julie the social director, aren't you?"

She swatted him on the arm. "I was just trying to be helpful. I am not the social director and I have no idea if this is the *Love Boat.*"

I only hoped it wasn't the *Titanic.*

✦ CHAPTER 3 ✦

Prissy's excellent French onion soup rolled on my stomach like a flimsy dingy on a stormy sea as Matt and I stepped into the wide hallway that led to Rose Sterling Advertising.

The agency occupied a seventh-floor suite of offices in the modern downtown high-rise. To our right were two doors, both with burnished wood plaques; one said Petry & Thomas, Certified Public Accountants, and the other Rose Sterling Advertising. Matt steered me in that direction, but there was a short line in front of us.

He leaned down and whispered in my ear. "Do you recognize these people?"

I looked around at the glitter of silk, satin, diamonds, and jewels, then shook my head. I kept my voice low as I said, "I don't know a single person. I think I'm out of my element, or my league, and I don't mean as in 'Junior.' "

"Don't you believe it," he said. "You're the most beautiful woman here."

I was wearing a very expensive beaded dress that I had bought in Dallas a few years before. Matt was in a dark suit; his white shirt had French cuffs held together by carved jade cuff links, and he wore a tie that had just a hint of the same color in it. He looked far more attractive than I did, but he didn't seem to know it. I whispered back, "You're prejudiced."

"I certainly am," he said, his arms resting lightly on my shoulders. I allowed myself to press closer to him for comfort.

The elevator doors opened behind us and a swell of people

poured into the area on a wave of chill air, expensive perfume, and laughter.

I closed my eyes and listened to the conversations floating toward me.

"We're glad you could be with us, Bill. Come in and make yourself at home." I could separate that voice out of the others. It came from inside the doorway, and it was Chester's. Apparently there was a receiving line, which accounted for the holdup.

The crowd moved forward. Another voice I recognized from those four years past became audible. "Willa, hello; it's so nice that you could come. This must be your handsome husband." It was Audry Sterling-Sherabian. I wondered if she still hyphenated the two names or if she used just Sherabian now. The office joke many years before had been that her monogram was appropriate, as in Audry SS.

I remember clearly the day that a videotape broke while she was playing a TV commercial for a client. Audry had been full of apologetic charm until the client was gone, then she'd marched into the creative director's office, slapped the tape on his desk, and said, "This tape broke in front of a very important client. I won't have that kind of incompetence around me, so don't let it happen again." With that she had stomped out.

In her defense, Audry had been young. She'd arrived from graduate school with a lot of theory but very little practical experience. Her idea of business chic had been to pull her ginger-colored hair back into a severe chignon and wear mannish suits with scarves tied into bows at the neck.

Interesting that, as I was about to face my own sins, I was spending time recounting hers.

Matt gestured toward a tall woman in mink in front of me. After I'd acknowledged seeing her, he whispered in my ear. "I thought furs were politically incorrect," he said. I turned around and saw the smile he was trying to hold back.

He leaned over so I could speak to him without being overheard. "Obviously a very brave woman," I said.

Matt just smiled and shook his head.

13

By the time I turned back around we were almost in the door-way, and another voice caught at me. A voice I knew all too well. And I knew the nuances it could contain, too. A shivery chill touched my skin.

"Richard, Pat, so glad you could come. Pat, you have to save me a dance later. Audry, you know Pat and Richard."

Michael at his most public and most gracious.

We drew closer and I could see the large Christmas tree be-hind where the front desk would be, had there been one. Then we were in the door and I was face-to-face with Audry. She was beautiful, no longer the awkward young woman I'd worked with. Her hair was short, sophisticated, and her makeup subtle, the perfect complement to her elegant features. It made her eyes ap-pear large and brilliant.

When she looked at me there was only the barest hint of hes-itation before she smiled and held out her hand. "Jolie, how nice that you could come. And this is your husband, Matt. Right?"

"Yes, of course, Audry. How wonderful to see you." The niceties slipped off our tongues as if they were truths. "Matt, do you remember Audry Sherabian? She managed the Atlanta office." Matt had taken me to lunch when we were dating, and he'd come into the agency, which is where they'd met briefly.

"Nice to see you again," Matt said, shaking her hand.

I thought I detected the tiniest narrowing of Audry's eyes as she gazed first at Matt, then back to me. Just the littlest ac-knowledgment of something that neither of us would admit to.

"I'd forgotten how handsome your husband is, Jolie," she said. "And you remember Michael." No question.

I got an impression of his suit, double-breasted, expertly cut, elegant on his tall, slim body. There was the scent of his musky aftershave that brought with it unwanted memories. I didn't quite look into his face. "Michael, hello," I said, shaking his hand quickly, then slipping my arm through Matt's. "This is my hus-band, Matt Wyatt."

"How do you do?"

14

I had to look. As I raised my face I saw those incredible eyes that could be playful, daring, sometimes compassionate. They stared into mine just a little too long before he flashed a smile. When E. M. Hull wrote *The Sheik,* he must have had Michael Sherabian in mind.

I nodded, tried to smile, then looked quickly at Audry, who said, "We'll talk later." She turned to greet the next couple.

With Matt at my side, I moved on—straight into arms that enveloped me in a bear hug. "Jolene Berenski, we've missed you around here. It never has been quite the same since you left." Chester was beaming.

I hugged him back. "I've missed you, too."

Chester Sterling had always been a big man, over six feet, with reddish brown hair like his daughter's and a round, slightly jowly face that reminded me of a happy sheepdog. He had lost weight since I'd last seen him, hastening nature's downward course, so that his face drooped into his neck. He now looked like a different breed of dog, more like a shar-pei. "And you remember Matt," I said.

Chester kept hold of me even as he stepped back to favor Matt with a welcoming smile. "Of course, Matt. What a lucky man you are to get our Jolie."

"I certainly think so."

"How have you been doing, Chester?" I asked.

"Fine, fine. Couldn't be better. And, Jolie, I want to hear everything you've been up to as soon as we get everyone welcomed. In the meantime, you just make yourself at home. Get something to eat, and something to drink; there are bars in every corner. Can't miss them."

He released me and we moved again. Someone took my coat, giving me a numbered ticket to reclaim it.

Inside the suite music from a live band played a bit too loudly. It was almost dizzying combined with the glitter, the lights, and the people. Luckily Chester favored wide-open spaces, so there were few real offices and only one massive conference room. All were being utilized tonight, and most of the desks and more

15

prosaic pieces of office equipment had been whisked away to some other place, as had the temporary cubicles.

Flowers blossomed everywhere. On the tables were trays of fascinating edibles and everyone seemed so sophisticated, an elegant garden of exotic humans.

"Would you like something to drink?" Matt asked me.

Bourbon straight up and make it a double. "Maybe a small glass of white wine."

"Well, I'll be damned," said a broadly accented female voice. "If it isn't Jolene Berenski and that good-looking husband she just snatched up and took off with her! How in the world are you, girlfriend?"

I turned to find myself facing a red strapless dress on a very tall woman. From the cut and the detailing I guessed the dress was expensive, but it was far too revealing for a woman who no longer had the creamy skin of youth. "Donna Katherine," I said as I smiled up into her face. "I'm fine. How are you?"

"Honey, I haven't been doing near as well as you from what I can see, but I'm gettin' along. You going to introduce me, or do I just have to sit here and drool anonymously?"

Matt was laughing as he held out his hand. "Matt Wyatt. Nice to meet you."

"I'm Donna Katherine Phennicie and I know that's a mouthful, but, honey, some women just are."

With a perfectly straight face he said, "You two used to work together?"

"For our sins," Donna Katherine said. "But I'm just a bookkeeper. I balance the checkbook and see that the bills get paid. Nothing exciting."

"And she's always done it exceedingly well," I added, trying hard not to glance toward the doorway to see where the Sherabians were now. "Donna Katherine, do you know what I can do with this?" I held up the package for Chester. Prissy had placed the mug and the tea on a bed of shimmery white grass in a white basket, then covered it with pale gold cellophane. A huge gold bow adorned the outside, and she had put some of the mistletoe inside, with another sprig on the bow.

Donna Katherine peered at it in the dim lighting. "Isn't that the prettiest thing! And look at the goodies inside. Girl, you always did have class. Here, give it to me; I know what we'll do." She took the basket from me and flagged over a waiter. "Here, darling," she said, handing it to him. "Put this on that side table in the conference room. It's one of the birthday presents for Mr. Sterling."

"Yes, ma'am." He nodded and took off.

"Quite efficient," Matt said. "We should have asked him for drinks."

"Don't you believe it. It would take an hour to get them. We've only got two waiters for this whole crowd."

"Then I'll go," he said.

Donna Katherine pointed the way, in fact offered to go with him, but he refused. "You stay here and visit with Jolie. Can I get you something?"

"Oh, darling, can you!" She stopped then and feigned disappointment. "Oh, you mean a drink. Well, I'll take a Scotch and water. The oldest they have."

Once, many years before, Donna Katherine had been a beauty, or so the story goes. I heard she had been Miss San Angelo, but that had been twenty-five years before. The intervening years had weighed heavily on both her face and body, leaving her with little of what had once been except the flaming red hair and not quite milky skin.

"Well, isn't he something?" Donna Katherine said, watching Matt walk away. "Girl, you did yourself proud. Now, what I want to know is, are there any more of him at home?"

"Sorry, just a sister."

"Damn. They should have made more of that model. It'd been a best-seller." She gestured at the offices. I glanced around, keeping my eyes away from the entrance, although I could tell by the movement of people that there was still a line at the door. It meant that Michael and Audry were still at the door, too. "How do you think the place looks?" Donna Katherine pushed. "Pretty good for an old ad agency."

This time I really looked at my surroundings. Chester likes color. Lots of color and lots of glass. There were hunter green accent walls next to navy blue ones, all surrounded by the glass exterior of the building.

Outside the lights of Austin shimmered seven stories below us. "I'd forgotten how beautiful it is. No wonder we never complained about working late."

Donna Katherine raised one eyebrow. "Honey, I don't think that's the reason, but I didn't say so."

I choked back a response. She knew. At least I thought she knew, but I wasn't sure. Luckily, just then we were joined by a few more of the old crowd.

I hugged Nola Wells. "Aren't you as gorgeous as always," I said, standing back to take a better look at her. Nola was about my height, maybe fifteen pounds heavier, with glowing ebony skin that looks like it's been brushed with peach.

Her black eyes sparkled. "I might say the same to you. And I love that dress."

"This old thing?"

"And speaking of old things," Nola said with a laugh, "you remember my husband, James?"

"Of course."

He had probably gained forty pounds since his college football days, but his smile still lit up the room. "How you doin', Jolie?"

"Fine, James. It's good to see you again." His big hand wrapped around mine in a firm but gentle handshake. James was in sales for an insurance company and he exuded trust, tempered with a little devilment that never went much beyond some sweet-natured teasing. "And how is Tisha?" I asked. "And James the Younger?"

He laughed. "Tisha is now seven going on seventeen, and James, Jr., well, it's hard to say."

"Problems?" I asked. "He's what, eight, nine?"

"Eleven," James said. "And that boy is something—"

"I'll say," Nola added. "He's either going to get himself elected as the first black president of the United States, or get a life sentence in Huntsville."

"I vote for president," I said.

"You and me both." Nola looked around. "Doesn't the old place look pretty? Although I expected more people."

Again I scanned the party. There were only fifty or sixty people, and I, too, had thought there would be more. At the front door a few stragglers were arriving, but they weren't being greeted. Chester was at one of the bars chatting earnestly with an older couple.

"I believe Miss Audry cut back on the guest list," Donna Katherine said with a wicked smile.

Nola looked far less amused. "Now, why doesn't that surprise me?"

Ralph Richardson joined us. "Jolie, hey, hi there." A smile peeked out from under his big gray mustache as he leaned over to kiss my cheek. The mustache had been brown last time I'd seen him.

I hugged him back. "Ralph, how are you?"

When I was up for the position of creative director, Ralph was the person who was brought in for the job. I should have disliked him. I'd certainly intended to; however, Ralph is a genuinely nice person. The kind who likes it best when everyone is working as a team, sharing both ideas and credit equally.

"I'm doing fine," he said. "Hey, I heard a rumor that you'd gone New York on us." He smiled. "Published a book and all."

"Sold one."

"That's great! I'm happy for you. Do you know Amber?" Amber was a young blonde who was hanging back just slightly. I smiled in her direction, but before I could respond, Matt was at my side, holding drinks for Donna Katherine and me.

Donna Katherine took hers and raised the glass. "Happy holidays," she said by way of a toast.

"Happy holidays," we all repeated dutifully.

"Enough of this holiday cheer," Nola said. "Ralph, did you say a book deal? Jolie, I thought you had a radio show."

This was my big moment, and I caught myself glancing around, wondering where Audry and Michael were. I wanted them to hear this, not as vindication, but as proof to them that no matter what I'd done in the past, I was beyond it now. It was some ridiculous need for both confession and absolution.

I saw neither of the Sherabians.

"Well, I did sell a book," I said. "My agent just mailed me the contracts, and we have a pub date of next September." I dropped the jargon as if it were part of my everyday vocabulary. Nola grinned at me.

"What kind of book?" Donna Katherine asked.

"A mystery. *Murder for Fun and Profit*," I said.

"A mystery? Really?" It was Ralph. "Do you kill off one of us?" he asked.

"No. It's not about—"

"Maybe you should hire the agency to get you some publicity." Amber, the only one of the group I didn't know, made the suggestion. She was wearing a burgundy crushed-velvet dress on a body that was fashionably pale and thin, like her hair. Her burgundy lipstick exactly matched her dress and the ribbon around her neck.

"I hadn't considered that." I didn't tell them that a first book advance wouldn't cover the minimum that Rose Sterling required of new clients.

"Can you send us some free copies, since you used to work here?" Amber asked.

"Actually—"

"Listen to this greedy little thing," Nola said. Nola's title was account executive and she was wearing a bracelet that probably cost more than my car.

"Well, I mean, I'd like to read it," said Amber, fingering the ribbon at her neck. "We could put a copy in the conference room and pass it around."

"Too many perks in this business," Nola said, with a quick shake of her head.

Donna Katherine hiked up the top of her dress where it had been riding dangerously low on her breasts, then put her hands on her hips as she stared at the group. "We are not going to set up our own lending library. You people can't even keep track of time sheets. Especially Ralph." She swatted him on the arm. "If I had a nickel for every billable hour you forgot to write down—"

"What a toughy," he said.

She waggled her hips at him. "And you love it . . ." She turned to me. "So, you'll have an author signing here in Austin, and you just let us know where and when. Y'all, this is a sales opportunity."

Sales opportunities were well understood by everyone at Rose Sterling, thanks to Chester's belief that every person in the agency was a selling representative of the firm.

"I'll make sure that you get invitations." All my senses were on hyperalert; things were going too smoothly to continue like this.

"I'll send out autographed copies of your mystery as Christmas presents," Nola said.

"And," Donna Katherine added, "I'll get the rest of these deadbeats to cough up the price of a book." She turned toward a makeshift dais at the other end of the room. "Oh, look. I believe the festivities are about to begin."

❖ CHAPTER 4 ❖

DONNA KATHERINE left us to take charge of the informal portion of the activities. At that point the Sherabians reappeared; they slipped in beside Chester, smiling graciously. There was the singing of "Happy Birthday," and at Donna Katherine's insistence, the opening of the few presents. Chester loved the mug and the tea, and beamed a smile at me from across the room along with his thank-you.

Next came speeches. About Chester. About the agency. About people present, and long gone. About triumphs and disasters. The drink I'd been sipping was still jittering around in my stomach. I was tensed for whatever was coming, a careless word from someone who'd known about me and Michael, or for the moment when Audry and Michael joined us, because I knew they would.

A thirtyish woman with sleek black hair, and an even sleeker black dress on her small, athletic body, stepped up to the microphone.

I leaned over to Ralph. "Who's that?"

"Desi Baker. Used to be Donna Katherine's assistant, but she's doing copywriting now. I'll tell you about her later."

Desi began to speak, her lovely voice shaky with nerves. "In my experience in business, Chester Sterling is absolutely unique. He is the kind of man who believes in people." She glanced at Chester and smiled. The smile turned into a grimace, and her right hand briefly touched her flat stomach.

Her face flushed lightly as she raised her chin and went on.

"Last week I checked the employment records of Rose Sterling and discovered that the majority of people in the agency have been promoted at least three times. Top positions are almost never filled by outsiders. To me that's proof that Chester Sterling is a man of unique vision. He believes in giving people the chance to move up, to try new things, to learn from their mistakes and to grow into the best they can be." She looked into the crowd, taking several quick breaths in succession. She smiled to overcome her stage fright, and again I saw how pretty she was. "I hope that all of us have learned this lesson as well. To give everyone a chance." She turned back to Chester. "And now I speak for every one of your employees, Chester, when I say 'thank you' to one of America's truly great leaders."

The applause was generous as she quickly hugged Chester, then stepped off the dais.

Nola's purse began to beep. She opened it and pulled out a cell phone. "Hello?" she whispered, already moving toward the front door to carry on her conversation less obtrusively. James gave us a wave and followed her.

Someone else moved to the microphone and spoke. Then someone else. It became a parade of speakers, all wanting to leave their mark on the occasion. Matt clapped politely after each; he does this sort of thing well. I began to feel sorry for him, knowing he must have felt like a stranger at a funeral. Even for me much of it seemed remote. Watching Michael and Audry on the dais was like watching a play. One I'd seen before; one I'd had a part in.

Then someone dimmed the lights, a screen came down from the ceiling, and a reel of the agency's award-winning television commercials began.

"Would you like another drink?" Matt whispered.

"I'd love one. Cyanide."

He winked and smiled as he moved away.

I turned back to watch the three shadowy figures sitting on the dais. I could see Audry, smiling as if she were responsible for all the award winners we were seeing. Michael was sitting beside his wife, but he was looking around the room, searching the crowd for something. Or someone.

His eyes caught mine and he smiled.

My stomach tensed. Once again I was reminded that if I go to hell, I will know why. Not that it was Michael's fault. I take full credit, with all due regret.

The truth is that I had never intended to have a relationship with Michael. It had started innocently. Accidentally. It was during that horrible time in my life when my father was dying of cancer, and my mother was in a state of denial that I'm sure was intended to be cheering. Unfortunately, there's no room for real emotions or real comfort when everyone is pretending that nothing is wrong. The problem was that I couldn't pretend, and it had left me bereft.

Once a week my parents would call from Dallas. Once a month Jeremy and I would drive up there to see them, but through all the conversations no one ever really talked. At first I asked for information, but I never got any. The few times I had the courage to say I was worried, or worse, scared, my mother would dismiss my feelings.

"Oh, pooh," Mom would say, "your dad will be fine. Fine. Don't mention the 'c' word to him; it would only upset him." I wasn't living close to my sister or brother, and Jeremy was only nine, far too young to bear the kind of grief that I was holding inside.

Then one day at work it all began to erupt, the hurt at being shut out by my mother, the anger at her denial, and worst of all, the fear that my father was dying. I'd run to the supply closet, the only place I could think of where I'd have some privacy. And there I'd finally begun to cry. Not a gentle rain of tears; no, this was an outpouring of gut-wrenching pain. Somewhere in the midst of it the door had opened and Michael had walked in. I'd tried to hide my face, but he hadn't let me.

"It's okay, Jolie." And with that he'd put both arms around me tightly. That physical contact, the closeness I'd been hungering for, broke down the last of my resolve to be strong, and the sobs

24

became even deeper until there was a physical pain to match the emotional one.

He had just held on to me, saying nothing, letting me cry, letting me draw from his warmth and his strength. When I finally began to calm down, my makeup was all over his shirt, my nose was running, and I didn't have a shred of dignity left. Michael had calmly reached for the Kleenex stored there, and held on to me while I blew my nose and wiped my face.

Little tears were still leaking out, and when I tried to bumble excuses, Michael tilted up my head and kissed first my cheeks, then my lips. I was as needy for the kisses as I'd been for the comfort.

And that was how it all started. Over my father's illness. Over my need. Over my own lousy weakness. Michael had just separated from Audry at the time, and might have gone right back if I hadn't been there. Seeing them together now brought it home powerfully.

The lights came up, startling me into the moment. Everyone was applauding again. Chester stood, and said into the microphone, "Thank you. This is a very special evening for me. I hope you all are enjoying it as much as I am." With that he helped Audry off the dais and they began to dance. The party went back into full swing. Michael looked out around the room. I ducked my head and moved a little closer to the windows, staring out, as if I could make myself invisible.

When I felt a tap on my shoulder I jumped. It was Matt. He handed me a tall cool glass of diet Coke. "How is this?"

"Perfect." We sipped in silence, then put our drinks down and joined the dancers. I ducked my head into Matt's shoulder like an ostrich. Through two songs I stayed focused on Matt, and then a realization hit me; I stopped in midsong.

"What?" Matt asked.

"I'm not having a good time," I said. "Are you?"

"I always have a good time when I'm with you."

"Liar."

25

He smiled. "Most of the time."

"We don't have to stay here. We can leave and no one will notice. Even if they did, they wouldn't care."

"Are you sure you want to go?"

"I'm positive. Let me just run to the rest room first and then we can disappear into the night." I gestured toward the glittering sky outside.

"I'll get your coat and meet you at the door."

"Great idea."

I gave him my claim ticket and headed straight out, hurrying between people, nodding at acquaintances without stopping to chat. Now that I had given myself permission to leave, I felt lighter, but I wasn't willing to slow down. If I did, I was afraid my past would catch up to me.

In the outside hall I sucked in the cold fresh air without stopping; I dashed down the hall and discovered a long line of women, all waiting to get into the ladies' rest room.

Luckily in a high-rise every floor has bathrooms. I went to the elevator and pressed the button. When it appeared, and the doors opened, there was a security guard inside.

"Is there something wrong?" I asked, stepping in.

"Oh, no, ma'am," he said, running his fingers over his brown crew cut. "We're just here to help the guests." His badge said his name was Ted Polovy. "Do you want the lobby or the parking garage?"

"Neither actually, I want to go to the next floor down and use the rest room."

He put his heavy thumb on the "door open" button. "I'm sorry, ma'am, but I can't let you do that. The guests aren't allowed on any other floors. Security. You understand."

"Actually, I don't. . . ." I said, but the look on his face told me very clearly that there was no point in challenging him. I could go to either the lobby or the parking garage, and neither had rest rooms.

"Thank you," I said automatically as I stepped off the elevator and turned toward Rose Sterling. I lurked at the door of the agency, and while I didn't see Matt, I did bump into Donna Katherine.

"Where you going, girl?" she asked.

"I was going to the rest room . . . but it's packed and the security guy won't let me on any other floors. I'm not happy."

"Then take the stairs down to six."

"Oh." Of course. The stairs. There wouldn't be anyone guarding the stairwell. "Thanks."

I turned back the way I'd come, pausing only briefly when I faced the door to the stairs. What if an alarm sounded? The doors hadn't been secured when I worked at the agency; I'd run up and down them fairly often because it was the only exercise I had time for. Michael and I had rendezvoused on the stairwell a couple of times, too.

With a quick shake of my head I popped open the fire door. Nothing happened and the metal staircase beyond was well lit, just as I remembered. I headed down quickly and dashed to the bathroom.

The lights inside were on, and I stopped in the doorway, assailed by an odor of perfume, urine, and vomit. It was enough to make me turn around and go back. Almost. Perhaps this was the reason they were keeping guests on the seventh floor—some kind of plumbing problem.

It was too late to worry about that, so I took a breath and entered. Inside the air felt chilly, perhaps because of the black and white ceramic tiles on the floor. I picked out the nearest stall, slid shut the bolt, and went to the bathroom.

When I came out I stopped long enough to wash my hands.

As I turned off the water, I heard a sound at the door. I expected the door to open, but whoever was outside changed her mind. It gave me an odd feeling. That was silly, because if I knew enough to sneak down one floor, there would be others. Donna Katherine was probably sending tours. I peeked around the tile wall so I could see the door and a movement on the floor caught my attention. At first I thought it was a bug crawling under the door, but with a second glance I saw it was a piece of paper. A note.

I walked over and picked it up.

The writing was as familiar to me as if I'd seen it yesterday.

Meet me in the lounge. I still love you. M.

Michael Sherabian was sending me notes like this was high school.

I would never deny that Michael had stood by me when I needed him, but some part of me, the portion that didn't want all the responsibility, always believed he should have reminded me that he was married, even if he and Audry were living separately. If I had been beyond rational thought, he shouldn't have been, and some portion of my being clung to that, maybe as vindication for what I'd done.

Knowing he might be outside the door made me feel trapped. I could not, would not, leave if there was a chance of running into Michael in the hall. I let out a breath. Damn it, anyway!

Now I had to wait, in a cold bathroom, with a disgusting smell. One more thing to blame on Michael Sherabian. In two minutes, I promised myself, I would go back upstairs, get my purse, get Matt, and get the hell out of the building.

I started pacing toward the large handicapped stall that took up the entire back wall. The tiles felt cool and slippery under the thin soles of my high heels as I marched to the far wall, whirled around, and walked back toward the exit door again. I stopped midway and faced myself in the mirror.

My party face was slipping; I no longer had the devil-may-care look I'd worked so hard to achieve for the evening. In its place was stress as evidenced by my unnaturally pale skin. Or maybe it was the lighting.

I wondered what Michael had seen when he looked at me.

While he had instigated our affair, I had been as much the seducer as the seduced, and I had loved having him in my life. Our relationship had gone on for five months of incredible highs when it felt as if I were flying on pure exhilaration, balanced with soul-wrenching lows when I admitted that it couldn't last forever. During all that time I knew that Audry wanted her husband and her marriage back.

I believe in love and marriage. I believe in families and loyalty, and all the old-fashioned virtues that were instilled in me during the more conventional era of my childhood. Maybe those values, combined with all the years of single motherhood, are why I cherish Matt so.

This time when I held up the note and read it, the memories touched me; the scent of Michael's musky cologne, the way he would begin a conversation by gently touching my hand, the chocolate Kisses he often brought me—

I crumpled the note and shoved it down into the shiny metal waste container on the wall beside me. If I could rid myself of the note, maybe I could rid myself of the feelings as well.

I whipped back around and began to pace again, back to the far stall. When I reached it I slammed my fist against the wall; my feet slipped on the tile and went out from under me. My shoulder banged open the handicapped stall door as I went down.

That's when I realized I wasn't alone in the ladies' room.

❧ CHAPTER 5 ❦

I GASPED and jumped up, stammering apologies. "I'm so sorry—"

There was vomit on the commode seat and inside it. Desi Baker was curled in a fetal position around the porcelain, her black dress twisted on her body. There was spit on one corner of her lips and her eyes were open, staring ahead. I realized she wasn't seeing anything.

The chill air seemed to permeate my being. I clung to the slick metal, afraid to breathe, too sick to move. I closed my eyes, willing her to be gone; when I opened them she was still there. My stomach lurched and for a moment I thought I was going to be sick.

Again I closed my eyes, only this time I twisted my head to breathe some cleaner air. When I turned back I saw again the once beautiful Desi Baker, still on the cold tile floor. With great care I bent toward her. Gently I felt the smooth white skin of her inner wrist. It was warm, but there was no movement of blood that created a pulse.

I straightened, stumbling backward across the tile. As soon as I reached the outside door I flung it open and sucked in air as I began to run. First to the stairs, then up toward Rose Sterling Advertising. All the way I prayed that someone would appear to help me. Someone who could work a miracle and bring Desi Baker back to life.

It was the security guard, Ted Polovy, who called both EMS and the police. Next he secured the area and me as well, insisting that

I stand just outside the rest room door while he guarded the elevator. I was too stunned to care, and too relieved that someone else was taking charge. I'm sure the emergency medical people were there in minutes, but it seemed like hours of waiting, shivering, and hoping for something that I knew wasn't going to happen.

When the EMS team did finally arrive they looked like kids, too young for the job. They moved past me quickly and efficiently, straight through the bathroom door that closed behind them with a heavy whoosh. Then the police arrived. First a patrol officer in uniform, then later two plainclothes officers accompanied by Polovy. They went by me without any acknowledgment.

I felt a million miles away from the party, and from Matt, as if I were in a cold, distant existence without a pathway back to the real world. When a plainclothes detective came out of the bathroom I stopped him.

"Excuse me," I said, my voice swallowed up by the emptiness in the hallway. "I need to go back upstairs. Could you tell me how she is?"

He looked me over curiously. "Who are you?"

"I'm the woman who found her. They, the security guard, asked me to stay."

He nodded, rubbing a finger on his chin. I realized that I could have left at any time and no one would have known or cared.

The officer looked me over again, assessing me. "Was she a friend of yours?"

"No. I never met her. She worked for the agency and I think her name was Desi Baker."

"But you didn't work with her?"

I shook my head. "No. I left the agency several years ago. They invited me back for the anniversary party, and Chester's birthday. Is she . . . ? Did she . . . ?"

His face was stolid, implacable. "I'm sorry, ma'am, but I don't believe she regained consciousness."

At first I could only stare at him while the confirmation of what I knew slowly filtered through my mind, numbing it. I suddenly needed Matt, and remembered that he was waiting for me one floor up. "I have to get back. My husband is at the party. I have to let him know I'm okay."

"Certainly. I'll need some information first," he said, as he pulled out a small lined notebook and flipped pages impatiently. He was a heavy man, heavy and big, somewhere in his mid-forties, with dark brown hair that came down to the middle of his ears. He had on metal-framed glasses that had worn a ridge in his temples.

His beefy fingers fumbled with the small notebook. When he finally found a clean page he asked, "Your name?"

"Jolene Wyatt. Jolie Wyatt."

"Your address and phone?"

"Route 3, Box 213, Purple Sage, Texas."

"Is that your permanent address?"

"It's where I live."

"Where are you staying here in Austin?"

"At my sister-in-law's." I gave him Prissy's name, address, and phone number, then said, "Look, I'll be right back. It'll just take five minutes. Or you can come with me—"

"No problem, ma'am, I'll come with you."

I was ready to head for the stairs, but he turned in the other direction. I had to trot to stay up with him.

"I didn't get your name," I said when we stopped at the elevator.

"Senior Sergeant Ray Bohles."

The elevator door opened and we faced another security guard. He nodded at Bohles and we rode up one floor to the agency. Music was still playing, but it was muted, as were the voices coming from the suite. A crowd of people was just inside the door. Donna Katherine was one of them. Her eyes widened as she saw me. "Jesus, girl, where have you been? Your husband's been looking for you." She glanced at the man beside me.

Sergeant Bohles wasn't touching me, certainly not constricting my movement in any way, but it was obvious that he was with me. At least it seemed obvious to me.

32

"Where's Matt?" I asked.

"He's in the conference room." She leaned over and said confidentially, "They said someone was hurt. Shit, I was terrified it was you. But then Matt talked to someone, and it just got so confusing. What in the world is going on?"

I shook my head as I moved past her. "I'll tell you later." I had to get to Matt and assure him I was all right.

He was in the conference room, along with at least a dozen other people. My coat and my purse were on the table in front of him; he forgot both when I entered.

"Jolie," he said, his arms going around me. "Are you okay?"

I mumbled yes and held on to him, feeling the texture of his jacket against my face, and the strength in his arms.

It was Senior Sergeant Bohles who spoke, over my head, directly to Matt. "Mrs. Wyatt was helping us with an incident downstairs."

Matt's arms relaxed their hard grip and I stepped back. A woman's life and death had become nothing more than an incident.

"Exactly what incident was that?" Matt asked.

The officer hesitated, looked around the room at the others gathered in it. "We need to find a place where I can speak with Mrs. Wyatt privately. If you'll come with us . . ."

"That's fine," Matt said, picking up my things along with his own overcoat.

We passed through the remaining partygoers, who watched our progress with curiosity. Some asked me what was going on, but I could only shake my head and keep on walking. Fortunately, Donna Katherine had abandoned her post at the door or I doubt that we'd have made it out. We headed for the elevator, and once inside, Senior Sergeant Bohles said to Matt, "A young woman died in the rest room downstairs. Mrs. Wyatt found her."

Matt's glance went from Bohles to me. "Are you okay?" he asked, again.

I nodded, but I didn't trust myself to speak just then. Matt must have sensed my feelings because he slid an arm around me. "You're cold."

Again I nodded.

Within a few minutes we were in a small windowless room on the ground floor that was apparently the office of the security guards. "I just need to ask you a few basic questions," Bohles said, holding out a chair for me in front of a dirty gray metal desk. "Mrs. Wyatt, are you okay with that?"

"I think so."

Matt gave me a quick glance. My face felt frozen, but whatever expression showed must have been enough. He nodded at Bohles, then his eyes came back to me as the policeman took out a notebook.

After that, time went quickly. I was asked some very simple questions about how I got to the ladies' room in the first place, how many other people I had seen, and exactly what I had done after finding Desi Baker. It didn't take long; that surprised me.

"That's it?" I asked.

He nodded, helping me on with my coat. "Yes, ma'am, that's all. If there's anything more I need to know, I can reach you at the numbers you gave me, is that right?"

"Yes."

"Then I hope the rest of your evening is more pleasant." He handed me over to Matt and opened the door for us.

Matt and I started toward the parking garage in silence.

A young woman was dead, I had found her, and now I was going home. It made no sense to me. I had agreed to attend the party to have some moment of glory; to recoup my losses from years past. In truth, there had been no losses. Very few people had known about my relationship with Michael, so there had been no disgrace. Now it was over. Sadly, horribly.

It was then I remembered the note that had been slipped under the bathroom door. The one that I had crumpled and shoved into the waste container.

"Jolie, what's wrong?" Matt asked.

"What?"

"You jerked away from me; are you okay?"

I looked down at my hands. "I think I left something upstairs." I turned toward the elevators. "I have to go back up."

"Jolie? What did you leave? You're wearing your coat, and your purse is over your shoulder. That's all you brought." He was watching me as if I might explode.

"It was, uh, the present. I left it."

"You gave it to Chester for his birthday, remember?"

I stared at Matt dumbly.

I couldn't tell him that I needed to find a note from Michael Sherabian; one that held his scent. I couldn't say that the police might be digging it out of the trash at that very moment. I couldn't say that I had picked it up, and crumpled it, getting my fingerprints all over it.

I could only say, "Of course. We should go home." We started walking.

Again he put an arm around me. "Some of Prissy's herb tea will help. And some sleep. Tomorrow this will all be behind you."

Even through the haze of my shock one thing was very clear to me—Desi Baker's death wasn't going to go away that quickly or that easily.

Prissy set a small bowl of fruit on my place mat. There were three different kinds of melon, along with grapes and strawberries. If anything could have tempted me to eat, that would have been it, but I didn't want food. I had barely sipped the tea she'd put in front of me earlier.

"Did you sleep at all?" Prissy asked, sitting across from me at the table in her breakfast nook. It was already midmorning, although the gray sky outside gave the world an eerie feel as if there were no time.

Matt had left hours before to attend a board of directors' meeting at a company he was heavily invested in. His parting remarks to me had been filled with concern, but I had assured him that

I would be fine. After that I had gone back to sleep, finally achieving the heavy dreamless state that had eluded me during the night. Now I felt drugged and slow.

"I slept a little," I said.

"Matt said you tossed and turned all night."

"Matt's a blabbermouth."

"It had to be hard, though, finding that woman dead and all. How are you feeling now?"

"Fine."

Prissy turned her gaze to the patio outside the French doors. "Matt said she was young."

I nodded, remembering her body in its short black dress, curled around the toilet. I tried to hide the shudder that grabbed me. "Late twenties or early thirties." I took a sip of my herb tea and the warm liquid slid easily down my throat as if it really might do some good.

I sipped some more, enjoying the companionable silence. I even tried a little of the fruit. My brain began to unclog and my thoughts converged. After I drained my cup I set it down, and Prissy went to the kitchen for the teapot. "You know what bothers me?" I said. "The police didn't do anything. That one detective asked me ten questions and then sent me away."

"What did you want him to do?" Prissy asked, returning to refill my cup. She looked directly at me.

"Find out how she died. I mean, what caused her to die? She'd been sick, vomiting. . . ." I didn't want to go into the details. "She was young and beautiful, and she'd just gotten the promotion she wanted. Writing copy. So why did she die? The police should have talked to everyone at the party. They should have sent for a lab crew—"

"Jolie, the Austin police force is made up of trained professionals; surely they followed the proper procedure. Besides, Matt said you left right after that detective questioned you. Maybe the police did do all the things you think they should have. Perhaps they did them after you left." She poured the tea, then went back to the kitchen.

I let out a long breath while her words settled into my brain. "You're right; I'm sure you are. Maybe *I* just need to know how she died. And somehow I think *I* should have done more. Something." I shook my head. "I don't know."

"I understand," Prissy said, as she sat down and touched my arm lightly. "But it's really not your fault. You didn't even know the woman, except for her name."

"Desi Baker."

It was an interesting name, and she'd looked like an interesting person. Young and smart, both in a fashion sense and intellectually. I wondered what Desi was a nickname for. Desdemona?

"Matt said he heard some gossip about her during the party," Prissy said, dropping her voice even though we were alone in the house.

"Really?" I felt a tickle of fear. Who was gossiping and what all had they been saying? "That surprises me."

"Well, actually he said some woman was telling him. He couldn't get away from her. Real thick accent?"

"It must have been Donna Katherine; I shouldn't have left him alone."

"He's a big boy, he can take care of himself. What he heard was rather personal."

I picked up my cup and inhaled the aroma, trying to appear casual. "What did she say?" I asked. I made myself take a sip of the tea.

"That this young woman, Desi, was having an affair with Michael Sherabian."

"What?" The word came out unexpectedly along with a shower of tea. I began to choke.

Prissy patted me on the back while I coughed and sputtered. She dabbed at my face with a flowered cloth napkin. "Oh, dear. Here, raise your arm, Jolie," she said, lifting my arm straight up into the air. "There, now take a breath."

I wheezed, and she pumped my arm until finally I could talk. "Sorry." I coughed again. "The tea went down the wrong pipe."

Voices and footsteps were coming from the patio at the back

of the house. Prissy jumped up and ran for the outside door.

I swallowed twice before I could say, "Who's here?"

Prissy grinned. "Remember we said there was a special surprise coming for you? Well, actually, a treat for both of us."

As I started for the French doors I could hear a little voice saying, "Surprise! Open the door. Grandma Prissy, Aunt Dolie, surprise!"

Before anyone could knock, Prissy threw open the door to the chill grayness. "Hello! Christopher, come in and give me a hug." She scooped up her three-year-old grandson and smothered his face with kisses as she pulled him inside to the warmth.

"Not so much kissing, Grandma Prissy!"

They were followed by his mother, Stephanie, carrying a small bag and a huge purse, which she dumped on the floor before reaching around Christopher to give her mother a hug. "Hi, Mom." She turned and I also got a big hug. "Jolie, hi. Merry Christmas!"

"What a great surprise! It's so wonderful to see you two," I said, putting an arm around Stephanie. "How are you?"

Stephanie has heavy, glossy brown hair and her father's long lean body; over the years she has developed some of Prissy's impish quality, as well.

She gave me a slightly weary smile. "We're fine. Mr. You-know-who had way too much energy on the flight." She poked at Christopher through his heavy coat. "But he finally settled down. It's wonderful to be here; we've missed you," she said, giving me another hug. "Haven't we, little bug?"

"Yes, we have," he said firmly.

Just then the phone rang. Prissy muttered something about turning all the phones off before saying, "I'll be right back." She held Christopher in our direction.

Naturally I took him. "You're getting so big."

He squeezed my neck with both arms. "Aunt Dolie, I missed you too much."

"Aunt Jolie," Stephanie corrected.

He grinned. "Aunt Dolie, Aunt Dolie!"

I had been the first person, after the nurse, to hold Christopher at his birth. He had been wrapped lightly in a thin blanket, still covered in blood and fluids, but I'd felt a bonding that I'd only experienced once before with my own son. Matt, who'd been standing beside me, had worn an expression of amazement and joy as he had stroked Christopher's tiny fist.

Perhaps it was so special for us because we were the only family with Stephanie during the birth. She didn't have a husband, and Prissy and Ross weren't there. I don't think they intended to miss Christopher's arrival; I've always thought their family argument simply got out of hand and no one quite knew how to put an end to it. It started when Ross and Prissy first found out that Stephanie was pregnant, and unwilling to get married. Unwilling even to tell anyone who the father of the baby was. That didn't sit well with Prissy's fundamentalist background, and since Stephanie can be as hardheaded as her mother, things escalated until Prissy and Ross left for a vacation in Europe. Christopher came almost a month early, a full week before they got back.

When Stephanie had gone into labor she'd called us and we raced in from Purple Sage. I remember walking into the birthing room and seeing Stephanie, all alone, her face mottled with tears and pain. Matt and I had both put our arms around her, and that awkward group hug had been the start of a long night, one filled with sweat and those primal emotions that pull us out of the nice civilized world where we usually live. I wouldn't trade anything for the memory.

When Stephanie reconciled with her parents a few weeks later, unreasonable as it was, I actually felt pangs of jealousy. Not that we were left out. Stephanie and Christopher visited us on the ranch as often as they could. It was Stephanie's hideaway, as she called it, and I got to take care of Christopher.

Then last summer, on the Fourth of July, Stephanie had announced she was moving to Phoenix. This was the first time I'd seen them in almost six months.

A clatter from the stairway announced Jeremy's arrival. "Hey, Christopher. Hey, Steph." He smiled.

"Hey, yourself, Jeremy," Stephanie said, giving him a quick hug. "My, how you've grown, and you're getting more handsome all the time." She grinned as an older sibling might. "I'll bet all the girls in Purple Sage are after you."

Jeremy actually blushed. "How come you're so mean to me?"

"Because I like you."

Jeremy shook his head and looked at Christopher. "Your mommy is silly. How are you doing?"

Christopher thought about it. "I'm fine, 'cept everybody's squeezin' me too hard."

"Oh, really?" I said, swinging him into the living room and plopping him on the sofa. "Then maybe I'll just tickle you instead!"

As I tickled he squirmed with giggles. "No more, Aunt Dolie!"

"Yes, more! Lots more." I pulled up his shirt and began to blow air on his tummy.

"Otay. More, more!"

"Actually," Stephanie said, the voice of reason towering over us, "we have to get the luggage in; the taxi driver piled it on the patio. After that we have to get Christopher fed because neither of us ate this morning on the plane. Did we?"

I stood up. "This is the nicest surprise—oh, but wait—I sent your Christmas presents to Phoenix."

"That's okay, because I brought them back," Stephanie said.

"Santa Claus is coming," Christopher explained, jumping up. "He's bringing baby Jesus."

"You're going to have to tell me that story," I said. "And I can tell you some Christmas stories, too. And then we'll drive around and see the lights, and we'll visit the tree in Zilker Park, and sing Christmas carols at the capitol building. . . ." I lifted Christopher up and swung him around. "Lord, you're getting heavy. If you keep on growing, I won't be able to pick you up."

"Is that bad?" he asked.

"No, sweetie, that's not bad. You're always good."

"How come you never said that to me?" Jeremy asked.

I heard the phone ringing again, or perhaps it was a second phone line.

"It's a generational thing," I said. "But I promise I'll say it to your children. And I'll spoil them rotten. Really rotten. You'll see; paybacks are hell. Uh, heck," I corrected, remembering that we weren't supposed to swear around Christopher.

"Lucky me." He headed for the back door. "Think I'll go get the luggage."

I turned to Stephanie, who was pulling off Christopher's coat. "I was beginning to think this was going to be a terrible Christmas, but you two have changed all that."

"Why would you think it was going to be terrible?" Stephanie asked, setting the coat on a chair.

"Well, something happened. Nothing to do with the family; I'll tell you later—"

"I have to go potty!" Christopher said loudly.

She grabbed his hand. "Come on, then. Hurry. Up the stairs." Over her shoulder she said, "It's always an emergency."

" 'Bye, Aunt Dolie!" Christopher put his hand to his mouth and blew me a kiss before he started up the stairs.

"Let me guess," Jeremy said, as he dragged in two suitcases. "If you ever have more kids, that's the one you'll have." He pulled in another bag.

After closing the door, I slid an arm around my son's waist, which is now higher than mine since he's a good six inches taller. "No, thanks. I adore Christopher, but I'm happy with the child I have."

Prissy returned holding out the cordless phone. "It's for you," she said to me. "Can you talk? It's Chester Sterling."

"Sure." I took the phone and said, "Hello?"

"Jolie, thank goodness I tracked you down. I had to call the radio station in Purple Sage to get this number," Chester said. "I hate to bother you, but I need some help."

Jeremy was watching me curiously, as was Prissy. "What kind of help?" I asked. I couldn't imagine what I could ever do for Chester Sterling.

"Jolie, you know one of our staff passed away last night; I was told you found her." He sounded like a man who was drowning, but still trying to be logical.

"Yes, I did."

"I'm sorry about that, and even sorrier that I have to disturb your vacation," he said, then swallowed. "Everyone is in a tizzy here, and I've got commercials that have to get written and produced before we can close up shop for the holidays. Jolie, would you consider coming in and working part-time for a couple of days? I'll pay you a freelance rate and a bonus, if you'll help."

I couldn't. I didn't want to. Stephanie and Christopher were here; it was Christmas, time for fun and family. Besides, I never wanted to go back to Rose Sterling. Not after four years ago, not after last night. "Chester, we have things planned. . . ."

"Just a few hours a day. Whatever you can spare."

"Prissy, my sister-in-law, needs my help with the cooking, and my son needs me to take him places—"

Jeremy shook his head no. He whispered, "I'm fine, go ahead."

But then, he didn't know what Chester was asking.

"Chester, I—"

"Jolie, please? I'm desperate right now, or I wouldn't be calling. Would you do it as a favor to an old friend?"

That stopped me. Back in my days at Rose Sterling, when I had needed an advance to cover new tires for my car, or to pay for a window that Jeremy had broken, Chester had never hesitated. When I needed time off for my dad's illness, Chester had simply said, "Go." Never a question, never a complaint.

In thinking it through, I realized that I had to be there for him, too. No questions, no complaints.

"No problem," I said. "I'll be happy to come in."

I could hear his huge sigh of relief. "Thank you. I really appreciate this."

"What time do you want me?"

"Right after lunch would be good. Say twelve-thirty? One o'clock?"

"I'll see you this afternoon." I pushed the button to hang up

42

the phone and handed it back to Prissy. "I have to go to Rose Sterling and write copy. Chester needs me."

She smiled sympathetically. "Christopher naps most of the afternoon, so we won't be doing anything special anyway. You won't miss a thing."

"Sure, Mom," Jeremy agreed. "Not a thing."

❧ CHAPTER 6 ❧

Ross and Prissy's house and outbuildings are a cream-colored stucco that passes for adobe, with roofs of red brick. The patio is Saltillo tile. In the center there's a fountain and at the back an atrium covered with wisteria and bougainvillea. Come spring both are a riot of greenery; additionally, the wisteria has fragrant clusters of lavender blooms that hang like impressionistic grapes. In the summer the bougainvillea flaunts scarlet petals that dazzle the eye.

But in winter the branches were like dried and twisted sticks of gray that clung to the trellis and snaked up the wall of the house that formed one side of the patio. At the top of the red tile stairs is the garage apartment where Matt and I always stay. The inside is beautifully laid out and decorated in a combination of styles that hint of French country and Victorian, with a splash of Southwestern for panache. Everything blends exquisitely despite Prissy's claim that most of the furniture is castoffs. It always makes me think her garage sales must be the events of the season.

"Aunt Dolie! Aunt Dolie! I need you."

I was in the bedroom of the apartment staring at the clothes I'd brought, trying to decide what in the world I was going to wear and wondering why in the hell it should matter.

"Coming, Christopher." I opened the front door and there he was, alone on the concrete steps, not wearing a jacket in the cold weather. I glanced at the patio and toward the house, but there was no one following him.

"What are you doing here, little bug?" I asked, pulling him inside and closing the door against the frigid weather. "And where's your coat?"

"In Grandma Prissy's house." He pointed in the vague direction. "I'm freezin'!"

"I'll bet you are. Come here and I'll bundle you up." With that I whisked him into the bedroom where I wrapped him in a quilt and set him up against the pillows on the bed like a big doll. I sat down close to him and hugged him once just for pleasure. "There you go; now you can get warm. Don't you know it's winter out there?"

"We don't have winter in Phoenix. But we have cold days."

"I've heard. So where's your mommy? You're not supposed to climb those stairs all by yourself, are you?"

Christopher's eyes were big and serious. "They're fightin'." He burrowed deeper into the quilt, like a little creature seeking protection.

"Who's fighting?"

He put a little finger against his lips. "Shh. No talking."

"Why can't we talk?"

"No talking about fightin'."

"Oh, right!" I said, laughing. "I'll talk about anything. Now, who's fighting? Is your mommy fighting?"

"Aunt Dolie!" His voice held an annoyance more typical of a forty-year-old than a child of just three. "I told you . . . no talking."

He was dead serious. It was a message he'd learned from someone, and whoever had taught him had done a good job. Christopher was watching me, but didn't volunteer another syllable.

"It's okay," I said. "If you can't tell me, then we won't talk about it."

He nodded.

"Instead, you can stay here and help me pick out something to wear. Can you do that? I need clothes to wear."

"Like Cinderella?"

I almost smiled, but didn't. "No, sweetie. I'm going to work today and I can't decide on the right outfit."

"Where do you work, Aunt Dolie? Can I work, too?"

45

"No, I have to go by myself. I'm working at the advertising agency."

He threw off the quilt and crawled across the bed to a royal blue sweater that I had been considering. "I like blue." It was lying there along with several other choices, none of which I had found suitable earlier. "It's pretty," Christopher added, patting the sweater with his little hand.

It looked particularly good with my black wool slacks and my fuzzy wool jacket. The outfit was a bit dressy for a copywriter at Rose Sterling, but I was going to wear it anyway. Somewhere I even had a gold pin with just that shade of blue enamel, if I had remembered to bring it.

I slid off my jeans and reached for the slacks as I asked Christopher, "Did you eat your lunch?"

"Yes. Tonight Mr. Javitz is coming."

And who was Mr. Javitz? A new cartoon character? Another friend of Ross and Prissy's? "Interesting." I slipped off my sweatshirt and hung it up with the button-down I'd had on under it. By the time I pulled on the blue sweater, Christopher had climbed off the bed and was poking at the computer Jeremy had transferred from Prissy's house.

"I like 'puters. Aunt Dolie, may you turn it on for me?"

"*Com*puters," I instructed. "Except I can't. Jeremy is working on this one and he gets very mad if we mess something up." He'd put the computer here specifically to keep it out of Christopher's reach.

"I won't hurt it." He was standing up on his tiptoes, his fingers mashing the keys.

"I know you won't, sweetie," I said, picking him up. "But what if *I* messed it up? Then Jeremy would be mad at me."

"Where did he go?"

"To his friend's house. W.D.'s," I said, carrying Christopher into the bathroom where I set him on the counter. "You don't know W.D."

A quick look in the mirror convinced me that my clothes would pass muster, and as I rummaged through my makeup bag for a lipstick I discovered the enamel pin. I slipped it in my pocket, then took the lid off the tube of lipstick.

"I can do that!" Christopher said, trying to get the lipstick from me. "I can do it, please, Aunt Dolie."

I moved the bag to the other side. "I know you can, but we're in a hurry. I have to go to work now, so you have to go back to your grandma Prissy's. I'll bet they're looking for you." I put the lipstick on quickly, then swept all my cosmetics into a drawer and out of reach of little hands. The nice thing about visits with Christopher and Stephanie, besides simply enjoying him, was that I could always send Christopher back to his mother. It was practice for when I became a grandmother.

"Come on," I said, lifting him again. "We'll go see what your grandma Prissy is doing. Besides, I think it's time for your nap."

"No it's not time for nappin'," he said very firmly. But he put his arms around my neck and hung on tightly as I went out the door and down the stairs. I almost lost my balance near the bottom of the steps and had to stop to regain my footing. "Well, that was scary," I said. Then I moved across the patio and heard the voices coming from Prissy's great room.

"Absolutely not!" It was Stephanie. "I won't. I mean it. This just infuriates me!"

Prissy's voice was battle-weary. "Stephanie, all I'm asking is that you—"

"You still aren't listening!" Stephanie snapped. "Every time I try telling you what happened, you blow me off like I'm some hysterical child. It's because you don't believe me, isn't it? I'm your daughter, doesn't that mean anything to you?"

"Of course it does. I just think—"

"Damn it, there you go again!"

"Stephanie, there is no need to yell. I'm sure the neighbors aren't interested in hearing about this." She lowered her own voice as I backed away from the French doors.

I couldn't help but wonder if this was what I had to look forward to with Jeremy, or if this only happened with daughters. And what kind of thing was this?

Christopher's arms were like a hangman's noose around my neck. "See? I told you they're fightin'," he said.

I rubbed his back. "It's just an argument. People do that sometimes."

"I don't like fightin'."

Before I could respond, Stephanie's voice came again, more sarcastic than before. "Oh, wait, I get it. You think because it's Christmas we can all kiss and makeup—"

I turned around and panted back up the stone steps. "We'll call your grandma Prissy on the phone and tell her we're coming down."

Christopher had goose bumps from the cold and he didn't need to be listening to the argument. I didn't need to be either.

Back upstairs I dumped Christopher on the bed and wrapped him in the quilt a second time. "There you go," I said. "Now you can be my little papoose while I call the big house."

Before I could move, Christopher said, "Aunt Dolie, I love you."

I stared into his big brown eyes, then leaned over and kissed his forehead. "I love you, too."

Christopher continued to watch me. I said, "Look, about this fighting—" I stopped. Whatever I said, Christopher would no doubt repeat to Prissy and Stephanie, and it was apparent that there were already firm rules in place when it came to fighting. My own philosophies, however right I might think they were, wouldn't necessarily fit the family mold. I smiled; what the hell. "Your mommy and Grandma Prissy still love each other, but sometimes people just forget that they can talk things out. That's when they start yelling. It doesn't make them bad. It just means that they disagree about something, okay?"

He nodded as if he'd understood every word of my little speech, and for all I knew, he might have.

"So, now I'm going to call," I said. I used the phone in the living room, which was on a separate line from the main house.

It took four rings, but eventually Prissy answered. "Yes?"

"Prissy, hi, it's me, Jolie. I have Christopher over here and I need to leave for the agency. Should I bring him back?"

"Oh, dear, I didn't even notice he was missing. I'll meet you on the patio." She hung up.

I hurried into the bedroom, grabbing my jacket from the closet and my purse from the chair. "It's all right, Christopher," I said, turning to face him. "They're all done arguing, and they're waiting for you. Are you ready?"

He considered the question with that serious, pensive expression, then said, "Okay. But may you hold my hand?" He climbed down off the bed and put his hand in mine before we headed for the stairs a second time.

Initially my title at Rose Sterling Advertising had been junior copywriter, meaning that I wrote television and radio commercials, newspaper and magazine ads, as well as press releases and industrial films. As time progressed I had moved up to senior copywriter, and then producer, a title that reflected new job duties including the casting and producing of commercials.

I should have been promoted to creative director. That's the top spot in the creative department, but Audry had seen to it that I didn't make the cut, all because of Michael. I could hardly blame her, and I had been as angry with myself as with her, because I had worked hard to get that job and knew that it was forever out of my reach.

After I had moved to Purple Sage I let go of any hard feelings, hoping that Audry would do the same. As I crossed the hallway from the underground parking garage I wondered if she had. The night before hadn't been much of a test.

On the drive downtown I had developed a strategy on how I was going to handle working at Rose Sterling. I planned to get copy notes and see what else was needed; then if I was uncomfortable at the agency, I'd work at Prissy's house and just fax things to Ralph, the creative director. All I had to do was get through this afternoon.

In the lobby I almost bumped into Ted Polovy, the security guard who'd called both police and EMS the night before.

"Good afternoon," I said.

He looked at me for a moment before he recognized me, then said, "How you doin' today?"

"Better thanks, and you?"

He fell into step beside me as I walked toward the elevators. "Can't complain." We stopped and he touched the button to get an elevator car. "That was a bad thing last night. Real bad. Sorry you had to get involved."

"Yeah, well . . ."

"Maybe you should've gone to the parking garage like it was suggested."

I stared at him for a moment before I realized he was at least partly kidding. "When you gotta go, you gotta go."

He smiled. "You must be one of the writers at Rose Sterling."

The elevator arrived and we both stepped in. I pressed the button for seven, while he touched the button for the third floor. The doors closed and we began our ascent.

"Actually, I used to be with Rose Sterling," I said. "Now I live in Purple Sage. I'm just filling in for a few days."

"Purple Sage? I've been there." The elevator stopped and the doors opened. As Ted stepped out he gave me a quick salute. "Stay out of trouble."

Then he was gone, and I caught myself hugging my fuzzy wool jacket around me while the elevator made another upward run. When the doors opened on seven I stepped out into the wide hallway that would take me back to Rose Sterling. My stomach tightened and my breathing quickened. As Yogi Berra said, "It's déjà vu all over again."

✤ CHAPTER 7 ✤

A LARGE Christmas tree glimmered with lights, and blue and silver ribbons and balls just behind the front desk. Sitting at the desk was Amber Hadley, the young woman from the party last night.

"Hi. I'm Jolie Wyatt. I think Chester is expecting me," I told her.

She blinked as if moving out of a fog into clear air. "I'm sorry, what did you say?"

She'd verged on beautiful the night before, but today her festive look was gone along with the burgundy crushed-velvet dress. In its place she wore jeans and a red sweater that only heightened her paleness. Her eye makeup was smeared and her nose red, both, I assumed, the result of crying.

"Jolie," I repeated. "Jolie Wyatt. Chester called me to come in—"

"Oh, of course, I'm sorry. We met last night. You're the writer. Right before he left, Mr. Sterling told me to expect you. He wanted you to meet with Ralph Richardson." She stopped and rubbed her hand across her forehead, brushing her eyes and smearing more makeup in the process.

Three workmen walked toward us on their way out of the agency. One was pushing a dolly stacked with blue quilting material; he stopped. "That was the last load," he told us as the other two men went out the door.

"What?" the receptionist said, her face still cloudy. "Oh, thanks."

51

He addressed the rest of his remarks to me. "All the furniture's back in place, and everything's hooked up. I left the invoice with your bookkeeper." He grinned and shook his head. "That's some lady."

"Yes, she is."

"Man, she went over that invoice with a fine-tooth comb. I thought she was going to get a magnifying glass!"

"That's Donna Katherine for you."

"And then she went through some desk drawers and some file cabinets." He shook his head. "I told her we're bonded, and besides, who would want papers? Diamonds I could see checking on, but papers?" He grinned again. "You know what she said to ol' Ernie, my buddy that just left? 'Honey, with you around, a girl better check everything she's got.' " He started laughing. "Well, you have a merry Christmas."

"Thanks, you, too." I held the heavy door for him as he whistled his way out.

Amber shook her head. "Donna Katherine will flirt with anyone. At least the furniture's back. When I walked in this morning I didn't even have a desk. It's been so crazy. It would have been bad enough with all the things we had to do to the office, but then with—" She stopped and bit her lip as a huge tear rolled down her cheek. She looked young and very unsophisticated. "I'm sorry, just give me a minute." She reached into her desk drawer and pulled out a tissue; the polish on her fingernails was half chewed off.

"It's okay," I said. "I'm in no hurry."

"You must think I'm nuts, but Desi was a friend of mine, and I just, I don't know."

"I'm sorry."

She nodded, causing more tears to fall. "We started working here at the same time, a year and a half ago. Then we started rooming together; she just moved out a couple of months ago. She was wonderful to me, like a big sister, only better." Amber blew her nose, threw the tissue away, and got a fresh one. "Wait, aren't you the one who found her? Did she—? Was she—? Oh,

God, I don't know what I want to know. Maybe nothing." Amber blew her nose again. "I just can't seem to stop crying. I was okay until I had lunch, and then I went down to the deli and the guy asked me where my friend was. He meant Desi, only—I just couldn't—" The words were choked out by her sobs. She put her head down on the desk and let the tears flow.

She seemed so young and vulnerable I couldn't stand to leave her. "I'm so sorry," I said, moving around the desk to put an arm around her heaving shoulders. Her pain was so intense I could almost feel it. She sobbed even harder and I mumbled soothing phrases, hoping she could find some comfort in knowing that she wasn't alone.

After a few minutes I took tissues out of a box on her desk and put them against her clenched fist. She raised her head slightly. "This is so awful."

"I know it hurts."

She cried some more, and eventually rose up and blew her nose. "I meant for you. I'm sorry. I hardly even know you and you've been so nice."

"It's okay," I said, patting her shoulder one last time before I straightened up. "Can't you go home?"

She shook her head, then wiped her nose. "Mr. Sterling wanted me to, but I thought it would be better if I was busy. You know. Some people are already gone, because of Christmas and all, so they need me. And besides, I feel closer to Desi around here."

"I understand."

"I don't even know what she died of. Someone said a heart attack, but that's just crazy; she was only thirty. I mean, she did have something wrong with her heart. She had some disease as a kid, but still, you just don't expect people to die." She blew her nose. "God, a heart attack."

"Is that what the police said?"

She shook her head and let out a long shaky breath. "No, it was just a stupid rumor. Donna Katherine's trying to find out."

I moved back to the front of the desk, and Amber straightened her body as if in response to our new positions.

"What about Desi's family?" I asked. "Surely the police will tell them."

"Her dad is dead, and her mom is in a home someplace in Kansas."

"She's sick?"

"Senile dementia. She needs someone to take care of her twenty-four hours a day, and, well, you know." She sighed again. "It really bummed Desi out."

"It must have been hard on her. And you, too. Did Desi have any brothers or sisters?"

"I don't think so. The only other person Desi talked about much was her ex-husband. He lives in Europe and he's a pilot with some airline. KLM, I think."

"The police will find out."

"Yeah. They took her employment file last night. That big cop."

"Senior Sergeant Bohles," I supplied, as I remembered again that he might also find my fingerprints on the note from Michael.

I was trying to push the thought away when the phone in front of Amber buzzed and she answered it with, "Yes?" Obviously an internal call. Then she said, "She's right here, Ralph. I'm sorry, it's my fault. I'll send her back." She turned to me. "Ralph's waiting for you. Down at the end of the hallway. On the right; it's the next to the last cubby." She pointed her index finger with its dark, chipped nail polish.

"Thanks. I'll see you later." I moved around the modular wall of navy blue that had closed off my view of the rest of the offices. I was keenly aware of my surroundings, and my muscles were tensed in the old fight or flight response. I wouldn't be fighting, but I would have loved to flee.

At first I saw no one, and there was a somber stillness to the office, with only a few floral arrangements serving as reminders of last night's party. This was a working office again, with the modular walls back in place, forming small, functional cubicles. Chester had never grasped the concept that floor space in an of-

54

fice was highly prized by his employees. Nor did he understand that privacy and real walls were much-sought-after commodities. We had accepted his idea of an office, but it may have been one of the reasons that employees were so motivated toward promotion.

Some video equipment was being loaded by a young man in jeans, and I nodded as I passed by him on my way to find Ralph. Ralph's cubicle was on the outside of the building, so one entire wall was glass. Beyond were the executive offices. First was Chester's in the corner, then Michael's, and finally Audry's. With a peripheral glance all I could see was Chester's empty office. I couldn't see into Michael's.

"Ralph?"

His body was hunched over his computer keyboard, and he was frowning. When I spoke he swung his chair around as if I'd surprised him. "Oh, Jolie! Come in."

There were plastic cartoon characters dancing on the top of his computer, four-color magazine ads pasted above his desk, and a large cork storyboard on the right-hand wall. It made the office seem young, hip, and busy, not the image projected by Ralph himself. In person Ralph's main characteristic was nice, but I'd never hurt him by saying so.

"Chester said you needed some help."

He grimaced as he stood up and hurried out of his office, returning with a second chair for me. "Here have a seat. I'm really glad you came. I'm in the middle of a twenty page newsletter for Bank of Balcones that has to be mailed right after Christmas, plus some year-end stockholder reports, so nothing else is getting done. There's a little backlog."

"Little backlog?" In advertising when you have a backlog you have real trouble. A client never hires you to do a campaign when you get around to it. They want it for their high season, their low season, a trade show, or whatever. But their request is usually that you have it done yesterday. It's an impossibility considering the limited availability of commercial advertising space with the major media, at least here in Austin, but we always did our best. *Backlog* wasn't a word I'd ever heard within the offices of Rose Sterling before. "So what exactly does that mean?" I asked.

He sighed and slumped in his chair. "We're in deep shit. My assistant quit a month ago and they haven't hired anyone to replace her. Audry thought she could save money, only with the party and the holidays and everything, we're so far behind it's not funny. We're short an artist and a layup person, and now our usual freelancers are gone for the holidays. With Desi dead . . ." The Ralph I remembered, a man who was easygoing, in charge, and always solid, had been replaced by someone who reminded me of Willy Loman. Tired, harassed, and frustrated.

"Can I see the hot list?" I asked.

He swung his chair around, and when he turned back he was holding two full pages.

"Are you serious?" I asked.

"At least we got all the Christmas campaigns finished in time; of course, I haven't seen my kids in a week, and my wife is so angry she refused to come to the party last night." He ran his hand over his head, rumpling his hair.

"So tell me what to do."

It didn't take him long to show me what had to be done immediately and what was only needed for tomorrow. We went through several client folders so I could see the most recent campaigns for each one. Then I stood up. I felt like a soldier thrust unexpectedly into battle. "Point me to a computer." There was no time to drive back to Prissy's.

He grabbed a pile of folders. "This way."

He trotted me to a tiny cubbyhole built with temporary walls of a rich red burlaplike material. There were no windows, and the secretarial chair was wobbly. "This was Desi's," he said. "You can work here."

I scanned the tiny space. The desk was clean, the same as the credenza since all of this had been stored elsewhere for the party. The only things in sight were those affixed to the modular walls: three snapshots stuck in the edge of one, a couple of Christmas cards, and some cheap plastic Mardi Gras beads held on with pushpins. There was also a small sign that read, "THE FIRST DRAFT OF EVERYTHING IS SHIT." ERNEST HEMINGWAY.

That is one of my favorite quotes, and it brought home to me that Desi Baker had been a living human being, and she and I had a lot in common.

Just Friday, two days before, she had worked here. She had typed on that keyboard, had looked at that quote. It was obvious she had not been ranked high on the agency's totem pole, but she was in the right space to move ahead. If Audry didn't block her way.

Again I remembered the note that had been pushed under the bathroom door. The one from "M" that was now at the police lab with my fingerprints on it.

It was only at that moment I realized the note hadn't been for me—it had been intended for Desi.

In a way I was relieved, but something else shivered through my body, too. Desi Baker and I had more in common than I'd known. What would the police think when they discovered that fact?

Ralph placed the large stack of files on the desk, then opened desk drawers, pulling out pens and pencils. He even put a box of white Posh Puffs on the file cabinet. "There. That should be everything you need," he said. "There are more client files in here." He pulled out a file drawer. "And if there's anything you can't find, I'll be in my office. Okay?"

I looked at him, seeing his discomfort.

"Ralph, it's okay." Only I wasn't sure it was.

"Oh, I know. I'll just stay long enough to get you started."

I sat down at the computer, which, thankfully, had all its cords reattached. I turned it on, then waited until it asked me for a password. "Any idea what that is?" I asked.

"She had two—I have a master one written down in my office. I'll be right back." As he whipped out, I typed in the word *Michael*. I don't know why; there was no premeditation on my part, it just seemed right for Desi.

The computer refused to let me in. I tried her first name, then *Baker,* and then the word *writer.*

The computer began setting up icons.

Apparently we'd had dreams in common, too.

Before the computer had finished loading programs, the phone rang. I answered it without thinking, my mind still trying to digest all this new information. "Rose Sterling, this is Jolie."

"Jolie, it's me, Ralph. The word is *bingo."*

"Thanks."

"I'll let you get right to work. And me, too. If you need anything, I'm at extension three-twelve."

"Got it."

"And don't forget the password."

"Bingo."

When I was little, third or fourth grade, I began making up stories. One summer in particular the neighborhood kids would gather in the evenings under a big pecan tree in our yard, and I would tell ghost stories. Not long after that my grandmother came for a visit, and one night when my parents were out and she was baby-sitting, I started telling her one of my stories. She responded with, "Jolene Berenski, if you think I have time for this nonsense, you're sadly mistaken. Any fool can make up tall tales, and if you don't believe me, you just ask your mama about your great-uncle Jack. Now, git. I'm busy."

It was a rude awakening, and I quit thinking that my stories were anything special. I still needed a creative outlet, though, so I tried out for the talent show at school where the teacher put me in a skit with some other girls. After the performance, while I was still backstage, Paul somebody-or-other's mother had looked straight at me and said, "It takes no talent whatsoever to act silly, and that's all you girls did up there." Paul played accordion.

It might not have been such a big deal except that my younger sister, Elise, played the piano and could sing. Beautifully. My older brother was an athlete, and wherever you found sweaty boys winning at any game, you'd find Win leading the way. Win was short for Winthrop, but nobody teased him about his name.

After that I made one last-ditch effort to find an arena where I could excel. I begged my mother to send me to a new art school. She finally relented. After only six classes the instructor took her aside when she came to pick me up. I'm sure I wasn't meant to hear, but I did. The instructor said it was a waste of money sending me to art classes—I had no visual artistic acuity and would be better off doing paint by numbers.

I retreated to my writing, only I didn't tell the stories out loud anymore. I wrote them on paper, and once accepted an F in English rather than turn in a story and let someone else judge it. Luckily my overall grade remained sufficient, because my test scores pulled up my average.

Writing was my joy, my solace, and even when I got over my shyness and early insecurities, which, of course, were replaced by adult insecurities, I kept my love of writing. I consider it a privilege to be able to put words on paper. Sometimes they aren't great words, or in great order, but I love the process even when it's a struggle and seems beyond my abilities.

My early training as a professional writer was in radio. When I discovered how fickle that world can be I moved into advertising, and my current job consists of writing and voicing radio news in Purple Sage. Everything is always on a deadline, and the one thing I had learned was that Jack London was right. "You can't wait for inspiration, you have to go after it with a club."

I stretched my wrists and started in. First I wrote two press releases, and admittedly they required more than one phone call to Ralph to ask questions and get a translation of someone's scrawled notes. And then I rewrote and rewrote them again. The third press release was for a client of Michael's, and his notes, written in heavy black ink, were easy to read. By that time I wasn't quite in the writing zone, but at least I knew there was one. I plunged into two radio campaigns, and realized I needed more information. I set the copy notes aside and dug into the folder for Bank of Balcones to see what they had done in the past. The first thing I found was a radio commercial written by Desi Baker.

It featured two squirrels discussing where to store their winter supply of nuts. One was partial to an old tree down on campus, while the other wanted a safety-deposit box at Bank of Balcones. According to Desi's production notes, the voices were to be sped up enough to make them sound cartoonish but still understandable. At the end, the bank president invited both squirrels and the listeners to drop by the bank, just to make sure it was secure enough.

Reading that script was like seeing into the mind of Desi. Clever and whimsical. I hadn't expected that humor, and it caused me to readjust my picture of her. She had been beautiful and funny. I sighed and plunged back into work. Using the same theme she had created, I wrote two more after-holiday commercials for the bank.

Next I turned to a magazine ad. It was complete except for the small square of body copy, so that was relatively easy. Everything I had written was still what I considered first draft, and I needed hard copies to edit. I sent all my work to the laser printer, then without thinking, pulled open a drawer looking for something to munch on. What I found was some trail mix. When I realized whose it was and where I was, I closed the drawer with a snap, almost catching my fingers.

I needed a break. My joints were stiffening; I stood and stretched. As I did I spotted the pictures on the modular wall. The first showed Desi with an older woman, presumably her mother, beside a wintry pond. Desi was younger, probably late teens, but much the same as the beautiful young woman I had seen. In the photo both mother and daughter were smiling, bundled up in winter clothes, their noses red from the cold. The second photo was of a tanned Desi, wearing short cutoffs, a tank top with a flannel shirt tied around her waist, and heavy hiking boots. Sunglasses hid her eyes but not the jubilant smile on her face. She was standing on what looked like the top of a mountain, deep blue sky behind her; her arms were raised in triumph.

The last picture was of a big yellow Labrador with his tongue hanging out and a bow perched incongruously on his head. A birthday cupcake was in front of him.

Desi Baker's life in three pictures.

A woman I'd never met was haunting me, perhaps because I was working in her office, touching all the things that she had touched, breathing into the same phone she had used just three days before.

I had to know more about Desi Baker, and if I could, I wanted to find out what caused Desi's death. There was only one person who might be able to tell me—good old Donna Katherine, our source of news and information. Better than a KSGE news bulletin.

❋ CHAPTER 8 ❋

Girl, i can't believe you're back here, just like you belong!"
Donna Katherine said when she saw me.

She'd been standing at a five-drawer filing cabinet in her office. Today her look was gypsy modern, a good choice for her tall frame and red hair. Her skirt was a wild print that reached almost to her ankles, which were encased in soft, black leather boots. With it she wore a deep turquoise sweater. On her ears were large gold hoops, and on her wrist were over a dozen matching bangles. Unfortunately her makeup was too heavy and it brought attention to the fact that she was no longer an attractive woman. "You thinkin' about movin' back in permanently?" she asked, a half smile on her lips.

I shook my head. "Absolutely not. I'll be here two or three days at the most," I said.

"That's because of that handsome husband of yours." She patted her chest. "Be still my heart."

"You are something."

She grinned, cleared her throat, and said, "Now, let's get down to some business. Chester told me he wants to treat you like contract labor. I have everything you need to get paid right here." Her bracelets jingled as she pulled three sheets of paper from her out box. "I filled them in since Chester said you were going to be so busy and all. All you have to do is put your John Hancock on them."

"What, you didn't sign them for me? Seems to me you used to forge everybody else's signature—"

"I never! Jolie Wyatt, there are some things it'd be a lot smarter to forget—if you get my drift." She gave me the evil eye.

"I've got it."

"Smart gal. Just sign here and here," she said, pointing to sticky tabs attached to the spots, "and we're all done but the crying."

I looked the papers over quickly, found everything accurate, and signed where she'd indicated. "That was easy." I handed her back the forms, which she slipped into a folder that was prepared and waiting.

"We aim to please." She pulled out the second drawer of the cabinet and filed the folder. "Fill out a time sheet when you finish. We pay in forty-five days, fifteen longer than we used to, and I'll just mail you the check."

"Fine," I said. As she sat down, I reached for a second chair. "Mind if I visit a minute?"

Donna Katherine used to be the chief source of information at Rose Sterling. For example, when a rumor was going around that the offices were to be remodeled, she knew who was doing the work and what the time schedule was. She also knew that Michael and Chester were selecting the colors and styles. Donna Katherine explained that Audry wasn't getting involved because that was stereotypically a woman's role, and Audry had refused to play it. By the time the memo about the remodeling came out, for me it was junk mail.

"What's on your mind?" she asked.

"Desi Baker. Have you heard anything from the police?"

Donna Katherine scooted her chair closer to mine and whispered, "Let's take a little break to the ladies' room." She looked around. "Even these temporary walls have ears."

The bathroom was almost identical to the one just a floor below, except that the accent tiles were black and deep rose. It was a nice change.

Donna Katherine walked along the row of stalls and peeked under each one, then rejoined me at the mirrors. "Don't sit up there," she said, gesturing toward the faux marble counter. "The faucets all leak. I reckon management doesn't get to the ladies' room on our floor, although you'd think Audry would have gotten it fixed. Woman gets everything else she wants. Maybe she's never noticed because she doesn't pee like the rest of us mortals."

I wasn't going to respond to that. "So tell me, has anyone heard from the police?"

Donna Katherine rolled her eyes. "They were here first thing this morning, and I'm tellin' you, it was not pretty. Not that I was in the room, mind you. It was a private conference with the royal family." Donna Katherine's office was next to the conference room, though. "First thing that cop said was that it wasn't a normal heart attack. He suggested that maybe Desi had committed suicide. Chester wouldn't stand for that. Not for one minute."

Chester believed in people. Suicide was something outside the world as he knew it.

"But what do you think?" I asked. "Did she kill herself?"

There was a long pause while Donna Katherine considered the possibility. Finally she said, "I don't know; but Desi could be moody sometimes." She shrugged the thought away. "Anyhow, I figure this Bohles was on a fishing expedition, as my daddy used to call it. When no one went for his suicide theory, he said it was more likely a drug overdose."

"Drugs? What kind of drugs?"

"He said he suspected cocaine."

"Cocaine?" It made no more sense than saying Santa Claus had slipped down the chimney and given her the drugs. "Cocaine?" I repeated. I had seen no signs of it in that other bathroom.

As I thought about it, there was something even more out of kilter—Desi Baker hadn't looked like a woman on cocaine. She had been poised and clear-eyed, and slender, too, but well muscled to the extreme, as if she worked out hard and was proud of the effect. Her black dress had skimmed along her body, and her arms had been taut and firm as she had stood up and delivered her speech about Chester. Drugs aren't part of that healthful regimen.

"Desi didn't look like someone who did drugs. Does it seem possible to you?" I asked.

Donna Katherine didn't even consider her answer. "Girlfriend, I know nothin' about drugs. I smoked pot once in my life and spent the rest of that night in the emergency room. I'm allergic to the stuff, and that one experience was enough to keep me real straight for a real long time. Like my whole life."

I was no more experienced than she was. I'd smoked pot with my first husband, Steve, a few times until I became pregnant. I decided that the natural high of having a healthy baby was far better than an artificial evening of silliness, so that was the end of my experimentation.

"When Chester and Audry heard that word *cocaine,* that's when Chester got real firm with the cop," Donna Katherine went on. "Chester told him he had friends on the city council, which he does, and friends high up in the police department, which he does, and that Sergeant Bohles better find out the truth about how Desi died pretty damn quick and stop trying to palm off these scurrilous rumors." She grinned. "Nice word that, *scurrilous.* I looked it up. 'Low indecency. Abuse.' Sure put that cop on notice."

"I guess."

"Bohles told Chester it was the medical examiner's office that had the final decision, and those folks usually take up to a week for an autopsy. Chester said something like, 'Perhaps you should try to hurry them.' Bohles was pretty nice about the whole thing when you figure the kind of pressure they were putting on him. He said he'd try to get things moving. Course, Chester called some old bud of his, anyway."

What little I knew of law enforcement and police procedure came from experiences in Purple Sage, admittedly a much smaller place than Austin. There, if the sheriff's office sent anything to the DPS lab, it could take up to a week for results. It wasn't because of lack of caring, it was simply the heavy workload. Apparently the medical examiner's office in Austin had the same problems, and this being Christmas week no doubt made things worse.

"This could take a long time," I said.

"Maybe not." She shrugged, then reached up to scratch her neck. The movement set up a soft clattering as her bracelets clashed together. "Bohles said he'd call or come by first thing tomorrow. I figure we'll see."

"How did the others take it?" I meant Audry and Michael, but I couldn't say names.

"I was real proud of Audry," Donna Katherine said with a grin. "She just told that policeman that she wasn't buyin' any of his conclusions so far, and that was that. As for Michael . . ." She lowered her voice. "He was all but silent when that cop was around, but I was standing near the water fountain in the hall about an hour later, and I swear the sounds comin' from the men's room made me think there was some new Wailin' Wall in there. Weepin' and gnashin' of teeth like you never heard. He hasn't been back since, so he must've left. I figure he'll just say he was seein' clients."

I was wholeheartedly glad I hadn't been at the agency that morning.

"Oh, and I was going to tell you last night," Donna Katherine said, "I think Desi Baker was special friends, if you get my meaning, with someone in the agency. But I figure you know that by now."

"Michael."

"Right."

I let out a breath. Donna Katherine hadn't known about Michael and me after all, or she wouldn't have told me about Desi. I hoped.

"So, Jolie," she went on, "you're a big mystery writer now, what do you think Desi died of?"

"Not a big mystery writer, just an aspirant." But I had been mulling over her question for some time. I always came back to the same answer, and I wished I could feel more sure of it. "I've thought of some kind of poison. You know, something that she accidentally ingested." I have read up on poisons for my writing, but it's a vast subject and almost anything can be poisonous if

66

given to someone who has an allergic reaction. "I suppose it could have been natural causes, like a brain tumor, but in the bathroom she'd vomited."

"Wait, how about this one," Donna Katherine said, leaning against the sink. "Maybe she was allergic to one of the hors d'oeuvres. Of course, we didn't have much but fruit, raw veggies, and cheese. And that steamship round of beef."

"There were rolls. And alcohol. I wonder if she had too much liquor and died from that." I hardly had to think about it. "No, couldn't be. She was perfectly sober, or at least she looked sober, when she was on the dais. How could she be dead drunk an hour later?" It was an unfortunate choice of words.

Of course, there was another option—someone could have purposely given Desi Baker a poison.

"Sorry, gal, but I've got to run," Donna Katherine said, looking at her watch, straightening up, and smoothing her skirt. "I'll let you know if I hear anything."

"Thanks, I'd appreciate it."

We left together and when we entered the agency, Donna Katherine went toward her office. The reception area was empty and I assumed Amber had finally gone home. There was a note on her desk with my name on it; I picked it up and began reading as I walked around the partition. It was from Matt, asking if I would give him a call at Prissy's.

Unfortunately with my head down, and my attention on the note, I walked straight into someone.

"Excuse me," I muttered, then detected a wave of the musky aftershave that pulled me into a distant past. I didn't need to raise my head to know that Michael Sherabian was right there, inches from me. "Oh. Michael. I'm sorry." And then I had to look up.

His normally dark skin seemed pale. He appeared stunned. Not from running into me, but I assumed from the bigger shock of Desi's death.

"How are you doing?" I asked. "Are you all right?"

He stared at me for a moment, then said in a low-pitched

voice, "Yes, of course. Why wouldn't I be?" Anger, sorrow, and resignation were all crammed into those few words, although on the surface he appeared poised.

"I'm sorry." It felt inadequate. "I didn't mean—"

"This is difficult for all of us. It's hard to lose someone you've worked with, especially because Desi was a unique person. Ask anyone at the agency, anyone who knew her."

"Well, if there's anything I can do—"

He stared at me for a long time, his eyes so intense I could feel a surge of heat that coursed through my body.

"Actually, it's like a miracle that you're here," he said. "Just when I need someone, you're at the agency. Come and talk with me?"

"Of course." Michael had been the one to help me through my father's death; I was obligated to be there for him. "In your office?"

He shook his head. "There's a new little coffeehouse not far from here. Very quiet and private."

Coffee with Michael? My warning sensors prickled.

There had been so many times in the past when we had gone off to have coffee together. Just the two of us, slipping out of the agency, pretending even to ourselves that it was business.

I brushed that aside; I had changed, grown, and so had he. There was no reason not to go.

"Now?" I asked.

"Yes. That would be good; I have the time." He tilted his head to watch me, our eyes held, and it was like the fleeting moment at the top of a roller coaster with all its quivery anticipation. Next would come the incredible downhill rush that no one could stop. "And thank you," he added.

Like a cobra he had me mesmerized; even my breathing was shallow. "Of course. I'll have to get my coat." But I didn't move, couldn't move. "Are you sure?" I asked, perhaps more of myself than him.

"Of course." He held me with his eyes, but didn't touch me again, he didn't have to. I could sense him as clearly as if our skin were touching in a thousand places.

I wanted to comfort him, but just to talk.

Just to talk, I reminded myself again. But would there be that moment when, just as in the past, our hands would accidently brush? Some part of me grew shivery at the memory.

"Would you like me to get your coat for you?" he asked.

If Michael went for my coat, I would be committed to leaving.

Once he returned with it, he would slide it over my shoulders, just as he had so many times in the past. It was impossible not to think of how his hands used to slide along the collar on the pretext of straightening it, and how my body would begin to vibrate in response to his fingers gently brushing my neck.

Clearly I saw that this was how all the problems had started the first time, but surely I was beyond that now. Stronger than that. I could talk to Michael without having anything happen.

I tried to break whatever mystical hold he had on me, but my body wouldn't respond. It was an effort to force out words. "No, I'll get my coat."

He nodded, his eyes still watching mine. "Then I'll meet you in the parking garage. Second level up by the elevator."

Just the way we used to meet.

He turned to leave, and the finality of his move jerked me out of whatever spell had held me captive. I thought of Matt.

"Michael," I called. He turned, and I spoke quickly. "I'm sorry, I've changed my mind. I don't have the time."

Confusion crossed his face. "Jolie, you said you'd go." It was voiced with innocence, as if he honestly couldn't understand my reluctance.

I looked away and forced myself back a step; it may have appeared to be a retreat, but it felt like a safety precaution, like moving away from a live bomb. "I'm sorry, Michael, I don't think I'd better."

His eyes searched my face, looking for something. He seemed to find it. "You're angry."

"No, not at all." I shook my head quickly. "I don't belong here," I said. "I feel like all of this, you, everything is from some dark part of my past that should never have happened. Even a conversation—" At the expression on his face I stopped. "Michael, I'm sorry. I know you must be in pain, but I'm not . . . it just . . . I can't do anything to help." I was stammering, and I knew it. "I have to get to work—there's just no time."

Michael stared in disbelief, then his elegant nostrils flared. "But there was time to gossip in the ladies' room with Donna Katherine?"

Before I could think of a way to escape, Michael's eyes went soft and his voice became gentle. "Jolie, I'm sorry. That was unforgivable." He reached for my hand, kissed the palm, and hurried off toward his office.

I probably stood there a solid minute, staring after him, before I realized I had to move.

As a child I had once seen a Hollywood film device for making people look like they were sinking into quicksand. The actor stood on a raised platform, and under him was a flattish box of mud, with a heavy rubber center that had two crosscuts. Initially the actor positioned his body on the center cuts, actually standing on the raised platform. Then slowly the platform would lower so that eventually the actor was "enveloped" by the muck.

I could almost feel the platform going down under me. Rose Sterling Advertising was sucking me back in. It mattered to me that the agency was behind in the work for its clients, and somehow it had become my responsibility to bail them out. And now Michael—

Coffee. Just coffee. But not with Michael.

I was having feelings for these people again. It was the last thing I'd envisioned when I'd accepted the invitation to the party.

The front door opened and the balls on the Christmas tree swung together in the whoosh of air. I stepped around the partition to cover the front desk, hoping my face didn't show all the things I'd been experiencing. It was Audry Sterling-Sherabian who'd come into the agency.

"Jolie," she said, when she saw me. "You're exactly the person I want to talk to."

✦ CHAPTER 9 ✦

I FOLLOWED her as she knew I would. With unerring accuracy, Audry skirted the cubicle where I'd been working and went straight to the laser printer in the hallway outside. She picked up all the copies in the tray, flipped through them quickly, left behind those with someone else's initials, and said, "Is this everything you've written so far?"

"That's everything."

I had to wonder if she knew everyone's working habits so well, or just mine. And how much more did she know of the things that went on in the agency?

"Let's talk in my office." She led the way.

Audry's office was large, but then, it needed to be to accommodate her massive desk, topped with a slab of black marble veined with white. Three walls were burgundy, the accessories all sleek and black, from the floor lamp to the bookends on the shelves. There was a splash or two of dark turquoise for accent, but very few; even her computer was black.

It would have been like a dungeon, except the back wall was glass with a view of downtown Austin. I could see the river as it meandered below us; even in winter there was an unspoken invitation in the running paths and biking trails along its banks.

Without a word, Audry gestured to a black leather visitor's chair while she sat behind her desk. She began reading through the pages in her hand.

Sitting there in my low chair with her massive desk in front of me, I felt like a child who'd been called to the principal's office, a child who was guilty as charged. Audry finished the first page, started on the second, and frowned first at the paper, then briefly at me. I wondered if she hated me. She had good reason to.

I'd even understand if she did, because I had hated my first husband's girlfriend.

I'd never even suspected her existence until, late one night when Jeremy was just a month old, Steve had come home and told me he was leaving. There had been no discussion, he was in a hurry. After all, Candy was waiting downstairs in the car.

With only the dim glow of the teddy-bear night-light to relieve the blackness, I had rocked Jeremy as I listened to Steve pack in the other room. I'd been at such a disadvantage suffering with postpartum blues, my pregnancy weight gain, and no job. I'd had no weapons to fight with, and so he'd walked out the door leaving $43.27 in the checking account, the rent due, and no car. But all those things piled together weren't as bad as the hole he had left behind. Jeremy had never had a father until Matt came along just four years ago. I'd done everything I could to make up for it, but I was afraid Jeremy had suffered in ways that I didn't even know about.

As for me, I'd never been the homecoming-queen type, but when Steve left, my self-image shattered. Even now, sixteen years later, I sometimes found myself reacting out of the old insecurities Steve's defection had caused.

Looking at Audry, so cool, so self-assured, I couldn't help but wonder if underneath there was proof of the damage that I had done to her. At that moment I would have given a lot to undo the past and erase my relationship with Michael, but my remorse wouldn't make a whit of difference to the pain I had inflicted. My only saving grace was that when Audry convinced Michael to try and repair their marriage, I had stepped aside. There had been a brief phone conversation between Michael and me, but nothing more.

I'd always wanted to apologize to Audry, to let her know how truly sorry I was, but I could never find the right moment. Certainly not when Michael first went back to her because then I had been the wounded party. Later it had seemed too late, like bringing up the past for no good reason. Yet even now, I could feel myself squirming with guilt.

Audry's expression changed as she went through the next several sheets of paper. At one point she almost smiled; twice she nodded. When she was finished she picked up all the sheets and handed them across the desk to me.

"Very nice," she said. We were back in the land of polite, where façades were kept firmly in place. "One suggestion—the press release on Mangason's charity Christmas gift is too terse. It reads like a news story."

"It is a news story."

"It needs lightening up. Add some humor, a twist of some kind."

Before I could defend myself further, she went on. "You're very good, but then you always were. I like that bank spot. Nola's out today, so I'll fax it to them this afternoon for approval."

"Thank you."

"I'm the one who needs to thank you." She leaned back in her chair and seemed to relax slightly. "You didn't have to work during your vacation; I'm sure the extra money won't even be noticed at your house." Her quick glance took in my cashmere sweater and the heavy gold balance bracelet that Matt had given me for our anniversary. "Certainly not like before."

"No," I said. "But when your dad called this morning he said he needed help. He'd do the same for me. He certainly always has in the past."

I thought I heard a touch of envy as she said, "He's wonderful with people."

"Yes, he is. Is he in today?"

"He's delivering Christmas baskets. He's almost completely retired now."

"And you're running the agency?"

She nodded. "We moved back from Atlanta last year. I think the change will work well, once everyone has adjusted."

"Who's running the Atlanta office?"

With the light behind her it was hard to tell, but it appeared she stiffened before she said, "We're downsizing Atlanta. There's no need for a full staff; what with E-mail and computers, almost everything can be done from here. We'll keep one account executive and one artist."

Downsizing, rightsizing, capsizing. Business as usual in the nineties. I was very glad that I was out of it, rather than a potential victim to the mercenary slashing that was going on.

I started to say something more, ask how business really was and how she was doing, but Audry stood up. Maybe she sensed that we were treading close to personal communication. "Thank you, again," she said with a quick smile. "Even if you're here just as a favor to my father, you're helping us all."

"You're welcome. I'm glad I could do some good for you."

The words only hinted at my regrets, and the protectiveness I felt toward her. There wasn't time for more, because she reached for the phone and began dialing; for all her toughness, in some ways Audry was very vulnerable.

I headed straight back to my little cubby, shifting all my attention to the offending news release as I went. It started out well enough, but as I went through it I realized Audry had been right, it was more like a terse news bulletin than an inviting story. Damn.

Many hours later I left Rose Sterling. I was feeling pulled in a dozen directions as I drove home through the dark sea of traffic. When I arrived at Prissy's I wanted to run up to our little apartment and shower, a long shower that would wash away all the feelings and needs of Rose Sterling Advertising, but unfortunately there wasn't time.

I hadn't seen Michael again, although Chester had stopped by late in the afternoon to give me a warm hug and a key to the offices since I would be needed again the following morning. The key felt as heavy as lead, weighing down my purse, a physical reminder that I was back at Rose Sterling whether I liked it or not. It took the entire drive to Prissy's to break free of the hold the agency had on me. The cold winter air helped, as did the walk from the drive to the patio.

Once there I stopped to glance through the French doors into Prissy's living room. A grouping of poinsettias brightened a corner of the fireplace, and pine boughs graced with glittering Christmas balls were draped across the mantel. It was like watching a play through a proscenium, a Noel Coward play, with Prissy and Matt looking elegant as they sipped coffee in the beautifully decorated house.

Prissy's husband, Ross, was sitting on the couch, his long rangy legs stretched in front of him. Beside him was another man I'd never met before. He appeared to be about the same age as Ross, possibly even a few years older, late fifties, early sixties, but of a totally different type. With his thick silver hair and tanned skin, he looked like an actor. His eyes were such an intense blue I could see the color from outside; they were set off by the pale blue sweater he was wearing.

Presumably he was the owner of the classic bathtub Porsche that was parked in the driveway, its smooth body shimmering silver in the streetlight. A rich man's car, my father used to call such automobiles. Not because the initial cost was so high, although it certainly was these days, but because the upkeep was tremendous and, according to my dad, you had to have a second car to drive while your expensive car spent most of its life in the shop.

With one last martyred sigh, I dashed across the cold patio. The house was warm inside and smelled like Christmas as I joined the gathering.

"Jolie, hi." Matt stood up, and I moved into the circle of his arms, getting a welcome-home hug that I needed. He gave me a quick kiss before saying, "How was your day?"

"Oh, fine," I said, trying to dismiss it with a shrug. "Mostly it was productive. And yours?"

"Okay."

As I slipped off my jacket Prissy began the introductions. "Jolie, this is a, uh, an old friend of ours. He just recently divorced. Peter Javitz—"

"I should have introduced you—" Matt began.

In the jumble of words, their guest, who was already up off the couch, held out his hand to me and said, "Just call me Pete." We shook. His grip was firm and his smile dazzling. "Matt was bragging about you earlier," he said.

"I pay him to do that," I said as I sat on the love seat beside Matt.

"He said you have a book coming out. Congratulations, that's a tough field to crack from what I hear."

"Well, I think so, but I may have done everything wrong at first," I said with a smile. "Do you work with Ross?" I asked.

"We don't work together," Ross explained, gesturing with one of his long thin arms. "But Pete is the one who got me started in consulting." He seemed annoyed about it, although Pete laughed.

"You love it. Fly in, work a few miracles, fly out. And get paid very well for it—I can't think of a better life. You've even built up a clientele right here in Austin, so you don't have to travel that much, you lucky dog."

"That's easy for you to say."

Prissy explained, "Pete is taking an early retirement, and while he's in the process of the sale, any of the clients he can't accommodate, he's sending to Ross."

"It's a mixed blessing," Ross said.

There was something going on. Pete's conviviality appeared forced next to Ross's barely concealed dislike of the man. I wondered what that was all about.

"Retirement," Prissy was saying. "I can't imagine people our age retiring. My father retired. My grandfather."

"Call it a lengthy sabbatical. From which I'm never returning."

Having done what she could to smooth the conversation,

Prissy offered me coffee. After I declined she said, "A glass of wine? I have a new white from Château St. Jean."

"That would be great."

"Are you starving?" She stood up, and I got the impression she was relieved to have an excuse to leave the room. "I have some hors d'oeuvres."

I followed her to the kitchen.

"I'm not really hungry." I was dying to ask what the story was on Pete Javitz. "Can I help?" I asked.

"There's really nothing to do." She seemed distracted as she scooped warm appetizers from the oven and slid them onto a red tray with bright green Christmas trees. She set them on the counter, frowned, then said, "Actually, you might get some napkins from the pantry while I pour your wine."

"Be happy to." I found some green napkins to complement the tray and placed them on the side of it. "By the way, where's Jeremy?" I asked. "And Stephanie and Christopher?"

"They should be back anytime. They wanted to let Christopher see the ice rink at Northcross Mall, and then they were going to rent a couple of movies for this evening. I think Stephanie wanted to supervise the movie selection, and Jeremy wanted to make sure they got something besides Disney films."

Now that I was at the back of the kitchen, I asked, "So who is Peter Javitz, besides an old friend?"

Prissy looked at me and I could see her weighing her answer. It seemed she was just about to talk when she tipped her head in a way more suited to a Barbie doll. "Oh, you know, just an old acquaintance." She turned to me, wineglass in one hand, tray in the other. "Ready?"

So much for that. "Sure." I followed her back into the living room with its crackling fire.

The men were talking about the company Matt had been looking at, and I sank onto the love seat, grateful that I didn't have to join in. Prissy handed me the wine, and I sipped it slowly, letting the conversation simmer around me.

After a few minutes, maybe it was longer, I wasn't paying attention, the front door opened and Christopher came toddling in.

"Hey, Christopher," Matt said. "Did you get some good movies?"

"The Rescuers—" Christopher stopped and looked around the room at the assembled group. "Oh, no. Peoples!" He ducked behind the Christmas tree.

Jeremy and Stephanie hurried in. Jeremy was carrying a sack of movies, and while he stopped to shut the door, Stephanie brushed past him. "Pete! I'm sorry we're late." She went straight into his arms. Before my mind could accept their very warm hug, she planted a kiss on his lips.

His blue eyes glowed as if he'd just spotted the seventh wonder. "Hello, beautiful."

I waited for Stephanie and Peter to break apart. To tell us that they'd been joking. For them to say something, as if they'd just mimicked a movie scene, but it didn't happen. Pete sat back on the couch, pulling Stephanie down with him.

"Christopher," she said. "Did you say hello to Mr. Javitz?"

He peeked around the tree. "Hello, Mr. Javitz."

Pete kept his arm around Stephanie's waist as he leaned forward to say, "How's it going, young man?"

"Fine."

I looked at Prissy to see what she thought about all this. It was obvious from her expression; she wanted to wrench her daughter away from Peter Javitz and send him packing. Permanently. But being the perfect hostess, she took a breath and her face became placid again, as if I'd imagined the anger.

Nevertheless, I was feeling angry. Angry at Pete for taking advantage of Stephanie, and at Stephanie for behaving so uncharacteristically. And all the while the word *trophy* was screaming in my head. As in trophy wife, or trophy girlfriend.

I am always appalled when an older man divorces the woman who'd had his children and helped make him successful, and then replaces her with a trophy wife. I've seen it happen to two of my friends, and in my opinion that's two too many. Both times when the husbands walked out, they walked almost directly into the apartments of young women in their twenties.

They act as if the practical lifespan of a woman is fifty. As if after that she is no longer up to the current standards. The worst of it is that it's the young women who perpetuate the myth in their quest for the money and reflected status of the older man. If only they realized that their time is coming.

I watched Stephanie pick a piece of lint off Peter's sweater. I couldn't dismiss Stephanie as if she were some little gold-digging bimbo. She might be acting like one, but I loved her dearly. She didn't need the money, so what did she see in a man the same age as her father? A father figure?

"Hungry?" Pete was asking Stephanie.

"Of course. Aren't I always?"

He laughed and gave her a quick hug. I wanted to slap him.

"Good. I have a wonderful new restaurant for us to try. I'd like your opinion of it." He glanced toward Ross and Prissy. Ross was poker-faced; Prissy was doing her best not to glower. "We'll see all you nice folks later." He stood up and grabbed his jacket off the couch beside him, then helped Stephanie up.

She went over to Christopher, who was now poking around under the Christmas tree. "You be a good little bug, okay? Grandma Prissy's going to put you to bed, and I'll bet Aunt Jolie would read you a book, too."

"I know," he said, hardly even looking at her.

"Don't I even get a kiss good night?"

He turned. "Good night, Mommy." He kissed her quickly, then scampered back to the far side of the tree.

"And stay out of those presents."

"I'm just hidin'! In case Madame Medusa comes here."

None of the other adults said a word, which made me suspect they were thinking about other things, primarily Stephanie and Peter.

Stephanie kept the mood light. "Well, don't let her find you and don't open any presents." She stood up, waved to the rest of us, but before she left she leaned close to her mother and said quietly, "I'll be home early. Remember your promise."

"I remember," Prissy said, a touch of annoyance lacing her charm.

Stephanie watched her seriously for a moment, as if judging her mother's truthfulness. Prissy added, "Don't worry, I'll be here the whole time."

"Thanks," Stephanie said, before she gave us all one last smile and swept out the door on Pete's arm.

"That's her boyfriend?" Jeremy asked, speaking for the first time since they'd returned.

I shot him one of those looks. Prissy glared at him, too, although her anger was more likely intended for Pete than Jeremy. "Unfortunately," she said, "it is. Temporarily."

It was later, much later when Matt and I were in bed, that I asked him what he thought.

"I don't know. I guess I think Stephanie's making a mistake. Maybe not."

"Remember Tom and Beverly?" Friends of ours in Purple Sage.

"It's Tom and Leigh."

I refrained from making a gagging noise. "Now it is."

When the divorce between Tom and Beverly had first occurred, Matt and I had had differing thoughts on it. He believed that Beverly had changed from a bright, funny woman into a shrew, and it was amazing Tom had put up with her behavior as long as he had. The fact that it was a hormonal imbalance as a result of menopause didn't sway Matt's opinion. "Does that mean Tom should have to take that kind of treatment? No, sorry. You can't condone verbal abuse for any reason, and that's what she was doing."

When I reminded Matt that Tom had a daughter two years older than his new girlfriend, Matt had merely shaken his head. I never could get Matt to denounce Tom as an idiot, which I was perfectly willing to do, although he did finally say, "I don't know how Tom communicates with Leigh. It's the ultimate generation gap."

Now we were looking at the gap, and a similar relationship, from another point of view. "Stephanie's perpetuating the obsolete-wife myth," I said. I was ready to fight this one all night if necessary, as if by convincing Matt, I could stop my own fears that someday I would be treated as if I were archaic. "She could do so much better. Someone younger. Someone willing to share her dreams and help her reach them."

Matt made a sound as if he were coming out of sleep. Or dropping off. "Maybe Pete can give her what she needs. He seems devoted."

"Lust and devotion are two different things."

Matt, who had both arms around me, snuggled my body closer to his. "How do you know that?"

"Because I'm very wise."

"Hmmm, I see. Well, I'm both lustful and devoted."

"So?"

"And you're very sexy."

"You're just trying to distract me."

"How am I doing?"

I didn't even have to think about it. "Keep working at it, I think you'll have it in a minute."

An hour later Matt was asleep and I was awake staring at the ceiling. I had come close to dozing off after we'd made love, but there was simply too much rustling through my head. Bits of anger mixed with worry about Stephanie refused to rest. Concerns about the agency and curiosity about Desi Baker kept after me, too. The more I tried to sleep, the faster the thoughts seemed to scurry through my mind.

As carefully as possible I slipped out of bed and dressed in clothes that were lying on the chair. I would make some warm milk in the house and perhaps that would help me sleep. Still in the dark, I took Prissy's house key off the hook near the door and slid outside, quiet as a ghost. It was colder than I'd expected, so

I moved quickly, silently skimming down the stairs. A night-light from Prissy's kitchen was on, and it dimly illuminated the patio so I could see the two tubs of pansies that flanked the back door, the start of the trellis against the far wall, and the dead leaves scattered along the tiles.

As I turned to make my way to the back door, I could see that a man was there before me. He was silhouetted in the weak light from the kitchen, and he was watching me.

❧ CHAPTER 10 ❧

Bᴇꜰᴏʀᴇ ɪ could speak, he opened the door and stepped out. "Hello."

After the initial jolt of finding a man I didn't know, I realized that his face was vaguely familiar. Not someone I knew . . . someone I had seen.

"I have an advantage over you," he said, moving into the reflected kitchen light. "I know that you're Jolie, but you don't know that I'm Todd." He smiled again, held out his hand, and said, "Todd Rainey. My mom was a friend of Prissy's."

He was in his mid-twenties, and the reason he looked familiar was that he resembled his mother, Olivia Rainey, whose smiling face I had seen many times in the picture on Prissy's dresser. Olivia had been Prissy's best friend all the way back to junior high school. She had died just eight months before of breast cancer. "You're Olivia Rainey's son," I said.

His eyes were much like his mother's, and at the mention of her name they briefly dipped closed, I assumed to hide his sadness. Then he looked at me and offered a simple, "Yes."

I remembered Prissy talking about how, after marriage, the two women hadn't kept in close contact until Olivia divorced maybe fifteen or sixteen years back. She'd been living somewhere in the East. Maryland? Pennsylvania? I knew, too, that Olivia had moved home to Texas for a while and then they had done some traveling together. Most had been around the state, but they'd also cruised the Bahamas. Ross had been working;

Prissy claimed it was better that way since he wouldn't want to know what kinds of things they'd gotten up to.

This was Todd's first Christmas without his mother.

"Hi, nice to meet you. Prissy didn't tell us you were coming; you're here for the holidays?" I asked.

Todd nodded. "It was kind of iffy until this morning. Work and school and all. Getting time away is tough sometimes, but you probably know how that is." He waited for my nod, then added, "I got here just after you and Matt went up to bed."

Ah. Something tickled the back of my mind.

"Where do you live?" I asked.

"Takoma Park in Maryland. I grew up there, then we moved out here for a couple of years, so I could go to UT." The University of Texas at Austin. "Only after mom died"—again his eyes dipped closed—"I've kind of been floating; you know, here, there. We . . . I still have the house in Maryland, but I don't stay there much."

His pain was still alive and I didn't know how to respond to it.

"Prissy's mentioned you." I wrapped my arms around my shoulders to hold the chill at bay, and still I shivered.

Todd noticed. "You're freezing. Were you going in?" He gestured toward Prissy's kitchen.

"I was, but I really should get some sleep. I'm working in the morning." I rubbed my forehead. "I think I just needed to clear my brain. This cold certainly did that."

He laughed, and I could see his breath in soft puffs. "I was clearing my head, too. I could give you my jacket—" He started to pull it off.

"No, thanks. I need to get back up to bed. I'm sure I'll see you later."

"You will." He put the brown leather jacket back on, and zipped it as he spoke. "Prissy made it sound like the holidays are going to be great. I have friends to see, too."

"And I have to work," I said, with a quick smile. "No rest for the wicked, I guess. Well, good night."

84

"Good night," he called softly, as I turned to go.

Todd Rainey, son of an old friend, spending Christmas with the family. Prissy collected strays for every holiday, at least that was my impression, and Todd would certainly find himself lonely this year, even among friends. However, I had this sneaking suspicion that Prissy might be doing some matchmaking, perhaps to ease old Pete out of the picture.

Interesting speculations were drifting through my head, but they were as soft and slow as my movements as I undressed, pulled on silk pajamas, and crawled back into bed. Matt didn't even stir when I slid the covers over me, and finally went to sleep.

The out basket on the credenza had been emptied once, and there were already three more scripts in it, ready for production. It was amazing what Ralph and I were accomplishing with me doing the writing and him producing.

Audry had come in like a whirlwind, grabbing copy, picking up phone messages, and issuing commands all at one time. Then she'd swept out with hardly a glance at me.

Michael had arrived shortly after that, and he had made a point of coming into my cubby to say good morning. His eyes had traveled around the small space, taking in the pictures on the wall and the Mardi Gras beads, but then he had focused his attention back to me.

"How are you this morning?" he'd asked.

"I'm fine. How about you?"

Michael had smiled gently, studying my face. "Still the same as ever; aren't we all?"

"Actually, I've changed a lot. I've grown up, sold a book—"

"So I heard. Congratulations. Am I in it?" He was teasing me, those playful eyes dancing with a mischievous joy most adults have forgotten.

"Guess you'll just have to buy several copies and find out, won't you?"

"Tell me the name and I will."

I gave him the name, even wrote it down for him. Michael read the slip of paper, then pulled over a second chair and sat down, resting his briefcase on his lap. "Oh, and here, I have something for you."

My heart nearly stopped beating as he popped open his briefcase. How often in the past had Michael done exactly the same thing, opening the briefcase and pulling out a Hershey's chocolate Kiss? He would place it on the desk in front of me, leaning forward to breathe softly into my ear, "For the real thing, meet me in the parking lot. Ten minutes."

I would always shake my head no, protest in some way, but Michael would touch my neck, or stroke my arm, and I would give in. He'd leave then, quickly, and I would check my makeup, my hair, and wipe off my lipstick. After a few minutes, which seemed interminable, I would scoot out of the office, saying breezily to the receptionist, "I'm running down to the deli. Be back in a few."

There was a second elevator in the far corner of the parking garage that had a small enclosed waiting area. Very few people used that means of access to the building, and so Michael and I would meet there. Our time together was always rushed, always breathy, as if we couldn't pause even to take in air. We would say those repetitive phrases that lovers always make new, then kiss and hold each other as if each moment might be our last. A few more kisses, then we would break apart.

"This isn't right," I would say. "I hate this."

"And I love you." Michael would touch my chin gently, kiss me lightly, before adding, "Maybe after work."

"No. Absolutely not." Then I would stop. "Maybe."

I was always fighting to get away, even as I was wanting to get closer.

Now I watched as Michael shuffled some things in his briefcase. He must have heard my intake of air, because he looked up and smiled. "I thought about bringing you chocolate, but—"

"But I'm happily married," I said quickly. "And so are you."

He looked sad. "Yes." Then he brought out two sheets of paper with notes for new commercials.

"And there was Desi," I added brazenly.

He paused, first puzzled, then there was another emotion I couldn't identify. "Desi and I weren't lovers. We never had been," he said. "It wasn't that kind of—"

"Don't, Michael. You don't have to tell me, and I don't want to know."

"I want you to understand, Jolie—"

"There's no need. Really." I had promised myself that for as long as I stayed at Rose Sterling, I would keep my distance from Michael Sherabian, and it should be easy to do. "It's better if I don't know." I reached out a hand and took the papers from him. "Here, I'll take them. When do you need these? Does it say?"

He stood reluctantly, an injured expression on his face. "I didn't mean to hurt you. I really—"

"Michael, it would be better if I could just write. Work. You know."

"Sure. Whatever you say." But he left with that sad look still in place.

I forced myself to focus on the writing. The notes he'd given me had everything I needed to know, and I placed them at the side of my computer while I went back to what I'd been working on. Just as I had placed Michael aside when he had gone back to Audry.

It's hell when the skeletons in your closet start to dance again.

Two hours later Ralph departed for a recording session at one of the TV stations, leaving instructions that if I had time, I was to help with the client newsletter that was consuming him. We both knew that was wishful thinking.

At least all of the copy I'd written the day before had been approved and turned over to the art director. There was still much to finish before I could leave, but the most urgent work was getting done.

"Hey, look at this. I heard you were back here." Nola, Rose Sterling's high-level account executive, stuck her head around the corner. "How's it going?"

"Good, thanks. Come on in." I smiled as she pulled off her navy blue cashmere coat and draped it over the top of the temporary wall. "I was here yesterday, too, but I didn't see you," I said. "So where'd you go the other night? After the phone call at the party?"

"It was the baby-sitter, and Tisha was sick. Stomach flu. We zipped home and by the time we got there, James, Jr. was sick too. Not a good evening. Yesterday I made chicken soup and dry toast and kept everyone in bed. Actually, yesterday was a pretty nice day." She sat down on the filing cabinet, spreading her wool skirt to avoid wrinkles, then shook her damp, frizzy brown hair. "It's misting."

Droplets spattered me and the computer. "That's the heaviest damn mist I've ever seen."

She flicked a few more drops at me, grinning her smart-aleck smile. "Did I get you?"

"Weren't you intending to?"

"Okay, first question," she said, signaling the beginning of an old game we used to play. "Best adventure movie of the nineties."

"The nineties? That's a tough one, I don't see many movies in Purple Sage."

"No excuses; I need an answer."

"Uh, *Jurassic Park*."

"Good choice."

"Thank you. Best political figure in Texas? In the nineties."

"Ann Richards. Here's one," she said, grinning. "Sexiest actor from the sixties."

"From the sixties? Are you serious? I can't even name an actor from the sixties." I stopped to think. "Wait—I've got it. Moondoggie!"

"From Gidget? No way! Did you see Sydney Poitier in *To Sir with Love*?"

"Yes, and I thought he was too schmaltzy."

Nola made a face. "And Moondoggie wasn't schmaltzy?"

"I liked his smile." This was the whole point of the game—to argue over the choices. It was something we'd done through lunches and breaks, on the way to visit clients, and even when we'd snuck out to smoke.

"It's nice to have you back," Nola said, the smile still in place. "Of course, you're still wrong about certain things like sexy actors, but I've missed you. It's been like a ghost town around here, and now with Desi dead—oh, crap, I didn't mean that. You know what I mean."

Open mouth, insert both feet, and then try to dance. That was Nola, but clients loved her.

"I know," I said. "The whole office seems empty. Are you short-staffed?"

She puffed out air in a gesture of disgust, then peered around the corner before continuing. "Who's here? Anybody important?"

"Besides us? Audry is out, Chester hasn't been in, and Michael is in his office. At least I think he is."

"Well, then let me fill you in on the situation." Nola lowered her voice. "Audry keeps letting people go, all the while telling us we're 'outsourcing' our work to get higher quality at a lower cost. So why does the client need us, that's what I want to know? Any of them could go direct to an artist and then to a printer without paying our commission. Chester always ran this place like a family business, and that included client service. I think it made a big difference. Well, you know; you were here."

Rose Sterling had for the most part been a big warm happy place, always busy, always buzzing with people, including clients. Sometimes tempers flared and there were loud arguments, but those had been like family flurries, too. It didn't take long for everyone to kiss and make up. When Audry had arrived the atmosphere had shifted, but the rest of us had usually banded together against her. Behind her back, of course.

Nola leaned even closer. "Audry's even been making noises

about cutting my commission on new accounts, but I'm telling you right now it's not happening." She turned her head around to check behind her before continuing her whispered diatribe. "She's already done it twice, and I'm not taking another cut. I'm working on a big new client and I'll blow this pitch before I let her keep all the money."

We used to have a saying at the agency, "Everybody makes their own deal." Meaning that everybody got something a little different depending on what they asked for. It hadn't been that way with Chester, but it certainly had after Audry started. With Audry's involvement absolute, it appeared Nola needed to be making a hard deal. Fast. And one that was in writing.

The front door opened.

"Look at me in here gossiping," she said, standing up. "Like you don't have anything better to do."

I heard Chester and Audry speaking as they walked to their offices.

Nola raised her voice to a normal level. "What I really came for was to tell you how much you're appreciated, Jolie. I was afraid I'd start losing clients, but with everything finally getting done, my clients are happy little people."

"All kudos gratefully accepted," I said.

"Oh, you're welcome. Just don't let it go to your head; we don't need any more people thinking they oughta just climb over everyone else to get to the top." She clamped a beautifully manicured hand over her mouth. When she pulled it away, she said in a soft voice, "Would you just listen to me? There I go again. If I don't watch my tongue, something evil is going to come after me."

"Wait, I don't get it. Who are you talking about? Who tried to climb over you?"

"I'm not saying a word."

"Oh, come on, Nola. It's me." We were speaking barely above a whisper, not that anyone was officed close enough to hear us. "If you don't tell me, I'll blab to everyone about the first time you—"

"Shh!" She lowered her own voice even more. "It was Desi Baker."

I glanced at the three pictures pinned to the burlap wall. "Are you serious? What did she do?"

"If I tell you, and vampires come to my door, will you be there to protect me?"

"All you have to do is call." But I wasn't feeling flippant.

"Damn. Just don't repeat it. See, I asked her to write a bank commercial, and she wants to see the whole place right down to the vault. Which I arranged. Then I figure out that she really wants to meet the bank president, and next thing I know, our Miss Desi is having drinks with the man. Pitching my account! That girl had designs on my job, and when Desi wanted something, she got it. There were times I was ready to shoot her!" Nola stopped and scrunched her face in disgust, and said, "You hear what I said? I'd better go."

"See you later."

She grabbed her coat and went out, leaving me with the realization that I was sliding even further into agency life. Nola was gossiping in my office again, only there was a difference. I didn't know the object of her gossip, not like the people she'd talked about in the old days. And I didn't want to know things that were detrimental to my opinion of Desi. She was dead, and by some strange quirk of fate I felt linked to her in her passing.

I shut it all out of my mind and turned around to work, but my fingers had barely touched the keyboard when I heard a deep male voice coming from the front office. Immediately I had a vision of the large police officer from the night of the party, Senior Sergeant Bohles.

I went back to typing, but when the conversation with Bohles continued for more than a few minutes, I paused, craning to hear words in the outer office. Before I could discern what was being said, Amber was hurrying down the hall and into my cubby.

"The police want us in the conference room," she said, her pale face almost ghostly. "They didn't say why, though."

"Do they want everyone?"

"Yes." She scraped at her nail polish with her front teeth, then pulled the finger away from her mouth. "This is scary."

I stood up and put my arm around her. "Not to worry. They can kill us, but they can't eat us."

She gave me a horrified look. "What?"

"It's an old expression. Never mind. It was supposed to make you feel better," I said. "Why don't you get Nola? Do you want me to call Ralph?" He was still at the TV station.

"No, I already did." She started toward Nola's office. "We're going to go ahead without him."

"Fine." While she went to gather the rest of the staff, I saved the document I'd been working on. Once it was safely tucked into the bowels of the computer, I headed for the conference room. Despite my assurances to Amber, my own stomach produced a sudden gush of acid. Whatever the police had to tell us would not be good news.

And then there was the little problem of my fingerprints on that note.

Even with the lights on, the pervasive gloom of the misty day made its presence known in the conference room. The faces staring at me matched that brooding sky.

Audry was standing at the far end of the table. Her black suit accented the creases on either side of her mouth. They were far more pronounced than when I'd seen her earlier, making her appear tired and angry. Chester and Donna Katherine were sitting together, both of them staring straight forward as if waiting for a funeral to begin.

Michael was also in the room; I didn't look at him.

Then there was Fred, the art director. He was a short, reedy man with thin salt-and-pepper hair pulled back into a ponytail. A leather thong around his neck had a shark's tooth on it, and a hand-tooled belt held up his well-worn jeans. He was typical of one segment of the Austin population, none of whom appeared to have realized that the sixties were gone.

Sergeant Bohles nodded as I came in and gestured toward a chair on the far side of the table. It put me directly in front of where Michael was standing. Michael didn't seem to notice; his eyes were glazed, and he stared out the glass wall as if he were alone, contemplating the growth of the city.

When Amber and Nola came in, Bohles asked them to sit as well. If this was the entire group, it was a very small staff compared to what the agency had employed before. We were down a good ten people, even if there were some employees out for the holidays.

Bohles waited until everyone was seated, then glanced around the room, taking in each one of us, and waiting some more. Another officer arrived and took a place beside Bohles. Both had their feet apart and firmly planted on the carpet; their shoulders were stiff with their hands clasped behind their backs. They looked tough, and maybe even angry. Perhaps they were.

It was Bohles who spoke. "I'm Senior Sergeant Ray Bohles with the Austin Police Department. Beside me is my partner, Senior Sergeant Billy Dempsey. For those of you who don't know, I was called to this building two nights ago as part of a routine investigation of the death of a young woman who was employed here at Rose Sterling Advertising. Her name was Desiree Ann Baker, Desi Baker as she was better known to you. She was found in the sixth-floor women's bathroom by Mrs. Jolene Berenski Wyatt." He nodded in my direction, never taking his eyes off the rest of the group. "Miss Baker was dead upon the arrival of the EMTs. Mrs. Wyatt did not know Miss Baker, but I'm sure many of you did."

There was no sound in the room except the distant hum of the central heating, which had just clicked on. All eyes watched Bohles.

He continued. "At the time I suspected that Miss Baker had died of a drug overdose. The assumption was based on the fact that a big party was going on, and it was consistent with what we found at her death scene. That assumption was wrong. The autopsy showed that Miss Baker had not taken any street drugs. We have subsequently learned she died from ingesting a poisonous substance. We do not at this time believe that it was self-administered, therefore we will be conducting a homicide investigation and request complete cooperation of every person in this room. At this time I would like to read all of you your rights so that you will understand what they are."

Hearing the Miranda rights on television or reading them in a book is nothing like having them read to you in real life. Bohles's deep voice was almost a monotone, yet his words hit like projectiles, tearing away at the veneer of politeness we all wore. There was fear underneath our façades, and my hands were suddenly icy.

Amber was so pale she was almost blue. Nola's upper body was rocking slightly side to side as she listened, openmouthed. Deep emotions were churning in Michael's dark eyes, and though I suspected one was anger, the others were a mystery. Audry had withdrawn to some mental executive suite where nothing touched her. Chester looked ill. Donna Katherine had taken his arm, I assumed to give him comfort. Fred merely looked surprised.

"Do you all understand these rights as I have read them to you?"

We all nodded or mumbled, but that wasn't sufficient. He went around the room, asking each person individually. Everyone said yes. When he was done he nodded, satisfied. "Good. Now I need to talk to each one of you separately.

"Mr. Sterling, I'd like to begin with you. The rest of you are requested to stay here. Sergeant Dempsey will wait with you."

There was more silence as Chester, looking old and confused, left with Sergeant Bohles. There was nothing for the rest of us to say with the watchful eyes of Dempsey on us. Even my thoughts seemed to halt until twenty minutes later when Bohles reappeared. He said, "Mrs. Wyatt, come with me, please."

✦ CHAPTER 11 ✦

Bohles took my fingerprints first. When he was finished he handed me a paper towel soaked in some kind of fluid, and said, "I appreciate your time, Mrs. Wyatt; I know this is difficult for you."

I said something nondescript and polite.

Sergeant Bohles was sitting on the edge of Audry's desk, while I sat in front of it. With the light behind him he was a faceless profile.

No doubt he had selected this office because it was farthest away from the conference room, assuring that our words would be private. Unfortunately, for me this was the least comfortable office in the suite. Bad vibes, as they say.

"Do you mind if I record our conversation? It will help with the transcription later."

"That's fine."

"Good." He started a tape recorder. "Now, would you tell me again about the night you found Desiree Baker's body. Please begin with the party and tell me why you were there."

"Of course." I took a breath, wondering how in the world I could explain my motives for some official report. How could I make him understand that I had wanted to brag about my book contract, and laugh with my old friends? That I needed a homecoming? Looking at the very sturdy Sergeant Bohles, I doubted that he would comprehend, even if I could get the words out.

I started slowly. "It was a combination birthday party for Chester and anniversary party for the agency. Rose Sterling has

95

been a big part of my life, and so has Chester; I felt it was important to be here. We combined the trip with my husband's business, and time with his family. For the holidays."

"Thank you. I understand that Mr. Sterling received some gifts; did you give him one?"

I told him about the mug and the tea.

"What did the box look like?" he asked me.

"The box?"

"The outside of the package."

"Oh, I see." I concluded he had a picture of the table that held the gifts and was trying to determine which was mine. "It wasn't in a box. It was in a basket." I told him about Prissy's fancy wrapping.

"So it was a white basket with gold cellophane."

I nodded. "And of course, it had a big bow, and I had brought some mistletoe from Purple Sage that Prissy put on the outside—and some on the inside, too."

Bohles's attention intensified as I spoke. The package was important, but why? I paused to consider the possibilities, then I stopped and looked straight into Bohles's face. A shudder caught me and my shoulders contracted with the chill of it. I knew how Desi Baker had died.

"It was poisoning from mistletoe, wasn't it?" I was appalled that I'd said it out loud.

He responded with a question that was asked as if the answer didn't matter. "Why would you say that?"

"Because. Because I looked up mistletoe in a book once. I'd been thinking of using it as a murder weapon. In one of my mysteries." My mouth felt very dry. "People can become very ill from eating the leaves. Or the berries." I felt nauseous as the vision of Desi Baker, dead on the floor, came back to me.

"Take a deep breath," Bohles commanded. "You may want to put your head between your knees. Go ahead."

I did as suggested and stayed down until I felt steadier. Desi Baker had eaten mistletoe, just like what I'd brought from Purple Sage. It might even have been the same mistletoe. Someone could have taken it off the package, and—

No, that wouldn't work. There was merely a sprig on the outside, and it was still there when Chester opened his presents. Besides, mistletoe was everywhere; there was no need to blame myself.

Cautiously I brought my head up, and when that didn't cause any adverse reactions I sat up. "I'm better." But I didn't nod my head or make any other sharp movements. "I saw the berries." They had been in the toilet.

"I'm not saying that you're correct in your assumption, but I would like you to avoid speculating out loud with the others."

Because I'd been right. "Certainly."

"So you left the party, went straight to the bathroom, and discovered Miss Baker upon entering. Is that correct? And why were you alone on that floor? I understand guests were not supposed to be there."

As a starting point for my explanation I used my encounter with the security guard in the elevator; from there I went straight through the story.

Except for the note, of course.

I faltered when I came to that part, but only for the merest second, and then went on until I reached the end. Bohles continued to watch me as if expecting more.

We stared at each other, and I was the first to look away. "That's all there is," I said.

He waited, then with the timing of an actor he slowly reached behind his back. His eyes never left my face as he brought out a clear plastic Baggie with a file label on the back. Inside was a piece of Michael's notepaper, creamy and rich, only this piece had been crumpled and smoothed as an afterthought, leaving deep wrinkles on the paper. I didn't have to see the handwriting, or read the words, to know this was the note Michael had slid underneath the bathroom door. Bohles continued to watch my face as he said, "You didn't say anything about this."

My reaction was the same as when I was a teenager and the police had caught a group of us toilet-papering a house. My blood seemed to stop in my veins and my body temperature dropped.

The note remained in the bag; Sergeant Bohles held it motionless between us like a battle flag. I couldn't deny seeing it before—my fingerprints were on it and I was sure Bohles already knew that.

"I forgot," I said. "I heard a sound at the door and when no one came in, I went to see what it was. That was on the floor."

"And you read it."

"Yes, of course. I couldn't help it. It was faceup, not folded or anything."

"Did you recognize the handwriting?"

The lie was conveniently close, but I knew I would be caught. "Yes. I've seen Michael Sherabian's writing many times. It's very distinctive."

"And what did you do with the note after you read it?"

"I, it seemed so strange. I didn't understand. So I guess at some point I must have thrown it away." The words were as new to me as they were to Bohles. "Yes, I remember that; putting it in that silver container on the wall."

"You crumpled it first."

I swallowed. "Yes, I guess I did."

"And you didn't go outside to confront Mr. Sherabian about the note."

"No." The temperature in Audry's office was as cold as her decor.

"And he wasn't outside the door after you'd found Ms. Baker's body."

"No."

"Why did you crumple the note and throw it away?"

"Why?" I frowned; it was a true reflection of what I was feeling. Why? Why? Why would anyone? I fumbled the words. "I knew that it, the note, wasn't for me, and I didn't want to leave it for just anyone to see. I guess."

Bohles waited, still watching. I waited too. Finally he nodded.

"I'd like you to do two things. Please write down your movements from the time you entered the offices of Rose Sterling the night of Desi Baker's death until you left to use the rest room. Please include approximate times." He handed me a fresh yellow legal tablet and a new number-two pencil. "Then draw me a map of this suite of offices."

"Now?"

"Yes, ma'am."

The term *writer's block* was the first thing that came to mind. Beyond that were disorganized images that would never translate to paper.

With a feeling of hopelessness I ducked my head and tapped the pencil eraser against my front teeth. I stared at the blank sheet of paper.

"What time did you arrive?" he coached.

"About seven-thirty or so. We didn't get in the door for a few minutes."

"Just start with that."

I did, and the physical act of writing the words broke open my thoughts. I listed people and conversations, because those were most memorable; exact times were more difficult. I had checked my watch once during the presentation, and once when I was getting ready to leave. In between I could only guess, so on the sheet of paper I left blanks rather than provide the police with incorrect information. "Is this okay?"

He glanced at the tablet and nodded. "We know when the video started, and the speeches, so if you remember any of those events, you might want to jot them down."

I did so quickly and realized that I had been alone for almost ten minutes, staring out the window, while Matt had gone for my drink. No doubt Bohles would spot that time period and question me about it, if not today, then later. "I'm done," I said, holding the yellow tablet up toward him.

"The map, please."

I sketched it quickly on a second page. I'm not a draftsman, which became readily apparent; the proportions were off in several places. "Not perfect," I said, standing up. I was grateful to discover that my muscles held me upright.

He glanced at the map. "Close enough."

"May I go?"

He answered by leaning forward. "Do you like writing commercials?"

"What? Do I like writing commercials?" This wasn't a cocktail party, and I tried without success to figure out where his question was taking us. "Um, yes. Sort of."

"It must be satisfying, seeing your commercial on television, seeing the end product."

"Yes. It is."

His nod was slow, almost lazy. "That's why I like being a detective. I like seeing the end product, but I enjoy the investigation, too. Getting to the bottom of things. Finding the whys, and digging out the truth. I always know the truth before it's over." There was a long pause, followed by a half smile. "You can go now." I started toward the door, but he called me back. "Mrs. Wyatt?" When I was again facing him he said, "I'll need to talk with you again. Save some time for me tomorrow."

It was like the dream where you run but don't get anywhere. "Tomorrow? Certainly."

"Good. I'll look forward to it."

This time I made it out of the room, but once outside the door, I stopped. I couldn't think where to go. I felt as if I'd miraculously escaped some brutal ordeal, and I wasn't certain how or why. The one thing I did know for sure was that Sergeant Bohles was going to keep asking people questions until he knew about my affair with Michael Sherabian. I could feel it coming like an arthritic person can feel the onset of rain; his persistence was going to make my transgression public knowledge.

Had the windows around the building been the kind you can open, I might have considered jumping.

Donna Katherine appeared beside me, chatting away as if it were normal to find me paralyzed in the hallway. "I was fixin' to make a cup of herb tea for Chester. They let me out because I was nice and said, 'Pretty please.' You look like you could use a cup, too."

"Yes." The act of nodding, speaking, and moving broke the feeling of rigor mortis. "I'd like that."

She led me into the little break room. It was outside this door that the dais had been set up at the party.

"You okay?" she asked.

"Sure. Fine."

"This is very hard on Chester. He had a heart attack a few years ago; I think it aged him. You maybe noticed how thin he is."

"Yes."

"I sure hope this mess with the police doesn't cause him more problems." Donna Katherine pulled mugs out of the cupboard and rinsed each with hot water before filling them.

"Is he feeling ill?" I asked.

"Says he's not, but I don't like his color. I'm making him some chamomile tea, that ought to help." She put the two mugs on the counter. Donna Katherine had always had a very special relationship with Chester. She did everything for him; picked up his laundry, his lunch, and his prescriptions. It was a platonic relationship, but she was combination mother hen and old-time secretary, always seeing to it that his needs were taken care of.

I waited until she was finished, then ran my hands under the tap, rubbing at them as Lady MacBeth must have rubbed hers.

"At least it's over," Donna Katherine said, opening the door of the large microwave oven. We were assailed by the nostalgic odor of the hundreds of once-frozen entrées that had been cooked in there. It was mixed with a dusty scent like weeds.

It brought me back down to earth.

"Smells like someone cooked a bush," I said as Donna Katherine placed the cups in the microwave and closed the door. "With marinara sauce."

"Always does," she said, setting the timer. Once the oven was humming she turned and asked quietly, "So really, you doin' okay?"

"I'm fine. Honest." At least I was breathing, and able to form short sentences.

"So what went on? Was it rotten?"

"Oh, not so bad." Or it wouldn't have been if I'd told the whole truth. "There were no bamboo shoots, whips, or chains."

"Damn well better not be. This is a polite society. What did he want to know?"

Some part of me didn't want to discuss it, as if my refusal would alter the fact that it had taken place. However, in an agency as small as Rose Sterling, I knew that wasn't going to work for long.

"Bohles seems thorough, and I guess that's good," I said. "He asked again about the things that happened before I found Desi's body. I've been over it with him several times now; I'm sure he just wants the timing straight. He had me write things down. I guess it's a way of tracking people."

"We all had to do that after you left the other night."

"Really? Did you have to draw a map, too?"

"A map? Of what?"

"Of the offices, and the rest of the floor."

She stared at me. "No way. Now, I can see wantin' to know where folks were, because obviously someone was doin' something they weren't supposed to be. But a map? Now, why would he do that? And did he say what killed her?"

"No." I lengthened the one-word response with a shrug. "The whole thing is a big mystery, I guess. Besides, you know the police, they don't give information, they just get it."

"I *don't* know the police except for a deputy I used to date, and it was never information that he was after, if you get my drift." She reached into a cupboard and pulled down a box of chamomile tea, then turned to me. "So you're telling me you spent all that time in there and you didn't—" She stopped, swallowed, and went on smoothly, "Buy a single thing? Honey, even if you had your husband with you, you should have taken a little time. A woman is supposed to shop till she drops. Haven't you heard that? Isn't that true, Sergeant?"

Sergeant Ray Bohles was in the door behind me.

Donna Katherine fancies herself an actress, and having gone to a few community plays to see her, I'm sorry to say she is terrible. She is of the "look, Ma, I'm acting" school of theater, so I was amazed at how smoothly she'd transitioned into the questions.

"Not my call, ma'am," the sergeant said. He reached beside the door and pulled up some yellow tape I hadn't noticed. Printed on it were the words POLICE LINE, DO NOT CROSS. "Didn't you see this? I'm going to have to ask you to put everything down and come out of there, please. Without touching anything else."

Donna Katherine stared at the tape, same as I did.

"I didn't notice it," I said, bowing my body away from him as I slid past him out the door. "I'm sorry."

"What I want to know," Donna Katherine said less than graciously, not even budging, "is how I'm supposed to make a cup of tea for Mr. Sterling."

Bohles shrugged. "That I couldn't tell you. The guys from the lab will be here any minute to examine this room."

"Well, then just help yourself to whatever you want," Donna Katherine said with exaggerated graciousness. "I'll skedaddle. And when Chester has a heart attack, or hyperventilates, we'll just call you so you can put up more of your little yellow tape. That ought to be real helpful." With that she flounced out of the room.

For the first time Bohles looked like he wanted to smile. He called after her, "We'd like to speak to you next."

"Well, I'm lookin' forward to it," she said with one more flip of her hip.

He turned to me. "Oh, and, Mrs. Wyatt, I understand you're working in Desi Baker's office." When I paused to listen he added, "You'll need to relocate temporarily; the staff from the lab will be going through that area as well and they may take a few things with them. I hope it won't inconvenience you."

"Certainly," I said.

"You can wait in the conference room, if you don't mind."

"Right."

As I passed Donna Katherine's office I saw she had pulled out wrapping paper and was wrapping a Christmas present. When I paused, she scowled. "Well, I've got to do something useful, or I'm fixin' to go downright crazy. You know what I mean?"

I knew.

✦ CHAPTER 12 ✦

THE MARBLED tile of the lobby floor was damp and smeared with footprints tracked in from the sluggish rain outside and I had to step carefully to avoid slipping as I moved from the elevator to the garage stairs. Ted Polovy was at the security desk, running his hand across the top of his short bristly hair; I slowed.

"Don't you ever get time off?" I asked, pulling my coat tightly around me.

"Why? You want to take me out?"

It took me a moment to understand what he meant, then I smiled, almost laughed. The smile felt like something I'd needed to do for a long time. I moved closer to the desk. "I think my husband would object. It's just a guess, of course. . . ."

"Yeah, well, you change your mind, and I'll consider it. I'm not saying yes, but I would think about it." He threw me an exaggerated wink. He'd changed from the grizzly he'd been the other night to a teddy bear.

"I'll remember that," I said. "You seem to be around a lot."

"Don't I know it. It's the holidays. We've got one guy out with his wife having a baby, and two others on vacation. I'm putting in some extra hours since we have to have three people on every shift."

"Really? That's a lot of security."

He cocked his head. "It's a tough world these days. There's more crime than there used to be, and with computers and stuff, one burglary could wipe out any business in the building."

"I see." After a pause, I said, "Ted, on the night of the party, could a stranger, you know, someone not invited, have gotten up to the agency and killed Desi Baker?"

His response was swift. "No way. I was in the elevator, and Lina was on the desk. You think I'm tough, you should meet her. I guarantee you, she made sure every person got on the elevator; we only had one running, and I took it straight to the seventh floor. Nobody was slipping around on their own."

No one could get in the building without passing this spot.

"What about when you two were on break?" I asked.

He gave me a look of disbelief. "What break? Does Superman take a break? No. And neither do we."

"Right, I'm buying that."

"Okay, so maybe once in a while. But Travis was our third that night, and this guy was on the Olympic karate team eight years ago. People don't sneak past him, either." Ted studied my face for a moment. "You're hoping whoever killed Desi Baker was an outsider."

"Is that wishful thinking on my part?"

"I'm afraid it is, kiddo. Besides, if you were going to sneak into a building during a party to kill someone, you wouldn't use poison. You'd get them to some empty spot and use a gun or a knife, and then you'd leave. Poison is for when you're hanging around and can't get away."

An interesting thought, and it made as much sense as anything I'd come up with. Unfortunately, it also limited the possible murderer to the employees and guests of Rose Sterling. Most likely to the employees. "And there were no other parties that night? No one working late?" I asked.

"Not on a Sunday night." When I sighed, he said, "Checkmate."

"It's not over till it's over." I hiked up my purse strap and waved as I turned toward the elevator. "Thanks."

"See you later," he called after me.

"Right."

Inside my car the air was that crisp cold that hasn't yet reached unpleasant, and it was tinged with the bayberry air freshener I'd put in a week earlier during my pre-trip car cleaning.

After the engine was warm, I put the transmission in gear and headed out of the garage. It was almost dark outside, with the lights of the city twinkling invitingly. Rose Sterling was located in the maze of one-way streets that run through downtown Austin, and as I turned in to it I began noticing Christmas decorations and lights on many of the stately buildings.

I rolled down my window as if to suck in the Christmas spirit.

It seemed unfair that Desi Baker was missing all this.

The traffic was heavy up to the freeway, and then stop and go on Mopac, the taillights in front of me a stream of red. My thoughts were a jumble of pictures and feelings, past and present woven together to form a rope that held me tight. I couldn't shake it loose and I hardly noticed the other cars as I drove.

Michael and Desi formed one picture. Donna Katherine with Chester in the conference room, another. There was a quick flash of Nola and James ducking out of the Christmas party, which was replaced by Nola and me ducking out of the office to smoke. God, had we ever been that young?

Eventually I exited, still fighting the past. After a few more turns I drove into the driveway. A car was there ahead of me and that's when I realized I hadn't driven to Prissy's, but instead had gone to my old house as naturally as if it were four years before.

I had no idea what my subconscious was suggesting, and I wasn't willing to dwell on it long enough to figure it out, but looking out at the houses in my old neighborhood was comforting. Jeremy and I had lived much of our lives here, and we'd had many good times. They seemed as vivid as the bright star on the roof.

What the heck, no one would worry if I was a few minutes late.

I backed out of the drive carefully and cruised the car-lined street until I found an empty spot, then parked and walked back to my old house. It was small, just two bedrooms, with a big den and a kitchen with lots of cupboards but no room for a table.

The yard looked as it always had in winter, the grass a golden color, the juniper bushes a soft gray-green in the reflected porch light.

The drapes were pulled back on the front window to show off the Christmas tree, which was flocked and decorated with a mixture of ornaments, beads, lights, and bows. It looked a little more sophisticated than anything we'd ever had, but pretty just the same. By moving a foot or two down the sidewalk I could make out the corner of the fireplace and see a stocking hanging there. It appeared to be a knit sock, long and striped, and it hung dangerously low, just missing the opening of the firebox.

It made me think of the time Jeremy's stocking had gotten so hot it had started smoking. Luckily it hadn't caught fire, but it was good that we'd been there to see it.

I shook my head at the memory. There were so many memories. Like the time Jeremy had hidden in the garage, working on a birthday present for me, a specially painted and lacquered computer disk box. I had noticed his absence and gone hunting for him. He was only eight and thoroughly disgusted with me for ruining his surprise.

And then there were those wonderful evenings when Matt had been our guest at the house. At first he had picked me up at the door, saying little more than hello and "How are you doing?" to Jeremy. But then, on our sixth or seventh date, when I knew I really liked Matt and was harboring some secret hope for our relationship, things changed completely. What a night.

I had agreed to let Jeremy stay home alone since it was summer, still light outside, and we were only going to be gone an hour or two. Except as I called good-bye he appeared in the hall doorway, looking waiflike. His voice had been barely a notch above pathetic as he'd said, "Mom, what am I going to eat? I'm starving."

I had tried to smile sweetly. "You can make a sandwich, we have cheese, and there's frozen pizza, or leftover spaghetti."

Pitifully he'd shaken his head. "Oh, thanks a lot—those really sound appetizing."

It was a ploy to make me look bad so Matt would go away. My son was being territorial, the age-old battle of male dominance; after all, he was the man of the house, and Matt a potential interloper. Jeremy had pulled similar stunts when he was younger, although they'd been less subtle.

While I recognized the reasons behind his words, they had left me in a stupefied silence. I debated whether to respond or just kill him on the spot, thus solving the problem permanently.

"I have an idea," Matt had said in an easy tone of voice that I have come to know, and usually love. "Jeremy, why don't you have dinner with us? I was planning on taking your mom to Chez Zee, but we can do pizza if you prefer."

Expressions flickered across Jeremy's face with amazing speed: shock, dismay, distrust, and finally, after a good thirty seconds, delight. He'd looked at me. "Really? Can I go?"

I'm not a suspicious person, but I'd had the horrible fear he was ready to take the battle for male supremacy to a public arena. And yet, if I said no, how would that look to Matt? "I don't know if it's a good idea," I'd said, giving Jeremy the beady-eyed stare mothers are renowned for. "Do you think we could all have a good time?"

He knew exactly what I meant, and he grinned. "Oh, sure we can." He'd turned to Matt. "And Chez Zee is cool. I'll have Sharon's Angel Hair Pasta."

My son the sudden gourmet.

Matt had nodded. "That's one of my favorites too." He was an innocent about to be cannonballed by an eleven-year-old.

"Cool. Be right back." Jeremy had raced out of the living room and returned in literally seconds wearing presentable jeans and a golf shirt with a collar.

I vividly remember locking the door as we left, thinking that I had made a terrible, horrible mistake and this night would live in infamy. It would have a special name in future annals, called Jolie's Last Date with that Wonderful Matt.

Once we were seated at the restaurant, Jeremy began some macho posturing unbecoming a boy of his age. I kicked him under the table several times until he gave it a rest. Matt and I chatted for a moment, then Jeremy started a new tactic: an interrogation of Matt.

"So what do you do in this Purple Sage place, anyway?" he'd asked.

"I have a ranch," Matt had responded easily.

"What's on the ranch?"

"We run cattle and a few sheep."

That had slowed Jeremy. "No kidding?"

"No kidding."

"Do you have horses, too?"

Matt had shaken his head. "No, I don't raise them, if that's what you're asking. I only have a few for work and for guests to ride. There are eight in the stable right now."

Jeremy's eyes had widened like sunflowers. "Are you serious? You have eight horses?" It was spoken with the same amazed admiration an adult might use on someone who owned eight Rolls-Royces.

"Uh-huh. Why?" Matt had said. "Do you like horses?"

"Oh, yeah!"

"Really? Would you like to come out sometime?"

"Oh, wow!"

"You and your mom can come spend the weekend anytime. I've got a big house, and I always need someone to exercise the horses."

I had jumped in then to stave off the inevitable questions from Jeremy, which would be, "Can we, Mom? And when?" But that was the end of Jeremy's skepticism toward Matt. The rest of that evening involved a swapping of information between the two, with a lot of "wows" and "cools" coming from Jeremy. He added a few stories of his own, and while most were wild exaggerations, it was fun. Back at the house we made popcorn and played Pente until I was falling asleep on the couch. Matt kissed me good-bye softly and Jeremy let him out, but only after making Matt promise to come back for dinner the next night.

It wasn't until months later that Matt admitted he'd been searching for a way to get to know Jeremy. In the country they call it salting the calf to get the cow. He told me he'd realized he was falling in love with me, and he'd thought that by winning Jeremy over, he'd have a better chance with me. That part always amazes me. I still can't believe that Matt could worry about such a thing, but he says that what with the distance between our homes and the slow build of the relationship, he was sure someone else would come along and sweep me away before he could.

And now we were a family. We appreciated each other in a way that natural families may not, and I was happier than I'd ever been. The only blot in my life at the moment was that damn thing with Michael. And Desi Baker's death.

As I stared at the house in the cold December air, I pushed those thoughts aside and let the other memories wash over me in waves of happiness, sorrow, laughter, and some regret.

Suddenly the front door opened and a woman stuck her head out. "Can I help you?"

It surprised me to be caught and it certainly must have startled her to discover a stranger standing on the sidewalk, staring at her house.

"Oh, I'm sorry," I said, keeping my distance so as not to concern her any more. "I used to live here and I just wanted to come back and see my old house."

She stepped around the door. "Are you Jolie?"

That surprised me even more. "Yes. Jolie Wyatt. How in the world did you know that?"

"How's Jeremy?" She was smiling now as she cut across the winter gold grass toward me. "Are you still in Purple Sage?"

I went to meet her. "Yes, but, uh, I don't understand. How do you know all this?"

"The present you left for us. Don't you remember?"

Present? "I don't know you, do I? Oh, wait. Of course!" I

hadn't given it a thought since the day we'd loaded the moving van for the trip to Purple Sage. "It was a candle, a housewarming gift for the new people who were moving in."

She nodded, smiling broadly. "It was the most wonderful surprise to find that huge, white candle on the mantel. It was just beautiful, and the whole house smelled like lemons. It was really nice of you."

"We'd just had so many good years in this house, we wanted to wish you the same happiness. Did it work?"

"You know," she said, after a moment's thought, "I think it did."

"Good; I'm glad."

"Me, too. And now I get to thank you. And please, thank your husband, Jeremy, too."

I laughed. "Jeremy's not my husband—he's my son. He's sixteen now."

"Oh, you're kidding! The card just had your names, and we assumed . . . Isn't that funny? I've thought about you so many times, and all these years I've had your relationship wrong."

"My husband's name is Matt. I'm sorry, I don't know your name."

"I'm Keri. That's my daughter, Hana Pearlson." She hugged her sweater tightly around her body, and pointed to a cherubic little girl peeking at us through the window. "Why don't you come in? Wouldn't you like to see the house again?"

"The inside?"

"Of course."

I stared at the front door, catching a glimpse of the tree and the stockings on the mantel. Inside that house were a million memories, but in fact, they weren't really in there; they resided in the house that still existed in my mind. It was decorated differently than this one, and it probably felt different, too.

I shook my head and took a step backward. "Thank you, that's really nice of you, but I need to be getting on."

"Are you sure?"

Again I glanced at the house, then back at her before I said with a firm nod, "Yes. I'm sure." I felt a compelling need to get to Matt.

"I was getting worried," Matt said as he gave me a welcome-home hug on the chilly patio.

"The police," I said, hugging him back. "They were at the agency, and it took up time we didn't have to spare. Are we going in or up?" I gestured to our apartment.

"In," he said, opening the door for me, so that I could smell gingerbread and pine mingled in a heady Christmas welcome. "Everyone else is getting ready to leave for the evening. We have a few minutes."

I could almost hear the hum of activity coming from upstairs as he led me toward the living room couch. I said, "Want to make out?"

He grinned. "On the couch?"

"Or the floor."

He started to laugh, then slid his arms around me and pulled me close. "Actually, when I start kissing you, I prefer to be in a spot that's a little more private. You never know where that kind of behavior can lead."

I tipped my head up to gaze at him. "Oh, yes, I do."

"What I want to know," he said, kissing me once lightly before setting me on the couch, "is what got you into this mood. I want to remember it."

"I went by my old house."

"Ah, I see, and how was that?"

I let the memory wrap around me, brief yet warm, before I said, "It brought back a lot of old memories. And it made me homesick for you." I curled back against him before I added, "It was a nice ending to a perfectly rotten day."

Matt held me tightly. "What was rotten about it?"

"The police came to the agency; they brought some bad news." I was serious now and Matt's expression changed to match my somber tone. "Desi Baker was murdered."

He nodded. "I heard."

113

"You did? How? Did Nola call you?" I slipped out of my coat, leaving it on the back of the couch.

"She didn't have to. The police stopped by here."

"You're not serious?" A burning log hissed from the fireplace as if in echoed protest. "What did they want?" I asked.

Matt shifted my coat slightly. "I had to give them a written schedule of my movements during the party, and then draw them a map of the Rose Sterling offices and the rest of the floor. It was a pretty sketchy map."

Maps and mistletoe, motives and—

"Aunt Dolie! You're here. Hip hip away! Hip hip away." Christopher plunged into the room from the staircase, ran across it, and threw himself into my arms. "I missed you too much."

"I missed you too much, too, but you aren't supposed to be running on those stairs," I said, pulling him onto my lap and kissing him on the head at the same time. He felt warm and cuddly, exactly what I needed. "Where have you been hiding? And where is everyone else?"

"Parties," Christopher said fervently. "Grandma Prissy and Grandpa are going to parties and my mommy's going to a party, too. They're gettin' ready."

"That's nice."

"No. I can't go."

"You get to stay home with us," Matt said, tickling Christopher. "We'll have more fun."

Christopher was unimpressed. "I can party."

"I'll bet you can," Matt agreed.

"So where's Jeremy?" I asked.

"On the 'puter, and I can't touch it."

"Poor guy." I hugged him again and smelled the baby-shampoo scent of his hair. "Sounds like you're having a rough day."

A timer went off in the kitchen and Matt rose, moving in that direction. "Jolie, would you like some tea?"

"I'd love some. The police cordoned off the break room this afternoon, so I haven't had any all day."

114

Tea and break rooms. There was something important in these associations, but I couldn't put it together.

"Christopher, would you like some juice?" Matt asked from the doorway.

"Nope. Thank you."

As Matt disappeared Christopher pulled a tiny plastic bag out of his pocket. "Aunt Dolie, look what I founded. It's for treasure." He whispered the last word, a grin on his face.

The bag was only two by two, and not something I could see Captain Kidd using. It was instead the kind individual servings of vitamins are packaged in at convenience or health-food stores. "Very tiny treasure; they must be worth a lot of money."

"Diamonds and gold," Christopher said, his eyes glowing. He hopped down off my lap. "May you go find diamonds with me?"

I smiled. "No, sweetie, I just want to sit down, relax, and drink some tea."

"I'll bring you some," Christopher said, racing up the stairs.

"Slow down on those stairs, and hold the banister," I called, watching him. Once he was safely on the second floor I pulled off my boots and wriggled my toes comfortably, then slumped deeper into the couch cushions.

Treasure and tea. Mistletoe. Again the words were pinging at me, but I was too tired to connect the dots.

Interesting that the police had come to see Matt. Had every guest been contacted, and had they all been asked to make a schedule and draw a map? I closed my eyes and let the thoughts drift away. At least we didn't have any parties to attend tonight.

I opened my eyes as I heard Matt approach. He was carrying two cups, one of which he handed to me. "Prissy would have done this better."

"Prissy does everything better," I said from my less-than-graceful position on the couch. I balanced the cup. "Matt, what did your map look like?"

"Like everyone else's, I imagine. Not very artistic, just a plain rendition of Rose Sterling's suite of offices." We were silent a moment, drinking our tea, before he added. "No, that's not true.

I wasn't sure about the location of some things, so my map may not have been completely accurate."

If this was important to the police, then I wanted to understand it, too. I sat up and pulled a pen out of my purse, along with the small notebook I always carry. "Could you redraw your map? I'm wondering what you saw."

He gave me a curious look, but said, "Sure. It was nothing fancy." With smooth, flowing strokes he outlined the offices, putting things pretty much as they'd been the night of the party, including the temporary walls and dais. When he was finished I studied his work. The scale was probably more accurate than I would draw, but as he'd said, it wasn't perfect.

"Close, but no banana," I said. "See, you're missing the supply closet." I pointed to the spot where the infamous supply closet should have been. Matt had distorted the dimensions in that area, leaving that and the break room out completely. "And you forgot—"

Tea and break rooms, mistletoe and murder.

"What?" Matt asked.

It fell into place as easily as a drawbridge lowering into position. Desi Baker had died from mistletoe, probably administered in the form of a tea, made in the little break room.

"Jolie?" Matt said again. "What?"

"The police think that someone, the person who killed Desi, made her mistletoe tea in the break room." I was breathing rapidly. "Except the door to it was closed and the dais was in front of it. Most of the guests don't even know that room exists. That's how they're narrowing the list of suspects. The police. If you didn't put the room on your map, then you're safe."

Disjointed as my explanation was, I knew I was right.

"Uh, Jolie, you know, the murderer could have left the break room off his map, too. Murderers have been known to be tricky like that." Matt had an amused glint in his eye.

"But he wouldn't. He wouldn't understand the purpose of the map. Desi didn't die in the break room. I'll bet she didn't even drink the tea there." I stood up and walked to the fireplace, then turned around. "But then why wasn't Bohles more upset that Donna Katherine and I were in there?"

"You were in where?"

"Oh, wait, I know! Because it's been two days since Desi died. Most of the evidence is gone, but he's hoping not all. Of course."

Matt rose and joined me in front of the hearth. "We have two choices here," he said, his arm brushing my sleeve. "Either you can explain what you're talking about, or I can leave and let you carry on the conversation uninterrupted. You choose."

So I explained what I was thinking, and as I did I realized that the cordon around the suspects was tightening. Audry and Michael were securely within its bounds, as were a number of other people. Ralph Richardson was such a nice man, but wasn't that what they'd said about Ted Bundy? Amber seemed too young and too naive to kill, but she displayed some hero worship where Desi was concerned, and it could have skewed toward hate; that happens sometimes. Donna Katherine, loose-lipped and loose-hipped, didn't seem a likely candidate any more than Chester Sterling himself, but both had opportunity. And what about Nola?

And then I realized that I, too, had opportunity. And, in the view of the police, I could also have a motive. As soon as Bohles learned of my affair with Michael Sherabian, I was in for some very intense questioning, if not something far worse.

It felt as if a ball of black tar were growing in my stomach. Fear can do that to me.

"Matt," I said, championing my courage. "I think there's something I need to tell you about—"

"I didn't stole it!" I heard Christopher's cry as he raced across the landing at the top of the stairs. There was a bump, then another cry, and he was on the staircase, falling toward the bottom.

❧ CHAPTER 13 ❧

M ATT AND I were up in a flash, running toward the stairs. We reached them just as Christopher bounced on the last step. Matt caught a leg, I grabbed a shoulder, stopping him before he hit the ceramic tile floor. We raised Christopher, turned him upright, and I wrapped my arms around him.

"Christopher! You have to be careful," I said as he began to cry. "Are you okay?" Cautiously I ran my hand along his arms, hoping I wouldn't find anything broken. "Where does it hurt?"

"I didn't stole it, Aunt Dolie, I didn't."

"I know, sweetie. Are you hurt?"

"No." But he cried even harder.

"It's okay; hey, it's okay." I rubbed his back, and my hand brushed Matt's. He was also trying to soothe Christopher.

"You scared us, Christopher," he said. "You have to be more careful on those stairs. You could have been hurt."

"But I, I, I not bad." He hiccuped twice through the faltering tears. "It was for treasure."

More footsteps clattered above us and Todd appeared at the top of the stairs. "Christopher—"

"I din't stole it!"

"It's okay," I said. "Relax, it's all right." I looked up. "Todd, what's the problem?"

He came down the stairs gracefully, his beautiful face showing a flick of anger, and something more that I couldn't define. "Is he okay?" he asked, gesturing to Christopher. "Are you okay, little guy?"

"He appears to be fine, physically." Matt said. "What's going on?"

Todd seemed reluctant, but said, "Christopher was poking around in my room, again. I told him this morning he wasn't supposed to go in there." I moved toward the couches to sit down and he followed along, explaining as we went. "I didn't mean to scare him, but I did tell him to stay out. Isn't that true, Christopher? Didn't I tell you that? Twice?"

Christopher rubbed a fist across his tearstained face and nodded; more huge tears fell down his cheeks. "I'm not bad."

"Of course, not," I said, hugging him tightly as I looked at Todd. "I know it can be frustrating, but he's just three. Little kids forget things. As the adults, we have to take responsibility for putting things up so that Christopher can't get them."

Todd twitched his shoulders, hesitating before he said, "I'm sorry. I overreacted." He was young, too; I could see that in his face. "You okay, little buddy?"

"I didn't stole!"

Matt took a relaxed posture, his voice easy as he asked, "What didn't you steal?"

"I din't stole—" Christopher began.

"It's okay, Christopher," Todd said, kneeling beside the couch so he could pat Christopher on the back. "I'm sorry you fell; I know you didn't mean anything." Then he looked up at us. "Christopher had one of my cuff links. Gold nuggets with a little diamond in it. My mom gave them to me last year for my birthday." He swallowed hard and stopped as if he couldn't say anything else.

I began to understand why he seemed young and upset. Some things have value beyond price.

I rearranged Christopher so that I could look into his face. "Christopher, you mustn't ever take Todd's cuff links again, do you understand?" I waited until he nodded. "Those are very special to Todd. Very special. You wouldn't like it if someone took something very special of yours. Like your teddy bear."

He sniffed and nodded. "No."

"And you can't go in my room anymore," Todd said. "You have to mind, don't you?"

"I know."

"One more thing," Matt added. "You cannot run on those stairs. Got it? You were almost hurt."

Christopher nodded again. "Okay."

I wondered how much of this a three-year-old could take in. I hugged him. "I'm glad you're all right. And we'll just forget the whole thing. Deal?"

"Deal," Christopher said, solemnly.

Todd stood up. "Deal for me, too." He patted Christopher. "Well, I guess I'd better go." He looked at Matt. "It's been a while since I've been in Austin. Lots of old friends to see." He trotted toward the front door as Prissy came down.

"Todd," she said, "did I hear Christopher crying? I had the blow dryer going—"

"He's okay, Aunt Prissy," Todd said. "He almost tumbled down the stairs, but Matt and Jolie caught him."

"The stairs? Oh, my God—" She hurried over and swept Christopher into her arms. "Are you all right, little bug?"

"I'm otay. Aunt Dolie saved me."

"And here I thought I was going to be the big hero," Matt said. "I didn't even get a mention."

Prissy was still clutching Christopher. "We're all so busy running around that we haven't been watching Christopher. And I promised Stephanie that I wouldn't let him out of my sight while she was in the shower! She made me swear, and he could have been killed. Oh, my angel." She squeezed him so hard he let out a squeak. "I could put up a baby gate, but I just hate those things. You have to step over them, and then if someone else fell and hurt themselves in the process, I'd feel terrible. I thought Christopher knew better. Don't you know better?"

"I know better, Grandma Prissy," he responded.

Matt took Christopher out of her arms and put him on the floor. "You're overdoing it, Grandma," he said to Prissy. "He's fine. Don't make a big deal or you'll s-c-a-r-e him. Go get ready, we'll baby-sit."

"You're just so pragmatic, Matt!" She looked at me. "Jolie, I feel so bad. I thought this was going to be a fairly relaxed holiday season, but I opened Ross's briefcase and he had nearly a dozen party invitations that he'd forgotten to tell me about! Can you believe that? And these are all clients. We have to show up."

"It's not a problem for me," I said. "I'd just as soon kick back and relax."

"You see, Prissy," Matt said, "Jolie doesn't mind, and she said that even before I told her that *White Christmas* is on TV tonight."

"Really?" I said. "That makes my evening complete."

"Jolie has this weird belief about that movie," Matt went on, getting the *TV Guide* from the television and handing it to me.

"It's not weird," I said. "It's very simple: If you don't watch *White Christmas* or *Miracle on 34th Street,* then Santa won't come to your house. If you watch both, you get anything you want."

Christopher jumped up on my lap. "I want to watch movies!"

"And I'd better go," Todd said. He went over to Prissy. "Good night, Aunt Pris. I'll see you later."

"Oh, Todd, I feel like I've been ignoring you, too," she said, putting an arm around his waist. "The holidays are almost too much. Have you even met Jolie?"

Todd smiled in my direction. "We met on the patio last night when I was getting some air. Don't worry, we're all fine and you're a wonderful hostess." He kissed her on the cheek and she flushed happily.

"Thank you."

A phone rang, and at the same time Ross called from upstairs, "Pris, which tie do you want me to wear?"

"See you all later," Todd said as he turned and headed out the door.

It was like prom night, only I was staying home, and grateful about it. Matt went for the phone, Prissy went upstairs, and I took Christopher to the kitchen. The refrigerator held the makings for some rather terrific sandwiches, leftover soup, and even a fruit salad Prissy had somehow found the time to make.

"Are you ready to eat, little bug?"

"Just soup. I don't eat fruit," he said as I fixed him a plate.

"Of course you eat fruit. Everyone eats fruit. Uncle Matt is having some. I'm having some, and your grandma Prissy made it special for you. So you can grow up big and strong."

"Call me Bernard. He's a Rescuer."

"Okay, Bernard, here's your plate. And just a little fruit. Rescuers need fruit."

He made a face, but once he was arranged on his booster chair, he began spooning soup into his mouth.

Food is imperative to life. And poison—poison could come in many forms. Most adults knew the difference and were careful not to ingest the wrong one. But mistletoe had been swallowed by Desi Baker. She had seemed like an exceptionally bright young woman, so she must have trusted whoever fed her the parasite.

"Mom, can you fix me a sandwich before I go?"

I looked at Jeremy, who had appeared in the dining room dressed in clean, ironed clothes. "Where are you going?" I asked.

"You know Alicia Willis? Remember, she was a friend of Suzie's when we were at Lucy Reed Middle—"

"Not really."

"Well, anyway, I ran into her at the computer store today, and we got to talking, and there's this big party tonight. She said I'd know almost all the kids that will be there, so she invited me. She's even taking me, because she has a car of her own." A pitiful yet accusatory stare was directed at me, apparently intended to make me feel guilty. "She's picking me up in ten minutes, so could you, like, make me a sandwich?"

"I didn't say you could go."

"Mother! You know her aunt. She's in the Austin Writers' League. She had a signing at Mysteries and More and you took me. It was right before we left Austin. Remember she wrote a book about something? There was a cowboy hat on the cover."

I did remember the aunt, although not the hat. Unfortunately I couldn't remember the woman's name, and even if I had, she wouldn't have had any knowledge of her niece's social plans.

"I just don't know—"

"Mother, I'm sixteen. You have to start trusting my judgment; it's just a party."

"Fine. Go talk to Matt and I'll make you a sandwich," I said, and he took off.

It was my way of bowing to greater wisdom; Matt was more evenhanded, perhaps because he was Jeremy's adopted father. Or perhaps because Matt is that way in all of life. Still it let me off the hook. If Matt said no, I was safe, and if he said yes, then I was being overprotective, which I suspected was the case.

"Good fruit, Aunt Dolie," Christopher said, bobbing his head up and down as he chewed.

I finished putting together a plate for Jeremy. "I'm glad you like it."

I tried to imagine Michael in this setting, but he didn't belong.

When Matt and Jeremy returned, Matt sat down beside me, while Jeremy merely snatched his sandwich off the table, almost at a full run, as he raced outside and up the staircase to the little apartment. I assumed he was after money—money Matt had promised him for the evening.

"Softy," I said.

Matt smiled as he reached for a plate.

Next came Stephanie, hurrying through on a cloud of Giorgio. She was in a festive red dress trimmed in black piping. Something by a designer, and probably borrowed from her mother's closet. It aged her, and at the same time softened her slender figure and added color to her cheeks. A good choice for business parties.

"Give me a kiss, angel," she said, bending over Christopher. After a quick kiss she took a bite of his sandwich. "Mmmm. Good stuff."

"Aunt Dolie made it."

"And she did a great job." Stephanie looked at me. "Are you sure you don't mind staying with Christopher tonight? Matt kind of volunteered you."

"I don't mind a bit," I said. "We're going to have a fun evening. Don't worry about us."

"But I do. Where is Todd?" She glanced around as if she might have missed him.

"He left a few minutes ago to visit friends," I said, wondering if the matchmaking was working.

"Oh." She ate a piece of Christopher's fruit, then said, "Pete has so many of these obligatory Christmas parties. You know. I'm surprised you and Matt don't have a dozen, too."

"Oh, we do," Matt said, then added with a drawl, "but not so many as you, bein' from Purple Sage and all."

Stephanie snorted, blowing her bangs off her forehead. "Uncle Matt, you can't even do a Texas accent anymore! You're going to have to practice. But I do appreciate your help with Christopher. You're not going to leave or anything, are you?"

"Stephanie, of course we won't leave Christopher alone," I said. "What is with you?"

"I'm sorry—"

"I have a plan," Christopher said. "We can make popcorn, and I can party!"

The doorbell rang and Pete was there, kissing Stephanie; I didn't look until he'd moved over to the table and was shaking hands with Matt.

"Matt, good to see you again." He leaned over Christopher. "Hello, young fellow."

"Hello, Mr. Javitz. I'm eating."

"So I see. Well, we won't interrupt your dinner. I'm taking your mother to a couple of parties. I hope that's okay with you."

Christopher looked at both of them seriously, as if weighing his options. Finally he said, "Okay."

There were more kisses from Stephanie, along with some final instructions for Christopher—instructions that were also aimed at us. "Christopher, you have to take a bath tonight, and don't leave a big mess in the bathroom. Also, you have to go to bed by eight o'clock. And no milk for your midnight snack because you know what happens. And you stay right with Aunt Jolie. No wandering around upstairs by yourself, because you get into things you aren't supposed to." When Christopher continued to eat without looking up, she added, "Do you hear?"

He looked at her and nodded. "I hear, Mommy."

"Good. 'Bye, little bug, I love you."

Finally they were out the door. Then Jeremy whizzed back through, clutching Matt's newly purchased duster, made of khaki canvas with brown leather trim. Matt had been wanting a long coat like this for years, not that he rides horseback a lot in the rain, but when he does, he says wearing wet jeans for any length of time chafes his thighs. I applauded fixing that problem; I wasn't sure I applauded Jeremy wearing the duster on its first outing.

Jeremy slipped it on, lounging in the doorway to give us the full effect. When he moved, the split in the back revealed his jeans. Apparently Jeremy's new persona was city-kid-gone-country. I shot a glance at Matt, who was nodding.

"Looks fine on you," he said very seriously.

Jeremy grinned. "Cool."

The doorbell rang, and he raced for it. I gave Matt one of those sidelong glances and he followed Jeremy at a discreet distance.

Matt discerned the young woman's name (by way of a simple introduction), as well as the name of the hosting family, where they were going (by cautioning of some road construction and discussing alternate routes), and approximately what time they would return. The last question he had to flat out ask, although Jeremy didn't seem bothered. Maybe because he was wearing Matt's duster and, as I learned later, carrying two of Matt's twenty-dollar bills in his pocket.

I was introduced from across the room. Alicia was a bubbly brunette with a sweet smile and dimples. I said hello without getting up, just to show how cool I could be.

After they left, Matt sat back down at the table.

125

"Big night," I said. "Are we the dorm parents?"

"Yes, we are," Matt said. "Luckily it's a very small dorm."

Next Prissy and Ross came down. Ross had misplaced his wallet and began hunting. Prissy tried to kiss Christopher and smeared her lipstick. Ross found his wallet while Prissy wrote down a list of phone numbers, ending with their cell phone. "Which I promise you Ross will keep with him all night." When they, too, had gone, I jumped up, saying to Christopher, "That's it! They're gone. We can party and trash the place!"

"Hip, hip, away!" he shouted, giving me a full view of his partially chewed bit of fruit.

"See what you started," Matt said.

So we partied, right up until eight-thirty when I fell asleep on the couch.

At seven-fifteen in the morning I quietly unlocked the door and stepped into the offices of Rose Sterling Advertising; there was an eeriness in the still empty suite.

The heat came on, and a gust of not-yet-warm air touched the Christmas tree, causing the ornaments to dance and jangle gently. I swore I could hear a soft humming that floated on the air current, but the very practical portion of my mind convinced me it was a mechanical sound and nothing more. The office was unpleasantly chilly; lower temperatures had blown in with an overnight cold front that left weathercasters predicting one of Austin's very rare snowfalls. Driving down Prissy's street, I'd seen plants shrouded in blankets to protect them from the frost.

Trying not to think about the temperature, or the solitude of the offices, I moved down the hall to the cubby that once had been occupied by Desi Baker.

When humans depart a company or the earth, they leave something behind them. I always expect some residual aura, intangible yet present, but I've never gotten it. Instead it seems that most people leave a legacy that is a reflection of what they did in their lives, like a happy family, a profitable company, or just a cupboard full of prescription bottles.

Desi had left unfinished business and unwritten copy, the result of a life cut short.

She had also left relationships incomplete, like the one she'd had with Michael. Luckily, that was not my problem. My only concern was the commercial work she'd left undone; my intention was to finish it so I could leave Rose Sterling with a clean conscience and a clean slate.

The police had spent several hours in Desi's former office just the afternoon before. I hadn't been close enough to see everything they'd done, but I knew they had gone through the files and the desk, removing whatever it was they'd thought important. I did see a young woman holding the trail mix in a gloved hand—no doubt that had gone to the laboratory. Then some computer person had come in and copied off the contents of the hard drive. Audry Sherabian had signed a receipt for all of the things they'd taken, and I had been allowed back in there late in the day.

Now as I stepped around the temporary wall that formed Desi's office, I stopped in surprise. The computer was already on and humming, drawers stood wide open, and file folders were everywhere. I had the eerie thought that Desi Baker had returned. Especially since I'd left the office in perfect order the evening before.

✦ CHAPTER 14 ✦

M Y HEART pounded and there was a metallic taste in my mouth as if my adrenaline had come from the superleaded pump.

Instinctively I backed away. I started to turn and rammed into something soft. There was a grunt at the same time as my own.

"Damn!" Nola was clutching the temporary wall. I had almost knocked her over.

"You scared the hell out of me!" I said.

Nola's normally dark skin had lost its glow. She took several deep breaths before she said, "It's mutual! What are you doing here at this hour?"

"I couldn't sleep, so I came in early. Did you do this?"

She glanced around at the mess. "I didn't realize it was this bad. I'm sorry; I'll clean it up." Without a word of explanation, she got down on her knees and began picking up folders, refilling drawers as she went.

"Here, I can help," I said, bending down and reaching for a stack of files.

She scooped them up first and shoved them in a drawer, saying, "No need, I've got it."

"Well, pardon me. What were you looking for?"

"What? Oh, nothing."

I stood back up. "There was obviously something."

"Just some copy I needed for a client, but it isn't here."

I glanced at my watch. It was barely seven-thirty, and to Nola that is like the middle of the night. Unless she had changed her habits drastically, this was not usual behavior. "I can't believe you did all this for a missing commercial, at least not at this hour."

"It's an important client."

"You could have asked me yesterday and I'd have helped you look. Or you could have checked with Ralph." I waited, watching her efficient movements. A sick feeling began in my stomach—Nola had been searching Desi's office. It looked suspicious and my mind made the easy jump to link her with Desi's murder.

Not Nola. Anyone but Nola. I couldn't keep silent. "Come on, Nola, this isn't your style; tell me what's really going on."

She stood upright, her arms full of papers. "You are so damn pushy."

"Then talk to me—"

"Do you mind?" She shoved the remaining folders at me. "Go flap your lip at someone else!" With that she whipped out. And not just out of my cubicle. I heard her slam a drawer in her own office and then head for the front door.

"Nola, wait a minute," I said, starting after her.

The clamor of the ornaments on the Christmas tree told me it was too late; she was gone.

I blamed myself; she wouldn't have left if I hadn't insisted on knowing what was going on. She probably had some perfectly logical reason for coming in so early. Maybe she really had lost some copy for a big client. I turned back to the office and looked around at the small cubicle. No matter how much I wanted to, I couldn't convince myself to accept that explanation. If there was a problem with a client, Nola would have said so. She would have asked for help.

Nola Wells and I had worked together for eight years, and she was probably the person I'd missed most when I left Austin. We had a history together; in fact, I had been the one who'd convinced her to go on her first date with her husband, James. She'd said no, and had been vehement about it when he first asked her out.

129

"He's a damn football player, and we know those guys are just raw-meat-eating animals. I don't need someone like that in my life."

"That was in college," I'd protested as we rode up in the elevator after arguing about it for most of lunch. "Nola, that was how many years ago? Give the guy credit for growing up."

"There are plenty of other men out there—"

"Name one who is as charming and good-looking *and* as interested in you as James."

"I don't have to answer that."

"Because you can't." I'd been at the media party where she and James had met, and I had sensed a spark between the two. Beyond that, I had liked James. There was something about him that just seemed right. "Look, tell him you'll go to dinner, but tell him you want to double-date. I'll come along and I'll bring the biggest guy I know with me. If James does anything he shouldn't, my date can corral him. At least you'll get to know him a little better."

It had taken a bit more talking, but finally she had agreed. "One dinner, Jolie, but it's just to get you off my back, not because I like James."

Less than a year later they were married.

We'd had some bad times, too, but while Nola could be fiery, her brand of anger was the get-in-your-face kind. I was the one who would sputter and dash out the door. Nola would plant herself in front of whoever had displeased her and vent until she was damn well through, thank you very much. Either she had changed a great deal, or something was very wrong.

I couldn't shake the worry as I began putting away the files I held in my arms. The client names on the bulging folders were some of the agency's old guard, familiar to me from my tenure at Rose Sterling: Bank of Balcones; Chez Zee Restaurant; Petry & Thomas, CPAs; the Travis County Zoo; Ant Computing; North and South China Restaurant; and the Austin Aqua Festival. It appeared Nola hadn't found what she was looking for here, so it didn't make much sense for me to go through these folders again.

What I really wanted was to help her. I pulled open the second file drawer hoping that something might occur to me. Desi had kept folders for dozens of clients, many I'd never heard of before. There was one whole section of hanging files bearing names new to me, each holding only a few pieces of paper. There were names like The Witch Stand, Iced Treats, Card Capers, and a business called Stuff 'N Puff.

Curious as to what that might be, I opened the manila file and discovered Stuff 'N Puff was a balloon company out of Friendswood, Texas. There was a print ad showing a teddy bear sitting on a nest of curly ribbon all inside a huge balloon. The next sheet of paper was a piece of radio copy that touted a holiday shopping fair held back in November. Stuff 'N Puff was one of the participants listed. The last thing I found in the folder was an eight-page newspaper called the *Holiday Bulletin,* obviously printed just for the fair. It was beautifully laid out with lots of graphics, and on the front page was a small article about Stuff 'N Puff. The other articles and pictures featured more sponsors of the event.

While it seemed likely that Nola had been through this section of hanging files already, or hadn't been interested in it, I put the folder on top of the desk and flipped through a few others. Most folders had three or four print ads for different fairs, and three or four pieces of radio copy, although a few had less. At the back of the hanging file I found full-page newspaper ads for the November Shopping Fair, a June Bridal Affaire, and a Spring Garden of Delights. Each had a special border around the outside, with the small client ads inside it.

As I closed the drawer I heard the front door of the agency open and the Christmas tree ornaments set up their holiday clamor.

I turned and jumped up, hoping it was Nola returning with a simple explanation. Instead it was Ralph Richardson who appeared in the doorway of my cubicle. I tried not to show my disappointment.

"Ralph, good morning."

"Good morning. You beat me here."

"Oh, not by much."

"It's still pretty early for someone who's supposed to be on vacation." He shifted his body and became more serious as he said, "I don't know if anyone's told you or not, but we really appreciate all the time you're putting in. I can't think of very many people who'd pitch in like you and be so serious about getting us out of our bind."

I responded lightly. "Well, you need to know I'm also serious about leaving here early today. Two o'clock at the latest, police or no police. I have a hot date with a young man named Christopher to do some heavy Christmas shopping, and I'm not letting him down."

Ralph appeared puzzled. "I thought your son's name was Jeremy."

"It is. Jeremy is sixteen and these days he goes off on his own to do his Christmas shopping. This is my three-year-old nephew. More dependent *and* he still lets me hug him."

Ralph grinned. "We're expecting our first grandchild next month, and Mary already plans to kidnap the baby twice a week and teach it quilting and gardening."

"Sounds like a great plan to me," I said, putting away the last of the folders. "And it's a small step from there to mud pies."

"As long as I don't have to eat them. Have you had your coffee yet?" he asked. When I shook my head no, he gestured toward the break room. "Come on, I'll make you some. My treat."

"Except," I said, following him, "that I quit drinking coffee almost a year ago. Only tea now, so I'll make my own."

"We have lots of different kinds. Donna Katherine thinks we're some kind of International Tea House; you can have your pick."

"Is the break room open again? The police had it blocked off yesterday."

We arrived at the door and the yellow police tape was gone.

"It was open last night when I left here," he said. "Guess that was around nine or so."

Advertising can be rough when the pressure's on, although usually our Christmas rush came earlier in the season. Then you had to deal with all the after-holiday sales, and before you knew it, it was time to advertise soft drinks and outdoor garden furniture.

Ralph flicked the light switch. In the fluorescent radiance, I could see that the break room was spotlessly clean.

"I'm impressed," I said, running my hand across a counter. It came up dust- and dirt-free. "I expected fingerprint powder and chalk marks, all kinds of things like you see in movies."

"Not a chance," Ralph said. "The janitorial service comes through around midnight, and I'll bet they cleaned it up. Not that there would be chalk marks. You're dating yourself, Jolie." By this time he had pulled open the cupboard doors. "What the hey?" he said, staring at the almost empty shelves.

"What?"

"Things are missing. The fancy tea that Donna Katherine collects for Chester is gone. All of it's gone." He opened the refrigerator; it was empty and clean. "Everything's gone. The police must've had some tea party in here yesterday."

Except it hadn't been held here. My guess was that the party took place at the lab where they looked for poison mixed in the tea tins. Most likely the search was still going on.

"Doesn't matter," I said. "I'll take whatever is available."

He handed me a brand-new, shrink-wrapped box of blackberry-flavored tea, and I proceeded to open it while he filled two cups with water and put them in the microwave.

"Did the police talk to you yesterday?" I asked.

"They tracked me down while I was in production at KVUE. I suppose it was unavoidable, but it was a bit embarrassing." His ears turned pink at the mention of it; most people would have complained loudly, maybe even rudely, but he wasn't that kind. "I thought about coming back here when Donna Katherine called," he went on, "but I felt like I had to stay. You know how it is. The station would have charged us for the studio time anyway, and you can't blame them. The biggest problem, though, was that I couldn't have rescheduled until tomorrow and then I'd only get an hour, not the whole day like I needed." He shook his head. "At least Sergeant Bohles came himself, and he wasn't in uniform."

"What do you think of him?"

"He seems competent."

"Except he didn't realize it was murder at first."

"But that's understandable. A young attractive woman dies at a big party? That scenario would indicate drugs to me, too."

I raised one eyebrow. "Oh?"

He looked embarrassed. "I was an MP in the service and I ended up doing a lot of investigative work."

"Really? I never knew that. And you gave it up when you got out of the military?"

"Sure. I never wanted to be a cop, and even worse is a private investigator. Who'd want to be one of those?"

I didn't admit it, but actually, I think I would. Or would have in my younger days. Not that thirty-nine is old, but I'm probably beyond the physical rigors of that profession.

By now I was dunking a tea bag in a cup that had an Austin Aqua Festival logo painted on it. The building was quiet, with only the creaks and groans that came with the cold winds outside. The break room was like a cozy retreat from the real world, and Ralph's presence was like the comfort of an older brother.

I took my tea and sat at the small table. "Ralph," I said, "what do you think of Desi's death?"

He spent some time formulating his answer while he pulled out a chair to join me. "It was a terrible thing," he said, when he finally sat down. "Desi Baker was a nice person."

Not the kind of in-depth response I'd been looking for. I wondered why he was being so vague. "Who do you think killed her?" I probed.

"I couldn't say." He became very busy pouring Equal and powdered creamer into his tea. Then he stirred, tasted, and poured some more.

"If you'd rather not talk to me—"

"It isn't that," he said, sniffing his tea as if it were a vintage wine. "I'd like to believe Desi's death was an accident. You know, she ate or drank something and had an allergic reaction."

"Wouldn't the police know that by now?"

"Probably."

"So you and Desi were friends?"

Ralph's eyes focused on something in the distance as he said, "I thought very highly of Desi. She was the kind of young woman I want my daughters to grow up to be like." He looked at me. "Sorry, it's just not something I can talk about easily." He took a swallow of his drink.

"Of course, I understand." In the past year I'd lost someone I thought a great deal of, too. Actually, he'd been closer to Jeremy, but it had disrupted our world in ways I hadn't expected and gave me an empathy with Ralph and what he was going through. Still . . . he seemed more than just a little reticent on the subject of Desi.

"Tell me about the fairs that Rose Sterling has been handling," I said, just to keep the conversation going. "That holiday gift fair and the Spring Delights sound like fun. Were those your ideas?"

His face brightened as he said, "I had nothing to do with them, although my daughters spend a lot of money at them. Actually, it was Audry who thought of putting them on, as a way to boost revenue. They're a quick influx of cash, from what I understand. Thirty clients at a thousand dollars each is a nice chunk of change. Not that we keep it all. We have to pay for the space and cleanup, and some ad placement, but it's still fast profit."

"Audry handled those?"

"Actually, somehow Donna Katherine got involved about three years ago, and she did the last couple of years practically on her own. Oh, she'd hire an intern to help and Desi worked with her on the last two, but they were Donna Katherine's babies. She designed the flyers so they looked like hometown newspapers with articles on all of the sponsors; it was a nice concept. And she grew the events into what they are today. Our first fairs only had fifteen booths, and some of those were comps to radio stations and such. The last fairs were at least twice that. In fact, I think she squeezed thirty-five or forty booths into the show right before Christmas."

"That's a lot of work."

"You're right, but you know Donna Katherine."

Donna Katherine had always been known for her efficiency. Deposits were made and invoices went out with the precision of a military drill unit. Donna Katherine could find something as small as a penny missing from a bank statement. When I'd had a problem getting my own bank account to reconcile, Donna Katherine had sorted it out, and had straightened out the accounting people at my bank, all in less than a day; before I'd gone to her for help I'd been struggling with it for weeks. She might be loud, and she might be brash, but she had a work ethic that was enviable. Whatever it took to get the job done was what she put into it. I couldn't ever remember her taking a vacation.

I started to say something about her, but another of Ralph's comments suddenly struck me. Fast profit. And here we were, sitting alone in the coffee room, without another employee in the office because of the pared-down staff. There was more to that theme, too. At the party, Donna Katherine had said something about cutting back the guest list, as if it were a money-saving measure.

There had always been ups and downs in the agency's fortunes, and I assumed it was that way with any business. You lose clients, budgets get cut, expenses go up, and then there are those times when the workload is heavy and the bank account is flush. Obviously this past year had been off, and it appeared to be by quite a bit. Odd considering all the production we were handling now.

I wanted to ask Ralph about it, but he stood up and gestured toward the door. "Guess it's time to get after it. Are you ready?"

"Is there an option?" I asked, rising to my feet and taking my cup with me.

"You could just leave, but then I'd be writing copy while other people were opening their Christmas presents."

"Well, we can't let that happen, can we?"

I followed him back to his office, keeping one ear cocked toward the front door. In part I was hoping Nola would return—another part of me was tuned to Michael's arrival. I wasn't sure what I was going to say to him, but I felt I had to say something to clarify things.

Ralph was talking and I paid closer attention as he went over everything I'd done the day before. He was generous with his praise before he portioned out another stack of work for me to start on. I went back to Desi's cubicle and did just that.

I'd been writing for almost two hours, glazed eyes on the computer screen, the keys almost like extended appendages, when I was interrupted by a young man in the doorway. I had to blink several times before I could refocus enough to recognize him. He was one of the men who'd returned the office furniture and equipment the day before; he'd left while I talked to Amber at the front desk.

"Brought back one more," he said, holding out a cardboard file box. "Where do you want this?"

"Here, set it here," I said, sweeping things off the top of the cabinet. "Where did it come from?"

He swung the box over and put it down with a thump. "When we brought all the other furniture back, someone must of missed this one. There weren't supposed to be boxes, anyway, just furniture. It wasn't on the instructions, so don't let your redheaded friend in there think she can take more off the bill."

I don't deal with billing; never did, never will. "Well, have a Merry Christmas."

"Oh, yeah. You, too."

"One more thing," I said, and he turned around, his expression saying he had known this was coming. "Did the receptionist tell you to bring this to me?"

"No, she didn't say nothing about that. I just knew where I got it from."

I nodded. "Well, thanks again."

✦ CHAPTER 15 ✦

AFTER HE left, I took the lid off the box. Four or five army green hanging files were lying flat on the bottom of it with an address book on top. More of Desi's things that were coming back to roost on my doorstep, just like her memory, adding to the subtle haunting that wouldn't release me.

I told myself how foolish I was being and turned to the more practical issue of the items in the box. Did the police need any of these?

Amber appeared in the doorway of the cubicle. "Uh, Jolie?"

I picked up the box and slid it back under the desk.

When I straightened up, I said, "Yes? What's up, Amber?"

Her eyes were wide. She said, "That policeman is here. He wants to talk to you. Again."

"Me?" And I thought of the note.

My stomach went into a tailspin. I'd almost forgotten about the note, or perhaps it would be more accurate to say I had conveniently repressed the memory of it. "Is it that big cop?"

"Uh-huh, that senior sergeant. He wants to see you."

This would be my third interview with Bohles. "Does he want to see me now?"

"Yeah, he said now."

Damn. There were too many things I didn't want to discuss with him. All those things that would lead him to my past relationship with Michael.

"Tell him I'll be right there."

"Sure, okay. No problem."

I slid on my jacket like some kind of protective armament and started after her. Bohles was waiting for me in the conference room. We finished with the niceties in a few short sentences, and when I was seated he began asking questions, covering the same ground we'd been over before. I might have been bored except for the little knot of fear that rested in the bottom of my stomach. It was coiled, waiting, just as I suspected that Bohles was waiting.

A couple more questions, and while Bohles didn't shift his large body, something about his eyes changed. They became tighter, more intense and focused, much like those of a bird of prey before an attack. He said, "Mrs. Wyatt, I've been going over your statement and I'm unclear about some things. The timing. Would you help me out?"

Only a fool would decline. "Yes, of course."

"Good. Is it correct that when you went into the ladies' room by the stairs, your first stop was a stall nearest the door?"

"Yes."

"After that you stopped to wash your hands and look in the mirror."

"Correct."

"You heard a noise near the door, went to it, and found the note from Michael Sherabian."

I was hardly breathing, so I merely nodded my agreement.

"Then you marched to the far end of the rest room, opened the handicapped door, and discovered Desi Baker."

"Yes." The word strangled in my throat.

"I see. Mrs. Wyatt, why did you walk to the handicap stall? Was there a sound? Was Ms. Baker alive? Did she do something to alert you to her presence?"

"Oh, no. I'm sure she was already dead." This was safe ground, territory I could easily tread. "I didn't do a lot to make sure, but I did feel for a pulse before I ran to get help. There was nothing, although her wrist was still warm."

"So you heard a sound near the door. You stepped around the wall, spotted a note that had been slid under the door. You picked it up and read it. You recognized Michael Sherabian's handwriting immediately, is that right?"

"Well, it took a second, but yes."

"Good. Then after reading the note, you crumpled it, pushed it down into the trash container, and then walked to the far end of the rest room, opened the handicapped door, and discovered Desi Baker. Is all of this accurate?"

"Yes. It's close."

"Where am I off? Explain it to me."

"No, I guess you have it all correct."

"Good. But none of it explains why you crumpled that note. Or why you walked to the far end of the bathroom."

I had no explanation—I merely stared at him. When that became impossible I lifted my shoulders and shook my head. "I don't know. I just did. And when I found her, I checked her pulse before I ran to get help."

He reached behind him on the desk and brought out the plastic Baggie with the note from Michael Sherabian.

He brought it up close to me so that I couldn't avoid the black pen strokes of Michael's writing. "Let me make sure I'm clear. This is the note, and you recognized the writing almost immediately?"

"Yes." I swallowed, my throat suddenly dry.

"And"—he paused—"you thought this note was for you, didn't you?"

"No, no."

"You crumpled it and threw it in the trash. Are you having an affair with Michael Sherabian?"

"No! The note was for Desi Baker. He was in love with her."

"Maybe. And maybe he was sleeping with you at the same time."

"That's crazy! I haven't been in Austin since last spring. I haven't seen Michael since I left the agency four years ago."

My voice was rising, and I was afraid it would become a hysterical wail. I stopped to breathe, to think. In my avoidance of the truth I had triggered an even worse suspicion. If I were to tell the whole truth right now, Bohles would have no reason to believe me, and he'd certainly try to verify anything I said with others at the agency. Everything would come out in the ugliest possible way. In desperation I said, "I'm very happily married."

Bohles continued to watch me, waiting for me to go on. I had no more to say.

After a time he nodded and said, "So tell me again how you found the note, and what you did after that."

As clearly as I could I told about hearing the sound near the door, finding the note, putting it in the trash, and discovering Desi Baker's body. The holes in my explanation were big enough to house a mausoleum.

"Again, please." His tone was deceptively gentle. He knew he had me.

I repeated my story. I still didn't say why I had walked to the back stall of the rest room, and I knew that was what he wanted to hear.

He asked me to tell it again. After that third telling he nodded. "Why did you throw away the note if you didn't think it was for you?"

I shook my head no.

"You won't tell me?"

"I, I don't know."

"Why did you go back to the handicap stall?"

There was nothing to do but shrug and look into those small intense eyes. He waited, stared, as if it were a game and he already knew he'd won. At last he said simply, "You can go."

I jumped up and almost fell over with the suddenness of it. "Thank you," I said, nearly running in my desire to be away from him. God, if only I had told the truth right away—but there was simply no way I could have. At the time I'd thought the note was for me, Matt had been there, and I hadn't wanted Matt to know about my past relationship with Michael Sherabian.

The phone was ringing as I hurried back into my cubby, and I grabbed it up as if it might transport me away from Bohles and Rose Sterling.

"Yes? This is Jolie."

"Aunt Dolie, come see us! We're playing."

Hearing Christopher's voice was like an invitation from another world.

"Christopher? Where are you?"

"At the Chirden's Museum. May you come and play? Here, Mommy wants to talk to you. 'Bye."

The phone banged against something before I heard Stephanie's voice. "Jolie?"

"I'm here."

"We're at the Children's Museum and we thought you might like to join us. It's just over on Fifth."

I glanced at my watch; it was after eleven-thirty. "I don't know that I'd be very good company—"

"Things pretty tense there?" she asked. Stephanie knew about the murder, but she wasn't aware of my personal link to it.

"Very," I said with more emphasis than I'd intended.

"Then this is exactly what you need, a hundred happy kids. Christopher begged me to call you. How about it? We can even have lunch later if you have the time."

I started to hedge some more and changed my mind. "I'd love to come over for a while. I doubt that I can take time for lunch, but a little break would be wonderful."

"Christopher will love it."

"I'll see you in a bit," I said as I hung up and reached for my purse.

I suspected the effect of the museum would be akin to the old veterinary cattle medicine, in that it would either "cure or kill in thirty minutes." Not that I thought I'd die from the noise and chaos, but if it didn't pull me out of my current mood, it would certainly send me screaming for the door, grateful to get back to the agency.

I hadn't taken more than five steps out of my cubicle when Bohles appeared. Stolidly he watched me, then gave me a noncommittal nod, accompanied by a flat, "Mrs. Wyatt." As if he were the new hired gun in town and I was—

I wasn't sure what he thought I was, so I nodded in return. "Good-bye, Sergeant."

He stared a few moments more before he said, "I may need to talk to you again. At your convenience, of course."

"Sure. Fine. Whenever." I left the building on automatic pilot. My mind was a canyon and Bohles's words continued to echo back at me. *I may need to talk to you again. At your convenience, of course. Why did you go back to the handicap stall? And maybe Michael Sherabian was sleeping with you. . . ."*

Had I thought it would do any good, I would have put my hands over my ears and shut out Bohles's words and their damning implications.

The absolute worst was that I had no one to blame but myself. I was the one who had decided to come back to Rose Sterling for the party. Had it not been for my own vanity, I would be in Purple Sage, contentedly swearing about my job, or at my writing, or at the fluorescent light in my kitchen that intermittently flickers. I would be worrying about normal, everyday, sane things.

Instead I was here in Austin, worrying over things that should have been none of my business. Things that threatened my happiness in a subtle, insidious way.

I arrived at the Children's Museum in just minutes and found a parking spot in front. The entire complex is one large, flat stucco building that rambles around a series of semiopen hallways, all one level down from the parking lot. It houses not only the museum but a dance studio, the Austin Writers' League, a recording studio, and many other small offices, most of a creative or theatrical nature. I went down the outdoor steps and hurried into the open hallway, grateful for some protection from the cold wind.

Rather than the happy shrieks of children, the first thing I heard was Stephanie's voice; it was loud and angry as it reverberated through the barren halls.

"Damn it, you have to stop following me! Do you understand? Stay the hell away from us!" To my left was the door to the

Children's Museum; Stephanie seemed to be down and around the corner to my right, but I couldn't be positive.

A man's voice responded to her, but I couldn't make out the words.

"Forget the justifications," Stephanie snapped back. "I've told you before, I want you to go away. I mean it. Now. Forever."

I'd determined she was somewhere to my right, and I was about to hurl around the corner to protect her from this intruder when she added, "And next time I'm telling everything. Do you understand? Every fucking thing!"

I stopped. This was someone she knew, and I wasn't sure I wanted to plunge into the midst of it; it also didn't sound like she needed me. With my coat wrapped tightly around me I edged nearer the museum door, just in case reinforcements were called for.

When the door eased open, I turned. Christopher was struggling to get out. "Aunt Dolie!"

"Christopher—" I helped him into the hallway, then bent down and gave him a hug. "How are you, little bug?"

"I'm fine. Where's my mommy?"

"I'm right here." Stephanie rounded the corner briskly, her face pinched and tight. I waited for the other person to follow her, but no one did.

"Are you okay?" I asked.

She flashed me a quick nod as she shooed us inside. "I was just in the bathroom. And, Christopher, you were supposed to stay in the museum. You can't go running off like that." She moved us both around the corner of the gift shop, and bent down to lecture him. "I mean this, and I want you to listen; it's important. A bad person could get you."

"I found Aunt Dolie—"

"Yes, you were lucky, but I want your promise that in the future you will stay just where I tell you to. Promise me."

He looked into her eyes, raised his hand, and said, "I promise."

"Thank you."

There were things going on here that I didn't understand. We do live in a world that is hazardous to children. The statistics are enough to frighten any parent: when children are abducted, they will never make it home alive unless they do something to free themselves. It makes sense to teach our kids ways to fight back, or at least protect themselves, but Stephanie's fears seemed rooted in a more immediate threat. My concern was, how immediate? And how dangerous?

I wanted to ask questions, but before I could formulate any, Stephanie stood up and said to Christopher, "So where do you want to go?"

"I know!" Christopher said, in a quick mood shift from the solemn promise he'd just made. "Let's play in the music room." He grabbed my hand and pulled me farther into the museum. "Hurry, Aunt Dolie, they have a whole bunch of stuff. You'll like it. . . ."

"Just a minute, I think I have to pay—"

Stephanie said, "You two go ahead, I'll take care of it."

"Good plan!" Christopher said, tugging me forward.

I went with him, but I couldn't help myself from turning around, just on the off chance that I would see the person Stephanie had been arguing with. Through the glass doors I glimpsed the hallway, but, it was empty. Stephanie saw my glance, and waved us on as if nothing had happened.

❧ CHAPTER 16 ❧

CHRISTOPHER BALKED as we loaded him into his car seat. He had played hard and run us hard as well, so now we were all showing signs of wear.

"Christopher, stop wiggling!" Stephanie snapped.

He slapped at the webbing as Stephanie pulled it over his head. "It's too tight! I told you, Mommy, it hurts me."

"And I told you that it doesn't hurt, and you have to wear it. It's a law, Christopher."

"Here, I have an idea." I jumped in and pulled at the underside to release the belt some, giving him an inch of breathing space. "It's the heavy coat—they take up so much room."

Stephanie looked annoyed. "Thank you. Now, Christopher, it's fixed; time to go home and take a nap."

"I want pizza! You said pizza."

"You can have soup at Grandma Prissy's and then you have to sleep. You're tired and you're cranky. You haven't been sleeping."

"Mommy—"

Before there was a full-scale outbreak, I leaned in and kissed Christopher. "I'll bring you pizza for dinner if you take a good long nap." I noticed Stephanie's scowl. "And if your mommy says it's okay."

Here in the gray light of the parking lot Stephanie's face looked drawn. Christopher wasn't the only one who was tired.

She shrugged. "Pizza's fine. Whatever."

I touched her arm. "Steph, look, I know it's none of my business, but it's apparent something's going on. You know I'm here for you and Matt, too. If there's anything we can do to help, we'll do it."

The sun broke free of the clouds and she blinked at the sudden brightness. For just a moment she looked relieved, perhaps expectant, as if we really could make things better, then something in her face shuttered and she flashed a determined smile. "I appreciate that," she said, turning to make sure the buckle had caught on Christopher's seat belt, "but everything's fine. Really. Except—" She stopped, and waved away her irritation. "Never mind. Okay, Christopher, time to go. Give Aunt Jolie a kiss."

Which meant I had to lean in and kiss Christopher good-bye, giving Stephanie a chance to get in the driver's seat and start the car. It was an effective escape method.

"We'll see you tonight," she said over her shoulder. "Don't hurry home on our account; we'll be napping until at least five-thirty." She put the car in gear.

"Have a nice rest." I closed the door; Christopher was already nodding off, and Stephanie was anxious to be on her way. Which left me with another load of concern and unanswered questions. Maybe I would detour by the mall on the way back and ask Santa if he could bring solutions instead of presents this year.

Matt called about three-thirty. My mind cleared, I had eaten a sandwich for lunch, and plunged back into work afterward. There was no need to rush back to Prissy's house with everyone else already occupied. Prissy had gone off with Todd to do some last-minute shopping; Jeremy was out cruising the city with Alicia acting as tour guide and chauffeur, while Stephanie and Christopher were sleeping. I hadn't known where Matt was until I picked up the phone.

"You were among the missing," I said.

Matt's normally easygoing voice sounded tense. "No, I'm not

missing. I've been working on Austin Edge. How is your day going?"

"Does the term 'like crap' ring any familiar bells?"

Instead of laughing, he responded with a terse, "Yes. That's how mine feels, too."

Not what I had expected. "Sounds serious. Can you talk?"

"A little." I heard phone rustles as if Matt were repositioning himself. "I'm at the CPAs right now, and we've found some financial irregularities that need to be straightened out. If we can get it done by tomorrow, then Trey will come back up here and address the management team with me. If not, it's going to have to wait until after the first of the year."

"I'm sorry." Matt is wonderful at both the financial end of business and dealing with people, but this didn't sound easy regardless of his skills. "Are you saying someone was embezzling money from the company?"

"Not outright; as of yet I'm not even sure what they've done is illegal. That's part of what has to be determined, and I'm meeting with some lawyers tomorrow morning. Apparently the management staff took out loans against the capital, and then used the capital to give themselves perks and bonuses. In effect, it gutted the company financially."

"Do they know you're on to them?"

"Not yet." The words sounded as hard as an ax hitting bone. "I may bring some of this home to work on, if you don't mind."

I had intended to talk to him about Stephanie, but it wasn't the time. "Whatever's best is fine with me. I'm just sorry this is going on."

"Me, too. I'll see you tonight."

"Okay. I love you."

"You, too," he said as we hung up.

I plopped down into my chair—Desi's chair—and my feet kicked at the box I'd tucked under there. I tapped my fingers on the keyboard and stood back up. As my friend Liz Street would say, "The vibes were all wrong." There didn't seem to be any peaceful haven this holiday season—no place where I could stop,

148

relax, and simply enjoy. Everywhere I went, every which way I turned, there seemed to be undercurrents of trouble.

The atmosphere at Prissy's was especially distressing because it involved people I loved. Stephanie could protest all she liked, but there was something wrong in her life. There had to be if she was being followed.

I rubbed my stiff shoulders and took a new position in the chair. Maybe my mood was all from unbalanced hormones; it was an encouraging thought, but unless menopause was striking ridiculously early, it wasn't true. What I needed was to get Stephanie alone and get her to talk. Or perhaps Prissy had some idea what was going on.

I fretted for a while, tapping the keyboard until a line of *j*'s appeared on the screen. Had Matt been there, he would have told me unless there was something I could do at that moment to solve the problem, my worrying wasn't helping her or me. Matt gives great advice, and sometimes I take it to heart, changing my outlook completely. At other times it merely leaves me more frustrated and wanting to clobber him.

Desi was grinning down at me from her picture on the wall, the one taken on top of the mountain. Today her smile seemed to hold more dare than triumph. It seemed personal, as if directed at me.

I jumped out of the chair and reached toward the box under the desk. Just touching the rippled cardboard made me nervous, and rather than pull it out, I left it where it was and started through the agency to see who was where.

"Everything okay, Jolie?" Ralph asked as I passed his office.

"Fine. Just stretching." I slowed. "I thought you were going to The Production Block?"

He looked at his watch. "I don't have to leave for another few minutes."

"How's the newsletter coming?"

"Very s-l-o-w-l-y. This computer barely has enough memory, so if I get too many pages opened at once, the whole thing locks up on me and I have to shut it down and start over." He made a crashing sound in his throat and aimed a karate chop at the air just above the computer. "My kingdom, such as it is, for more RAM."

"I'm sorry I asked."

"I should have this finished by tonight. If not, I'm quitting my job and moving to the outback."

"Out back of your house?"

His grin was rueful. "That's about all I'll be able to afford."

"I won't keep you, then. See you later."

I kept moving. The place was like an abandoned ship; there were two empty cubicles before I found another human, and that was Fred, the graphic artist. He was hunched over his drawing board making tiny marks on a poster for a local bed and breakfast.

"How's it going?" I asked, lingering in the doorway.

Fred started, clutching his shirt near the region of his heart. "I was concentrating."

"I'm sorry, I didn't mean to startle you."

"That's okay, come on in."

"I'm Jolie Wyatt; I don't know if we've officially met. I'm writing copy and I used to work here."

"I know." He held out his square hand and his shirtsleeve pulled up to reveal a woven copper bracelet tarnished with patches of green; I wondered if it really did help arthritis, as I'd heard it was supposed to.

As we shook hands he said, "I used to work for Mickie Bellah Advertising when you were here. We pitched a couple of accounts against you."

"Did we win or lose?"

"A little of both."

"Well, that's good, I suppose." I stared at him a moment longer. "Oh, yes. I remember, you were, uh, uh, the artist." The word *artist* was in lieu of what had almost slipped out; I'd been about to say he'd been slimmer, and when I realized that was unacceptable I couldn't think of anything to replace it except younger, or cleaner-looking. I vetoed all three.

"Right." He laughed, as if he suspected what had been on my mind.

I moved closer to the drawing table. "I didn't see you at the party the other night."

"I was out a week for the holidays," he said, as he turned back to his work, shading in a pale green on the stalk of an iris. "Missed the whole thing."

"You must have celebrated early."

He looked up. "Hanukkah. I'm Jewish."

"Oh, damn. I mean, of course." I was beginning to bumble like Nola. "I'm sorry, I live in a small town now and it's so firmly fundamental I forget there is anything else. That's what happens when you move off to the Hill Country."

"No biggie. But don't tell my mom." He smiled and he looked both younger and happier. "I'm trying to talk her into moving to Fredericksburg."

"She'll love it. How was your vacation?"

He laid down the green pencil and picked up a lavender one, which he used to shade the tip of the flower. "I don't know if I'd call it a real vacation." He shook his head and turned to face me. "Ten full days at my mom's house in Cleveland was a lot of time; I mean, I could have gone on a cruise to Alaska with all that time."

"But I'll bet you made your mom happy."

"Yeah. I did." He grinned as he tugged at the shark's tooth around his neck. "She say's I'm a good boy."

"You see? Now, there's an endorsement."

"For what it's worth. Except I really wish I'd been here."

"May I?" I asked, gesturing to a tall stool opposite him.

"Sure."

As I sat down I said, "Why? Too much work when you got back?"

"No. Because . . ." His face grew long and sad. "I didn't get to say good-bye to Desi. Desi Baker. I guess you didn't know her."

How could I explain she was a specter haunting my office? "I heard her speech about Chester. It was very effective."

151

"Was it? I'm glad. She was nervous about that speech. She practiced it with me a couple of times before I left." He stared out the window. Then he said, "How'd she look in her black dress?"

"Gorgeous."

He nodded and smiled. "Yeah, I knew she would. She was tellin' me about that dress; she'd bought it special for the party. She was pumping weights a lot and eating special stuff so she'd look extra hot. Crazy kid. She was a knockout anyway, but she just didn't get it." He shook his head, for once looking straight at me. "I miss her. She was a real different kind of person, if you know what I mean. And honest. If I asked her something she didn't want to tell me, she'd just say, 'Fred, there are some things I can't talk about.' Like about her mom. Or one time this fall she was real stressed, and she never did tell me what it was about. She just wasn't the kind to cry on anyone's shoulder. I like that in a woman." He shook his head as if to shake away the memory.

His next thought was brighter. "Oh, and she did funny stuff. Like she dressed up as a pumpkin for Halloween, and went around the building giving out apples and oranges. That was really nice, you know?" His grin faded and his face aged in the process. "And then some asshole comes along and kills her."

I nodded, thinking again how unfair life can be. And death. "At least she was happy about getting to write copy. Wasn't she?"

"Oh, yeah, she was real happy. Man, she hated that accounting stuff, but it was the only job she could get in advertising. It's tough right now."

"I've heard."

"It wasn't until about a month ago that she got to change jobs, and she was like a little kid, she was so excited. It wasn't because she couldn't do the accounting; she could. Desi worked hard at it, you know? She was just that way. Real hardworking, straight-arrow kind of person. Like she was John Wayne inside. But female and hip. Didn't smoke, was a vegetarian, worked out all the time. A real straight arrow."

My brain was busy digesting all this new information on Desi

Baker. "I guess I'd better get back to work. . . ." I said, sliding off the stool and moving toward the doorway.

"Yeah, me, too. But hey, thanks for listening to me." He appeared sheepish. "I didn't mean to dump on you like that, but Desi, she affected people. I guess she got to me, too."

"That's okay. And I do understand, because I've been affected by her, too." I waved and started down the hall toward the front office, trying to fit these new facets of Desi's character into the picture I already had. I'd made some assumptions about her and now I had to question them.

"Whoops, excuse me." Ralph whizzed past me carrying a battered briefcase and a folder of copy. "See you tomorrow. Half day—your last day, I promise."

Before I could say good-bye the tree ornaments clattered and he was gone.

Who did that leave in the building? The Sherabians? Donna Katherine? Nola?

When I reached the front office Amber had the receiver to her ear taking a message, and Donna Katherine was standing in front of the desk, tapping her foot, like a mother waiting for her teenager to get off the phone.

"Leaving early?" I asked. Donna Katherine was wrapped in a full-length coat and carrying her big black leather purse.

"Christmas shopping. I swear, I haven't had a day off in years, so I'm heading out now. I'll be back in the morning." She jerked a thumb in Amber's direction. "Tell her when she gets off the phone, will ya?"

"Sure. Have fun."

"Fun? Darlin', this is going to be like rounding up livestock at the rodeo. A timed event. I don't have even seconds to spare if I'm going to get everything done before Christmas!" Then she whipped out.

Amber thanked the caller and hung up. "I don't know why Donna Katherine thinks I'm deaf if I'm on the phone. I heard every word she said. They probably heard her in Louisiana!"

"Then you know she's out."

153

"Right."

"So where's everybody else?" I asked. "This place is like a—a library."

Amber counted off the staff on her fingers. "Chester went to a thing at the Headliners Club, Nola is working out of her house because now James has the flu, and the Sherabians are looking at new office space." She scrunched up her face and then smiled weakly. "I didn't say that, okay?"

"Didn't say what?"

"Thanks."

New office space. Smaller offices? Probably, and most likely in a less expensive building.

I hated that things were so rough, not so much for Audry or Michael, but for Chester. He and his wife, Rose Sterling, had built this agency from a little mom-and-pop shop that consisted of a typewriter and a copier on their kitchen table, to a viable and respected agency. They'd weathered the economic storms of the eighties, which made it especially unfair that they were facing trouble in Austin's affluent nineties.

While Amber took another call I thought about that. Beyond unfair, it seemed odd. The agency should have been prospering, especially with their experienced staff. There were ways an advertising agency could get in trouble, but they seemed unlikely with Chester at the helm. Underbidding jobs or undercharging for work could cause problems, but you caught those mistakes and corrected them; you didn't continue them until the business faltered. Bad debts could also hurt, but Rose Sterling had a pretty solid client base, at least from what I'd seen. Most of the businesses had been around a long time and were fiscally responsible. They paid their bills, something that's considered a nice quality in a client.

I thought about what Matt had said, management borrowing against capital and using the money on themselves. There were only two people in the agency in a position to do that—Audry and Michael. I found it hard to believe they would do that to Chester. Sort of.

154

"Are you leaving or what?" Amber asked, punching a phone button with finality and putting down the receiver.

"No, just taking a breather. I was beginning to feel permanently hunched over the computer, like a mannequin in a store window."

"I saw a movie like that once."

"Sounds like science fiction—I only write mysteries."

Amber made a sad little face and said, "Like Desi's murder. That's a mystery." Her eyes reddened as if she might start crying again.

"There are a lot of mysteries around here," I said, intending to distract her, then realized how suspicious it sounded.

"Oh, yeah? Like what?"

I had to think up an answer. "Why the copier is always out of paper just when I need to use it." That got a weak smile out of her. "Why it never rains until it's time to go home."

"Yeah, I know about those. Like, why I always get a zit just before a big date." The phone buzzed and Amber reached for it. "Rose Sterling Advertising." After a short pause, "Oh, hi, Mom. What's up?"

I turned away to give her privacy.

Outside the tinted windows the winter sky looked ominously dark, while inside, the agency was almost empty, the kind of quiet that creates intimacy. I looked back at Amber, who was saying into the receiver, "Of course, I'm fine. A little depressed, but I told you all that last night. No, I don't think I'll get there in time for dinner. Probably not until seven or so."

Today Amber was dressed in black with burgundy lipstick and fresh nail polish. Her straight hair was clean and shiny as if she'd made the effort to pull herself together.

I wondered if she was strong enough to talk about Desi. Something was bothering me, and Amber was probably one of the few people in the agency who could explain it to me.

"Okay. Okay. Sure; I'll see you Christmas Eve. 'Bye. Okay, Mom. 'Bye." She put the receiver back.

"Amber," I said, wondering if I was doing the right thing,

155

"there's something about Desi I don't quite understand. Would it be hard for you to talk a little about her? Just to help me on this?"

She looked puzzled and bit her lip. "Yeah, I guess I can. What is it?"

I paused to phrase my question delicately so as not to distress her. "I've heard some people say that Desi was very straight. Honest—"

"She was. That's exactly the way Desi was. I mean, she would tell you the truth no matter what." She gestured with her hands as if trying to make the picture of Desi clear enough for me to visualize. "Like this one time, she saw this kid, and he was like a big kid, you know, maybe fifteen or sixteen. She saw him steal some stuff from a store, and she grabbed him and said that either he could put it back, or she was calling the police and the store manager." Amber rested her hands on the desk, shaking her head in amazement. "He could have pulled a knife or something, but Desi said it was important that he knew he'd been caught. And I said she could have called the police, but she wanted the kid to have a chance to make restitution. That was important to her."

Straight arrow and moral. Although that was with a stranger.

I asked, "How was she with people she knew?"

Amber answered instantly. "The same. Honest. Last year I was going out with this guy, and he was real scum, but I didn't know it. Well, Desi saw him out with another girl. Even though she didn't want to hurt my feelings, she told me because she thought I needed to know." Amber lifted her shoulders in a gesture of resolution. "She was just that way. She said I should date people of a higher caliber."

Which brought me right where I wanted to be. I reached for the stapler and picked it up, opening and closing it casually, as if to make my words less important. "So tell me, who was Desi dating recently?"

⇻ CHAPTER 17 ⇺

Desi used to be married. Did I tell you that before?"

"I think you mentioned it."

Amber nodded solemnly, her fingers tugging on a lock of hair that swung forward. "He was a pilot for some airline. They divorced about three years ago. Bastard." She leaned forward to add, "He was one. A bastard. She never came right out and said it, but I think he used to hit her. He'd be like gone on a trip, and then he'd come home and accuse her of fooling around."

The heat in the building suddenly came on. "I'm sorry for Desi. He must have been a jealous man."

"A horrible man," she corrected. "I mean Desi wouldn't do something like that, so he couldn't have known her very well, and he was gone a lot, anyway. But from what she said he was older, you know? And here he had this young beautiful wife—well." She shrugged.

Trophy wife, like Stephanie. I wondered if Desi would have been considered a trophy for Michael. While he was older, it wasn't by that many years, and he was simply incredibly handsome, which seemed to alter the circumstances.

"Some women like older men," I said. "Apparently Desi was one of them."

"Not after that," Amber said. "She didn't like older men at all anymore. Except for friends, like Fred, who's kind of strange, but really a nice guy." She jerked her thumb to indicate his not-too-distant cubicle. "But she wouldn't go out with those kinds of men. She said you should only date younger guys, because then

157

you could train them right." This time Amber laughed. "Only I was dating an eighteen-year-old, and Desi said maybe I had gone too far. Then I was going out with—"

"Wait." I held up my hand to stop her, and my own confused thoughts. "I'm sorry, I was getting lost. You said that Desi only liked younger men, but she wasn't actually dating any, was she?"

Amber pulled on the blond lock again and thought about the question. "Sure. Well, no. Not now. Last summer she was dating two guys; one was some kind of engineer at some computer company. Real cute guy; I can't remember his name, but I think he was about my age. I'm twenty-three. And then there was Rudy. He was older, well, older of the younger ones, maybe twenty-eight, only Desi couldn't get serious about him. I'm pretty sure he moved to L.A. around Halloween."

The thought of the cardboard box under my desk tickled my brain. That was now a more potent pull. So I hurried the conversation.

"Amber, was Desi dating anyone recently?"

She didn't have to think about that. "No. She had some guys who asked her out, but Desi could afford to be picky, because she was really beautiful, and she had that great bod. In fact, she was taking something new to pump up her muscles; it was kind of like"—she rolled her eyes—"far out, and she was going to tell me about it—"

"I heard she was going out with an older man."

"You did?" Amber stopped and cocked her head to the side. "How old?"

"Thirty-eight."

"Ooh, that's just icky!"

"I heard he worked here at the agency, too."

For a moment she looked like an angry child, and I half expected her to jump up and stomp her foot. "I sure would like to know who's badmouthing Desi that way! I heard that rumor, too, that she was going out with Michael Sherabian, but beside the fact that he's too old for her, he's married. Desi wouldn't do that!"

158

"I'm sure you're right."

But who can say what any of us would really do? Matt would probably swear that I wouldn't date a married man, either. Even one who was separated from his wife.

I looked at Amber, knowing that these were lessons she would learn somewhere along the way, just like the rest of us. It wouldn't help to tell her, she wouldn't listen. I did give her a hint. "Sometimes life isn't the way we think it ought to be."

"Yeah," she said, then added, "Death isn't much of a picnic either."

I was torn between laughing and patting her hand in sympathy. Neither felt appropriate, so I glanced at my watch. "Guess I'd better get back to work."

Amber was staring intently out the front door as I left; I couldn't begin to guess what she was thinking. I, on the other hand, had a very focused thought and it was finally time to act on it.

Back in the office I shared with Desi's memory, I pulled out the cardboard box and put it on top of the desk. Once the lid was off, I peered inside. It appeared to me that Desi had packed the bottom of the box carefully, then at the last minute, shoved in those things that might get lost somewhere else. There was the small brown teddy bear that probably sat on her computer. I put it aside. As my skin made contact with the fuzzy body I thought for the first time about fingerprints. They weren't going to appear on the bear, but they would show up on any of the paper I touched.

While it felt silly, I got my leather gloves from my coat pocket. They were tight-fitting, and in other circumstances, not too clumsy. I just hoped no one would see me digging in the box with them on.

After one more peek into the empty hallway, I went back to my exploration. I removed a small bag of red jelly beans that Desi had tucked away, no doubt to avoid temptation. A wrapped present with a tag that said it was for Amber was next; I would let the police deal with that. There were two bottles of nail polish, a bottle of glue, a wrist brace like those used to avoid carpel tunnel, some blank postcards from various cities in Colorado, a stapler, a porcelain pitcher with eight or nine pens and pencils, and a basket containing potpourri. None of it seemed important. This was simply the stuff she'd had on top of her desk or file cabinet, and had ended up throwing it all in a box for safe storage.

Even surmising that, I handled everything as gingerly as possible, touching as little of each surface as I could.

Next came the hanging folders, and while not as interesting to look at, they were more intriguing to me. After all, words are my life, and they were Desi's, too.

Touching only the edges, I went through the papers, careful to keep them in order. The first file was overstuffed with a hodge-podge of old commercial copy. Some of the radio scripts covered end-of-summer sales, and there was one for a spring closeout. By rifling through I discovered that most were over six months old. I suspected what I had just found was Desi's filing. That had been my job when I'd first started as a copywriter, and as I remembered, they'd saddled me with almost six months worth of stuff that no one else had bothered to put away. I set the whole stack back in the folder. I wasn't going to file it either.

The next folder was labeled PLANNED PURCHASES. There were maybe eight pieces of paper inside. On top was an order form from an herb company. There was a page torn out of a magazine that showed a model wearing a short, lime green skirt with a skinny white T-shirt. There was a catalog from one of those specialty houses; one page was dog-eared and on it were various types of decorative fire logs and fireplace accessories. Desi's new apartment must have a fireplace.

There was also an ad for an Exercycle and a catalog with personalized stationery. My mind went nuts making up all kinds of stories about that. Was Desi planning on getting married? Was she looking for new thank-you notes with her married name? As I flipped through the catalog I found a circle around some return-address labels. New apartment, new address, new labels.

The third folder was simply marked FUN STUFF. There were

cartoon clippings from half a dozen strips ranging from Garfield to Kathy. There were E-mails with jokes. There were Crash Jet advertising slogans: *First with nonstop flights into the Grand Canyon.* I found lawyer jokes: *"As medical examiner, how many autopsies would you say you have performed on dead people?" "I would say I have performed all my autopsies on dead people."* Even a sheet labeled PHILOSOPHICAL SAYINGS: *Eat a toad first thing in the morning and nothing worse will happen to you all day.* The eclectic bits of trivia that every office collects. At least mine always does.

By this time I was wondering if I could make some copies so I could share the humorous items with my friends back in Purple Sage. I was beyond hope of finding anything that might point to Desi's murderer, but not quite ready to put everything away. As I picked up the next page, it slipped between my gloved hands and floated toward the floor. The print on it was slightly fuzzed and curved as if it had been photocopied from a book. I picked it up and was about to flip it aside when a word in the heading caught at me. *Mistletoe.*

My brain went on red alert.

It was a portion of a chapter about how mistletoe as a food could be a foundation for any bodybuilding routine. ". . . The study showed that mistletoe when taken in large quantities acted as a natural hormone. . . . helped build muscle rapidly . . . burned fat . . . turned into essential proteins to rebuild cells damaged from environmental factors and poor eating habits."

I couldn't believe anyone had written such a thing! It was wrong, flat wrong. Mistletoe was a poison. Everyone knew that; certainly anyone who grew up in this part of the country. I grabbed the dictionary from the side drawer and flipped to *M.* I was sure I was right.

The dictionary said mistletoe was a parasitic evergreen with waxy berries. There were also two mentions of its uses in certain customs, one being for kissing at Christmastime, while the other was in Druid ceremonies. There was nothing about its poisonous qualities. It didn't prove a thing.

Still outraged, I set the paper aside; I was going to do some further research on the subject as soon as I finished with the box.

The next piece of paper was a copy of an article on mistletoe torn from a newspaper. On the photocopy the ragged edges showed up like the dark outlines of a map. It said that scientists at Sloan Kettering in New York had discovered that this common parasitic plant, "once thought to be poisonous," actually did a number of beneficial things for the human body. "Mistletoe increases the metabolism, burning unwanted calories even while the body is at rest." Additionally the story said it was a muscle builder. There were several paragraphs more, including research statistics and some very impressive reasons to eat mistletoe if you wanted to strengthen and build muscles quickly, with less workout time and less concern about caloric intake.

My brain continued to fight against accepting these purported facts. Mistletoe grew like the parasite it was on half the trees on our property, and while it looked festive, it was nonetheless poisonous. I had researched mistletoe for a manuscript, and according to every source I had checked, including the Poison Control Center, mistletoe could be lethal.

So where had these articles come from? And why were they here?

The answer began to filter slowly through my anger. These articles might induce anyone, even Desi Baker, to drink mistletoe tea. What a perfect way to commit murder, and how insidious.

I picked up all three sheets of paper and held them close to my chest as I whipped through the hall to the copy room. The police needed to see these, but I wanted my own copies first.

As I placed the sheets in the automatic feeder, I realized that if I were caught, I was going to have a hell of a time explaining just what I was doing. Especially with gloves on.

The machine whirred and a light told me to wait while it warmed up.

I waited. I breathed. I worried.

The light went off and I pressed the button for one copy. With the slickness of modern technology, the machine clamped down all three pieces of paper, and whisked one off the bottom to send it into the entrails of the machine where magic would take place and a copy would be made. The moving light spilled out from the flat tray on top, and then a paper ejected from the side of the machine. It was my copy and I grabbed it up and flipped it over, putting the original facedown beside it.

By this time my heart was pounding as if I had been eating mistletoe with the results predicted from the articles.

While I waited the machine stopped its work and a new light flashed. *Original jammed.*

My gloves caught on the metal as I pulled open the front of the machine and stared into its bowels. Damn thing—where was that paper? With great haste I pulled out a metal rack, looked behind it, and shoved it back in. I shut the door with a snap. Work now, damn it.

But the machine refused to operate and the light flashed again. *Original jammed.*

Original, original. Not the copy!

I lifted the lid of the feeder and saw my original stuck in a white belt.

"Son of a—"

I pulled it out, placed it facedown on the glass, closed the lid, and hit the start button again. The familiar whir started up, and the light began to move.

The heat came on, blowing from an air duct above me. It was totally unnecessary since I was already sweating. There was also a tear in my good gloves. That would teach me to dig in copy machines, except I knew it wouldn't.

My second copy ejected and then the third; I practically fought the machine for the paper as I ripped it out of the feeder. I counted the copies and the originals twice. Three of each. Then I ran back to Desi's office.

Once there, I couldn't even stop to breathe. What I had found could be important to the police investigation. These could be the very leads that would take them to her murderer. There were two more files in the bottom of the box; one was labeled ABSCAN. I flipped it open and found a fact sheet for writing copy. Something about a computer company here in Austin. The next folder contained a couple of invoices. The top one was a November bill for Stuff'N Puff in the amount of two thousand dollars. I was beyond reading anything more.

I began putting things away in the box, just exactly as I remembered they had been. The fun-stuff file went in on top of AbScan and the invoices, with the mistletoe stories last in the file. On top of them went the jokes, and finally the cartoons. I closed the file, sucked in air, and stacked the planned-purchases folder and the old commercials on top.

My hands were actually shaking, something that rarely happened to me, as I hastily deposited everything else in the box and replaced the lid.

I was trying to get the gloves off my sweaty hands, my teeth clenched on the tips of the right-hand fingers, when Amber walked in.

"Did you hear someone running in the hall?" she asked.

"Uh . . ." I took my teeth off the glove. "Yes. That was me. I was leaving, but then I remembered something."

"Oh, yeah? What?"

Like everyone ran through the hall with their gloves on. My hands were feeling claustrophobic, and I grabbed the fingers again and ripped it off.

"Damn, it's hot in here," I said, pulling the second glove off.

"It's always that way. Or cold. I think some gremlin in the basement controls the temperature."

Actually there was a thermostat in Audry's office, but I didn't have the patience to explain heating and cooling.

"Listen," I said, trying to gesture casually to the box that now sat innocently on the desk. "Some guy brought this back this morning. He said it was Desi's."

She nodded in agreement. "Oh, yeah, I remember."

"Well, I think we need to call the police and have them pick it up. They took some of her other things. They will probably want this, too."

"You really think so? What's in it?" She pulled the lid off before I could stop her.

"No! Don't touch anything." I grabbed the lid out of her hand and replaced it. "I'm sorry; I didn't mean to yell. It's just that there could be fingerprints, and you don't want to mess them up. Or add yours."

She brought her hand up to her mouth as if it had been burned. "Oh, wow, I didn't even think about that. You better call that Sergeant Bohles. I'll buzz you with his number."

"Why don't you make the call?"

She pointed to her watch. "It's five o'clock. I leave at five."

❧ CHAPTER 18 ❧

"So the box was delivered by some man, and you don't know his name or the name of the company he works for."

It's the details of life that will trip you up every time. I had thought Bohles would find me a hero, but instead he was asking questions I couldn't answer. I began to wonder if he suspected me of filling the box myself, just to move his suspicions elsewhere.

"Sorry. I'm sure if Amber had stayed, she could tell us. Or Donna Katherine. I could have them call you in the morning."

He shook his head as he eyed the box carefully, then removed the lid. "You think this was some extra stuff that was in Desi Baker's office?"

"Right." I had expected him to heave the box up on one large shoulder and walk out with it first thing. Instead he dawdled. He asked how things were going and if Desi had left behind a lot of work. He wanted to know if she had been any good at her job. Interesting questions that I would have preferred to answer at another time.

Without seeming to touch things, he rearranged the contents of the box so that he could flip open the folders with a pencil. "These are commercials, right?"

I peered in as if I hadn't seen them before. "Yes. We call that copy."

He went through a dozen or more sheets of paper, lifting them so I could see what was printed on each one, and what was underneath. "Why do you think she put them here?" he asked.

"Well," I said, "I think that copy should have been filed and she didn't get around to it."

"Like hiding the laundry?"

"Something like that."

He opened the next file, and we looked through the planned purchases, both of us peering into the box. When he got to the lime green skirt he made a sound, something soft and unhappy. I looked up to find that he was shaking his head sadly. Without my asking he said, "She had a skirt just like that in her closet. Still had the tags on it."

"Oh." Before his comment, Desi Baker had become like a new pen pal to me—someone I was just getting to know and whose messages I enjoyed very much. Now I remembered the reality of the situation.

Bohles opened the next file. I tensed in anticipation of what we were to find; it was like knowing the scary part of a movie was coming, but pretending you hadn't seen the film before.

"That's great." He was grinning openly at one of the cartoons and he looked up to share the laughter with me. I tried my best to laugh, at least to grin, but the skin on my face felt too tight to let the muscles move naturally. I grimaced instead, hoping he'd buy that.

Next were the jokes and finally the articles on mistletoe. His eyes moved quickly to capture my response. I felt my stomach quiver. "Mistletoe." I breathed the word; my voice sounded sick.

It must have struck him as a natural reaction, because he went back to scanning the article, frowning as he did. "You ever read anything like this on mistletoe?" he asked.

"Never." I shook my head, vehemently. "I think I read it was supposed to prevent abortions, or maybe cause them. But I've always heard it's poisonous, especially in large doses." I stepped back away from the box, as if disavowing any association with what it held. "What about you?" I pointed but kept my distance. "Have you heard anything like that?"

He shrugged a big shoulder. "I leave all that to the experts." He slipped over the next two articles and went directly to the last green hanging folder. "What's AbScan? Do you know?"

I peeked into the box, then back up at Bohles. "It's a computer company here in Austin, isn't it?"

"Sounds right; that's probably where I've heard of them. Are they a client?"

I shook my head. "Not that I know of. Of course, I don't know all their clients anymore. And it could have been a pitch they made that they lost. It happens." With three or four agencies going up for every account, it happens on a regular basis. You get used to losing, although it's never enjoyable. I started to add something more, but Bohles was again poking in the box.

"Why would she have invoices?" he asked.

"I don't know." The telephone rang, the sound echoing from several phones around the agency. I hit the speaker option and said, "Rose Sterling Advertising."

"Hi, Aunt Dolie!"

"Well, Christopher, how are you?"

"I'm very hungry. May you bring my pizza?"

"Oh, no!" I looked at my watch; five-twenty. "I'm sorry, sweetie, I'm running a little late. Let me talk to your mommy, okay? I'll have it delivered right to your door. You could eat some fruit while you're waiting."

"I don't eat fruit. Here's Mommy."

"Sorry," Bohles said to me, as if he were responsible for my neglect of Christopher. He began putting everything back in its place. "I didn't mean to keep you."

Stephanie's voice sounded less strained than earlier. "Forgot us, huh? Christopher never forgets."

"I got tied up. How about if I order pizza, or you do that, and I'll be home in time to pay for it. Would that work?"

"Actually, I already ordered it. Take your time." She was definitely her mother's daughter; well organized and still silly enough to call and give me a hard time just for the fun of it. Actually, that reminded me more of her grandfather, Matt's dad.

"Good, then traffic notwithstanding, I'll be there in twenty minutes."

Bohles waited patiently until I hung up. He handed me a sheet of paper. "That's a receipt for the box and the contents, just to keep this on the up and up. I'll walk you out."

"Sure," I said, slipping on my coat. I left the gloves in the pocket. My luck, Bohles would notice the rip and then find matching leather DNA on the paper. Assuming there was such a thing.

We walked together toward the front desk. Fred was still there, still hunched over the drawing board, and I called a quick good night as we passed his cubicle. We stopped twice on our way to the door, once so I could turn off the copy machine, and once to check that the coffeepot was turned off.

"Just like home," Bohles said as I dropped the receipt on Amber's desk and we exited the offices. "Do you need to lock up?"

I shook my head. "No. Fred will do that."

"But you do have a key."

"Chester gave me one on my first day back. Does it matter?"

"Nope." We were at the elevator, and after I pushed the button he said, "Not near as much as why you walked back to that handicapped stall the night of the party. Or why you crumpled that note from Michael Sherabian and threw it in the trash." He smiled. "You ever going to tell me that?"

It was like a joke shared with a friend, but something inside me stiffened. This man was not a friend. He was like a crocodile, circling playfully, and I knew that the unwary who played back could be in trouble.

Instead of smiling, I shook my head seriously, pensively. I lifted my shoulders in a shrug. "It's the oddest thing, I guess we'll never know. What does Michael say about that note?"

He watched me carefully, the wide eyes shrinking. "He says he never wrote it." He blinked as we entered the already-packed elevator. "I have my own theory. Maybe I'll tell you about it the next time I see you."

169

The thought of telling the truth about the note, and my reaction to it, wasn't so frightening now that I knew Bohles a little better. If I were honest about it, and honest about why I'd been circumspect initially, my gut feeling was that he would use the information to help with the investigation, but would also protect the confidentiality of it.

I glanced over at him. I was pretty sure my secret would be safe. By the time we arrived at the lobby level and were propelled out of the elevator by the crush of people, I was actually on the verge of asking him to come back upstairs so I could tell him the whole story but we were stopped by Audry Sterling-Sherabian, who planted herself directly in front of us.

Amber had told me the Sherabians were out looking at property; the angry set of Audry's face, coupled with the fact that Michael was no longer with her, made me suspect things had not gone well. Audry took in me, Sergeant Bohles, and the box in his arms in one agitated sweep.

"You're taking more from the agency?" she demanded.

"Yes," Bohles said casually, moving out of the way of the stream of people hurrying through the lobby. "A box of Desi Baker's things was returned by the storage company. Apparently it was overlooked earlier."

"And how did you find out about it?" she asked him, throwing a sharp glance at me.

"Mrs. Wyatt called me. There's a receipt upstairs, and if you're concerned about the contents, Mrs. Wyatt went through the box with me."

"Oh, really?" She paused and in that instant she transformed back to the old Audry I had known too well. "As if you didn't know, Sergeant Bohles, Mrs. Wyatt is not an employee, nor a representative of Rose Sterling Advertising. She is merely contract labor who happens to be working out of our offices, using our equipment. Furthermore, Mrs. Wyatt does not have the authority, or the power, to turn our records over to the police. Nor does she have permission to act on my behalf."

170

I had wondered if Audry held a grudge against me, and now I had my answer. She did indeed, and this was my punishment for what I'd done to her. It may have been well-deserved, but as I stood there in the lobby with people scurrying around us and Christmas carols playing in the background, something shifted inside of me. I had been punished enough. Even if Audry had never said a word to me, I had browbeaten and bludgeoned myself for years over my affair with Michael. It was time to get over it and move on.

Time for both of us to move on.

I looked squarely at Audry and said, "I'm sorry. I'm very sorry."

Her eyes told me she knew exactly what I was talking about. She watched me to be sure, then her mouth moved as if she had much more to say, but this was not the time or the place. After one last angry look at me she spoke directly to Bohles. "I think we should go upstairs and you can go through that box again. With me."

Bohles had been observing the two of us with an expression of smug fascination. When Audry rounded on him he lifted an eyebrow in surprise. "We can do that," he said.

"*If* I don't think the contents are crucial to the business of the agency, then you may take it with you." She tilted her head like a queen who'd just chewed up and spat out a peasant. "Of course, if you have a warrant, I suppose you can take it regardless."

"No, ma'am, I don't. I didn't think that was necessary since you were so anxious to help clear up Miss Baker's death."

It was time for me to make my exit. "It appears that my presence is superfluous," I said. "If you will excuse me, I have a dinner engagement. Good night." I added as gracious a smile as I could muster and headed for the garage. On the way I passed Ted Polovy at the security desk. He winked.

When I arrived at Prissy's my intention was to tell Matt the whole story and get it over with once and for all. I'd already thrown out my original agenda for the evening, which had been to go by the central library and research the articles on mistletoe. My curiosity wasn't as strong as my desire to spend time with my family.

The whole plan went out the window, though, because Matt wasn't there. He was still working with lawyers and CPAs, according to Prissy, who'd spoken to him on the phone not ten minutes before I arrived. She said he'd gotten three other large shareholders involved in the irregularities at Austin Edge, and while that meant shared responsibilities, it also meant more opinions to be heard and researched, with more suggestions to be weighed.

Jeremy was also out, ice-skating with Alicia. Todd had spent the afternoon with friends and wouldn't be returning until late, while Ross was attending a cocktail party on the way home, then picking up Prissy before they proceeded to two other client affairs.

Lucky for me I still had Christopher.

"Aunt Dolie, eat your pizza," he said, gesturing to my plate. "Todd will eat it all."

"Todd isn't here," Stephanie said. She looked around the table. The bowl filled with greenery, red balls, and two tall slender candles had been pushed to the side along with the lace tablecloth. In its place were two pizza boxes, both half-full. We were drinking our diet drinks out of plastic glasses and using paper plates, while paper napkins from the pizza parlor littered the table along with the crumbs.

"Civilization has finally left my mother's house," Stephanie said. "Or do I mean it's finally found my mother's house?"

Prissy frowned. "I wish you wouldn't talk like that. You make it sound like I'm living some slick plastic life, and it's just not so."

"Slick crystal life," Stephanie corrected. "Do you know this is only the third time I've ever seen a pizza box on this table?"

"Get used to it," Prissy said as she got up, taking her paper plate and a couple of crumpled napkins with her. "I'm getting old, and I'm getting tired, and frankly, my dear, I don't give a damn."

"Whooh!" Stephanie made a face and grinned at me. "For my Mom that's heavy swearing."

I was tempted to say it was because she'd been goaded into it, one of the things that happens during the forced togetherness of the holidays when there are too many people jammed together in the allotted square footage. And perhaps it wasn't the closeness so much as it was the niceness. I certainly didn't feel free to swear or yell, or just be my normal self. I'm sure the others were experiencing the same constraints, including Prissy. It was like living on a sitcom.

"Looks like it's just us women tonight," Stephanie said, closing a pizza box. "Except for you." She stood up and popped Christopher with her finger.

"Ouch. You hurted me."

"Oh, Christopher, don't be a baby." She made a swipe at the table with her napkin. "Jolie, do you want any more?"

"No, thanks, I've had my fill."

"I'm filled, too." Christopher said.

He started to climb down from the table, but Stephanie grabbed his arm. "You're not going anywhere until you wash those hands. I don't need red sauce all over Grandma Prissy's house."

I picked him up. "Come on, I'll wash you."

As I carried Christopher into the guest bath to clean him up, the phone rang and Stephanie jumped for it. I was hoping that after we got Christopher to bed there would be time to go through Prissy's library to see if she had anything on mistletoe. I seemed to recall that she'd been very involved in the herb society when I'd first met her. She might even recognize the articles I'd brought home.

"All clean," Christopher said, holding up soapy hands.

I rinsed them off, handed him a towel, and when he was dry, herded him back into the great room. Prissy was straightening the kitchen and Steph was still on the phone.

"I'd love to go, Peter," she was saying, "I really would, I just can't leave Christopher again. Of course, you're more than welcome to come over here."

Christopher walked over and tapped his mother's knees. "Aunt Dolie can baby-sit me."

Stephanie put a hand over the mouthpiece of the phone. "No, little bug, we can't ask Aunt Jolie to stay home with you again."

"Aunt Dolie loves me," he said firmly. "We party."

Stephanie threw a questioning look at me. Damn. I didn't mind taking care of Christopher, my hesitation came because I appeared to be encouraging Stephanie to go out with a man her father's age. I wasn't, but what were the alternatives?

"I'd love to take care of Christopher," I said.

"Are you sure?"

"Of course." It was that nice quotient again.

"Peter? I can go."

I had thought, or perhaps just hoped, that the relationship between Peter and Stephanie was one-sided, but there was too much excitement in her voice for that. "What time will you be here?" she asked.

When she was off the phone, Prissy said, "Why don't you bathe Christopher before you go, so Jolie can relax for at least a few minutes?"

Stephanie saluted. "Consider it done. Come on, bug, we have things to do."

They went up the stairs, and I found myself on the couch being served hot tea by Prissy. "Thought you could use this," she said.

"Oh, thanks."

"How was your day?" she asked.

I raised an eyebrow and we both started to laugh. "Sorry," she said. "I'm so used to saying that to Ross after dinner, I guess I'll ask anyone who sits on the couch." She sat on the love seat and actually let herself loosen up a little. "But seriously, how are things at the agency?"

"Fine, I guess."

"You guess?"

"Oh, it's that murder. . . ." I remembered the copies I had folded in my purse. "Something came up today that has really piqued my curiosity." I couldn't resist reaching for my purse and pulling them out. "Prissy, you used to be involved with the herb society, weren't you?"

"Second vice president, but I dropped out before they could move me any higher. Why?"

"Would you look at these and tell me what you think?"

She took the papers from me and moved over to a spot on the couch under a good light where she began to read.

✦ CHAPTER 19 ✦

Prissy turned the page over, probably knowing full well that it was a copy and there was nothing on the back. Then she peered at me over her glasses. "The byline says this is an AP story, but what newspaper is it from?"

I could only shrug. "I don't have any idea. You have everything I know about the copies right there."

"Very odd." She pushed her glasses back up on her dainty nose and, after a puzzled glance at the first page, went on to the second.

I was close enough to see that she was reading the magazine article. Her frown grew even deeper. *"The Herbal Medical Journal?* I've never heard of such a magazine; is it new?"

"I can't answer that; I've never heard of it either."

She went on to the book excerpt. Then she took off her glasses and brushed her bangs off her forehead, prior to giving me a very perplexed stare. I could certainly identify with her reactions.

"Well?" I said.

She dropped the copies into her lap. "Jolie, where did you get these? While Arundales is an authority on herbs, I've never heard anything about mistletoe being a muscle builder, or a fat burner, or any of these things. If it really works, I want some."

"Don't we all. So do you think the information is accurate?"

"I wouldn't have questioned it if you'd just given me this," she said, holding up the book excerpt. "but there's something about these other articles that bothers me. For one thing, they're writ-

176

ten in a style that smacks of sensationalism, like one of the supermarket tabloids." I didn't ask her how she knew that. "I'd like to do some research, but what's this all about?"

I had expected that, and I was prepared. "Just one of those interesting little turns that life takes," I said, then gave her a quick and dirty version of where I'd gotten the copies.

"The police could arrest you!" she exclaimed once she heard the story.

"If they do, I think it will be for something more than just making copies."

That gave her pause. "Like what could they arrest you for? I thought you didn't even know the woman."

"I'm kidding," I said.

Prissy and I have never spent much time together, nor have we been through anything emotional that would help draw us closer. Thanksgiving dinner with its obligatory football games has not been a bonding experience for Prissy and me. I didn't think telling her about an old affair was the place to start.

"Does knowing where these came from change your opinion?" I asked.

She picked up the copies and again read them over. "Wait a minute!" She jumped up. "I think I have an herb book upstairs. Come on."

I followed her up the stairs and down the hall into the library. That sounds more grand than it was, but there were a lot of books. Two walls were completely covered with books, plus there was a small book stand next to Prissy's desk, which had been overrun with electrical equipment. On it was a computer with a twenty-one-inch monitor. There was also a laser printer, a scanner, and two telephones. A second desk, which was a new addition since my last visit, was shoved up under the window and it held more computer attachments.

"And you know what else?" Prissy said. "We could also look it up on the Internet. I'm a whiz at that." She began scanning the bookshelves. I would have helped, but I suspected she knew exactly what she was looking for and where to find it.

Instead I gawked at the computer equipment. "How many modems do you have?"

"What? Oh, two, I think. I keep trading up, but they keep getting faster. And then I had an entire hard disk crash a couple of months ago, but everything off it was retrieved, including files I'd erased months ago. Isn't that amazing? Now, where is that thing?" She pulled a thick, pea green book from the shelves and held it up to show me. "Voilà! Let's see the copyright date." I peered over her shoulder as she flipped to the title page. "Great," she said, the irony apparent. "It's already two years old."

"We could at least see what it says."

She thumbed through the pages until she found mistletoe. We read it silently together, and neither of us was surprised to discover that mistletoe was listed as a poisonous parasite.

Prissy closed Arundales. "But this is two years old, and new information is always coming out." As she returned the book to the shelf she said, "Amazing when you consider how old plants are, and how long they've been used by one culture or another. You'd think we'd know all there is to know by now."

"We have to keep relearning. Rediscovering. Like teenagers."

"Isn't that the truth. We certainly can't take anyone else's word for anything. And neither can our children. What we ought to do is access the word *mistletoe* on the Internet and just see what comes up." Prissy glanced at her watch. "Darn. Ross is going to be here any minute, so we'll have to do the computer work later. Actually, if you want, you can use this computer while Ross and I are gone. Or I can do it tomorrow."

The front door opened and after a moment Ross called up the stairs, "Anybody home?"

"We're up here," Prissy responded.

"Hi, there," I called out.

"Prissy, are you ready to go?" he asked.

We were already on the landing. "Let me grab my coat. I'll meet you downstairs."

I waited while Prissy went to her room. Across the hall from the master bedroom was a full guest suite with a tiny sitting room. It was easy to tell by the scattering of toys, children's books, and kids' paraphernalia that this was where Stephanie and Christopher were sleeping. Next to them was the office, then the smallest of the rooms, which was being used by Jeremy. Across the hall and on the other side of the landing was a room with its door closed. I assumed that was Todd's.

Prissy emerged already pulling on a beautiful long black coat.

Ross was at the bottom of the stairs. "Your chariot awaits, my lady."

I followed her down.

It may have been all the activity, or the sugar in the hot chocolate that I had given him, but whatever it was, Christopher became rowdy when I tried to put him to bed. I couldn't even call for reinforcements because everyone else was gone.

"It's very late," I said, firmly.

"Aunt Dolie, I'm not tired." He was squirming and fighting as I tried to get him dressed for bed. He kicked away the pajama bottoms.

"Christopher, don't do this. You have to put these on." I grabbed his leg and thrust it in the bottoms. He was wriggling so hard I was afraid he was going to fall off the bed. "Stop it!"

"I'm not tired." It was the whine of an exhausted three-year-old. There can be no more aggravating sound to an adult, simply because the cure for it, sleep, is what the child is fighting.

I lifted him physically into the air. "I'll read you a story, but I can't until you have these on. Stop wriggling."

He kicked harder until I put him down on the bed, then he thrashed his arms, too. "No, no! I'm not nappin'! I'm not."

"Christopher!" The loud commanding voice from the doorway scared us both. It was Todd, his face both older and fiercer-looking than usual as he strode into the room. "You settle down now."

Christopher stopped moving immediately, and I took advantage of it to yank up the bottoms and then sit him upright.

"You worked some magic," I said to Todd as I pulled the pajama top over Christopher's head. When his sullen face popped out of the neck I kissed him, then put an arm into the sleeve. "You see how easy it is if you'll just hold still?"

"I didn't mean to scare you," Todd said, moving to a rocker where he sat down. "My dad always said a man's voice is more commanding."

Christopher started to cry. "Aunt Dolie, I'm tired."

"I know you are, sweetie." I got the last arm in place and picked him up, hugging his stiff little body against mine. "Now you can get some sleep, and when you wake up it's only two more days until Christmas."

"A story. You promised a story."

"Christopher," Todd snapped, "you are pushing the limits again."

I held up my hand. "No, he's right, Todd, I did promise him a story." I smiled at him. "It's important to teach by example, and promises have to be kept."

Todd looked straight at Christopher. "You have too many women spoiling you, do you know that?"

"No," Christopher said, still hugging me. "Aunt Dolie, read me *The Cat in the Hat,* please."

Round one to Christopher, not that I wanted him fighting me, but I didn't like Todd walking in and being bossy, either. "Okay, little bug, you find the book, and I'll read." I set him down and he grabbed my hand, pulling me into the sitting area.

I seemed to remember that this had been Stephanie's room before she left home. There were still some signs of that, a pair of pom-poms with their handles tucked behind the mirror, a shelf of stuffed animals on one wall. Now several suitcases were stacked in the open closet, and a tennis bag of toys spilled over on the floor.

In the corner was a large wicker basket filled with children's books and tapes. Christopher headed straight for it. "See, Aunt Dolie, it's here. We can pick it out. Or we can pick two books. I like books."

Todd had followed us, and now he gestured down the hallway. "I'll be in my room if you need me."

"Sure, and thanks again," I said as he turned and left.

Now that Christopher had settled down, tucking him under the covers, reading him a story, and then saying a bedtime prayer with him became a treat. It was like having Jeremy a baby all over again, only better, because I wasn't responsible for his every move, and I wasn't nearly so worried about how he would turn out.

"Good night, Christopher," I said, giving one final tug to his covers and kissing his forehead.

Todd's radio came on, and after a short blast he turned it down to a white noise in the background.

"May you stay here with me, Aunt Dolie?" Christopher said. "We can make a pallet on the floor by my bed."

It actually sounded inviting, but I said, "No, thank you. I have to go, so you can sleep."

"I'm scareded of the dark."

"No one can hurt you while I'm here. I'll tell you what I'll do, I'll leave the door cracked so you can see the light. Will that help?"

"Where you goin', Aunt Dolie? Are you driving away?"

"No, of course not! I'll be right across the hall in your grandma Prissy's office. You'll hear me working on the computer; if you need me, all you have to do is call and I'll run across the hall so fast I'll be here before you finish saying my name. What do you think about that?"

"Real fast?"

"Real fast. And if the door is closed, I'll run so fast I'll knock it down and put a great big hole in the wall!"

He giggled. "Can you run so fast I can't see you?"

"Yes, I can. And I'll come in and check on you, too. So now do you feel better?"

He nodded. "Otay."

I kissed his forehead again, tiptoed out, partially closed the door, then popped it open. "Hello! I'm checking on you!"

"Aunt Dolie, you're silly."

"That's right, I am. And I'll be right across the hall. So good night again. I love you."

"I love you, too."

Austin is a computer mecca. Admittedly there are others around the country, but that doesn't dim the reality that Dell Computer began in Austin, that IBM has a major presence here, that Samsung, Apple, Power PC, Motorola, and Austin Computer employ thousands of citizens. The University of Texas plays a part by having what they call the Incubator, a program for start-up computer companies. The saying is that even if you're at the back of the pack in Austin, computerally speaking, you're still ahead of most of the world.

I am not at the back of the Austin pack. Unfortunately, I'm behind even in Purple Sage, so you can judge where that put me with all of Prissy's equipment. I could, and did, turn her computer on. Since I use a computer every day with my writing, I just assumed I could take a little extra time and walk my way through getting on the Internet. That was delusional thinking.

I pointed at icons with the mouse and ended up in bizarre locations within Prissy's computer, rather than where I intended to go. I couldn't even get the machine to hook up with the Internet; instead it gave me error messages.

Finally I stepped back mentally and started over. When all else fails, you check hardware. Are the plugs in correctly? Was there even a modem attached to the machine? I studied all the wires leading into the computer and determined, at least to my satisfaction, that they were properly, or at least firmly, attached. Next I got on the floor and started following wires to see where they went. It didn't take long to discover they went everywhere.

Above the music coming from Todd's room I heard a door open somewhere in the house. I waited, listening to see who it was, then Matt's voice called, "Hello?"

"Up here," I yelled, momentarily forgetting that Christopher was trying to sleep.

182

I found what I was sure was a modem and followed the phone plug to a multiple jack in the wall. Four lines, just as Prissy had told me earlier in the week. I touched all of them, pulled a little on the plugs, and decided everything was secure. I followed a second wire out of the wall socket and discovered it was attached to a small black box that was tucked unobtrusively behind the leg of the desk. At first I thought it was another modem, or some kind of surge protector, but on closer inspection I recognized the little machine, and would have even without the label: TELE-RECORDER. It was a microcassette recorder, which seemed a very odd thing to have attached to a computer. Not only that, a few feet away, an identical black box was hidden behind another leg.

"Well, now, that's what I've always wanted," Matt said from the doorway. "A beautiful woman on her knees to me."

I raised my head and smacked it on the underside of the desk. "Ouch."

"Are you okay?"

"Fine. Confused. Lost." I turned around and sat on the floor. "How are you? You look tired."

Matt let out a sigh and rubbed his face. "Let's just say this hasn't been my favorite day. So what are you doing?"

"Well, I was trying to do some research on the Internet, but I couldn't get the computer to sign on. Come here and I'll show you what I found."

I crawled out from under the desk and knelt down at the far side of it where Matt joined me. I pointed to the small recorder that couldn't have been over six inches long and two inches wide.

"What do you think of that?" I asked.

❧ CHAPTER 20 ❧

MATT CROUCHED down. "Let me get in there a second."
I scooted out of the way and he proceeded around me until he
could touch the box. Gingerly he pulled it toward him. "Amazing. Did you see what this is? A tape recorder, and it says that it's
voice-activated."

The tapes themselves are only a little over an inch wide, and
not quite two inches long, and the recorders are two by five. I
carry a similar one in my car to talk out story ideas when I'm
traveling. It's a great idea in theory, but the batteries are always
dead on mine.

"It's attached to the phone jack in the wall." I said, pointing.
"So where does it go? It can't be plugged into the computer.
Wait, I'll check the other one."

I got around to the far side, and without touching the
recorder, followed the thin wire up to the phone that was on top
of Prissy's desk. "I don't like this," I said.

Matt was tucking the small black box back where it had been.
"I can't say that I'm crazy about it, either. Did you notice? These
are new. There's no dust on them like there is on the modem."

"I hadn't gotten that far." Great detective that I was. "What is
yours attached to?"

"Apparently it's recording the other phone line. The one that
goes to our apartment."

I shivered. "That's nice. And they're new devices." I stood up
and dusted my hands off, as if something ugly had gotten on
them. Todd's music was a steady background noise, assuring that

184

he couldn't hear our words. "What do you think this is all about?" I asked. Who in this house was tapping the phone lines, and why? I could hardly believe it, let alone understand it.

"I'm not sure, but it's not the kind of thing you expect to find in the house of a loving family." He stood with his hands on his hips, his focus on the black recorders. "At least I wouldn't think so."

I turned off the computer; I wasn't in the mood for research anymore. "Let's go downstairs, Christopher is supposed to be sleeping."

"Just let me wash my hands."

While Matt did that, I went to check on Christopher. I found him with his eyes wide open; he watched me come into the room. "You're supposed to be asleep," I said, sitting beside him on the edge of the bed.

"Aunt Dolie, I had a dream and now I was thinkin' about something."

"What are you thinking about?"

"Well, what if a bad person comes here, and takes you away, and I can't hear you?" The question was phrased very seriously.

I put my hand on his arm. "First of all, no bad person can get us. I have all the doors locked, and your grandma Prissy has an alarm system, so nobody could get in without a key."

"Some of the times bad people get you because they aren't scareded of alarms."

"Well, this alarm rings at the police station, so the police would come right away. Not only that, Todd and your uncle Matt are here, and they won't let anyone get you, either."

I heard Matt come out of the bathroom and make his way through the little sitting room, only tripping once over the things that were scattered on the floor. He didn't even swear. "See, here's your uncle Matt," I said.

"Hello, Uncle Matt."

"I thought you were asleep."

"I think Christopher had a bad dream," I said, making room for Matt to sit beside me.

He held out his arms and Christopher climbed into them, saying, "I missed you today. Were you working harder?"

"That's exactly what I was doing. I didn't get to have fun, like you."

"We went to the Chirden's Museum, and I worked on the computer, and I bought groceries."

In the dim light I could see Matt smile. "Sounds like what your aunt Jolie does, only she doesn't think it's that much fun." With his free arm he pulled back the covers on the bed to make room for Christopher to lie down. "I'm sorry that you had a bad dream. Are you better now?"

"I'm better."

"Good, then I think you need to sleep so you can play some more tomorrow. How does that sound?"

"I could go with you. I'm not tired anymore."

"Yes, well, that may be true, but I think you should rest anyway. You want to get lots of sleep so that when Christmas comes you have the energy to play with your new toys."

"What new toys?"

"Oh, the ones I think Santa is going to bring you."

"I like toys!"

"So I've heard." Matt put Christopher down on the bed and gently pulled the blankets up around his chest. "Now, how about going to sleep?"

Christopher reached out a hand and caught hold of Matt's arm; I could see the tiny fingers tighten on the tanned skin and blond hair. "Uncle Matt, if you and Aunt Dolie go away, will you come and take me, too? Please."

Matt placed his hand gently over Christopher's. "We aren't going anyplace tonight. And if something should happen so we change our minds, I promise we'll come and wake you up and take you with us. But you have to go to sleep now. Is that a deal?"

"Deal." Christopher nodded his head, then looked at me. "Aunt Dolie, when I grow up, I want to be Bianca in the Rescuers."

"Honey, Bianca's a girl."

"No, Aunt Dolie, Bianca's a mouse."

186

I exchanged a smile with Matt, then said, "When you grow up, Christopher, you're going to be a man, like your uncle Matt."

He thought about it. "Oh. Well, otay."

"That's good to hear," Matt said. "We'll be right downstairs; can you sleep now?"

"Yes, please."

Matt and I both kissed Christopher on the forehead, and then the two of us headed out of the room. In the doorway I stopped to look back. Christopher had his eyes open, still watching us. On impulse I said, "Would you like to come and sleep in our apartment?"

Christopher sat straight up. "Yes, please."

"Then come on."

Matt didn't question the suggestion; when I grabbed an extra blanket and started to hand it to him he said, "You get those, and I'll carry Christopher."

"I'll get his coat, too."

I turned on the light, then went around the room collecting a teddy bear, a pair of Christopher's tennis shoes, an extra pillow, and his heavy coat. I don't know why, it wasn't rational, but I felt an urgency to get Christopher, in fact to get all of us, out of the house. When I had everything, I headed for the door and turned off the light. Matt was waiting for me on the landing, Christopher in his arms. "Go," I said.

"I like this, Aunt Dolie."

"I know you do, but you have to go right to sleep when we get there."

A door opened down the hall and Todd came out. "Hi, what's going on?" he asked. When he saw Christopher he looked concerned. "Is everything okay?"

"Fine," I said. "We're going over to the apartment and I thought we'd take Christopher with us."

"Oh, that's cool. I was just going out," he said, and I realized the music was turned off. He leaned over and touched Christopher on the cheek. "You get some sleep, little guy; it's way past your bedtime."

"I know."

We went down the stairs together, Matt in the lead. At the bottom I bundled a quilt around Christopher, grabbed my purse and keys off the couch, and we all went out the back door at the same time.

"See you in the morning," Todd called as he went around the corner of the house.

"Good night." We started up the stairs.

Matt put Christopher in our bed, firmly tucking him in with instructions to go to sleep. Christopher nodded, his little body seeming more relaxed now. "Otay."

"We'll be right on the other side," I said, as Matt pulled shut the white folding doors and we moved into the living room.

I felt better to be in the apartment, too. Normally when we spent a weekend at Prissy's we had a wonderful time, but this wasn't a normal trip and it was longer than a weekend.

"Does it feel like there are undercurrents around here?" I asked Matt, who was pulling off his boots.

"Yes, not that I've been here much to notice. But those recorders bother me." He placed the boots neatly beside the couch, leaned back, and put his feet up on the coffee table. "This feels good."

"It's like the whole trip is off kilter." I stretched out the length of the couch and put my head on Matt's lap. "And you know when I said Christopher had a nightmare? Matt, I don't think he'd gone to sleep. He was lying there with his eyes open, watching the door. He was scared about something else."

Matt stroked my hair and said, "Do you think it could be the movies he's been seeing?"

"I don't know." I took a breath. "There was a whole conversation that you missed earlier, about bad people taking me away. And he said something about being left alone, too, just like he did to you." I could feel my frown, a reflection of the concern that was building inside me. "That's a terrible thing for a child to even think about; why would he worry about that?"

Matt took a moment before he responded. "That might have something to do with Stephanie being out with Peter Javitz all the time. I don't know what we can do about that; parents do have to go away."

"You're right, and that's better than anything I've come up with. But still, I don't like it." I thought of something else. "And then there are those damn tape recorders."

"That doesn't work for me. I'm going to talk to Prissy about those tomorrow."

"You think she hooked them up to check on Stephanie?"

"I don't know what to think. It, it, I . . ." He stopped. I had rarely heard Matt at a loss for words before. "I hate to think that my sister would stoop to something like that. Stephanie is a grown woman, and monitoring her conversations that way is wrong. The other part of this is that Prissy's violated our privacy, because she has our conversations on tape, too."

"I know." I was getting a headache and I rubbed my forehead. "You realize that it might not have been Prissy who put the recorders there. It could have been Ross, or even Stephanie. I can't think of why either one of them would do that, maybe checking on Prissy. You said the recorders are new, at least not dusty, so there's the possibility that Stephanie brought them with her."

Matt shook his head. "I don't like that any better."

"Matt, I keep wondering how long Stephanie has been dating Peter Javitz. I mean, if she lives in Phoenix, and he lives here . . . and how did that get started?" I didn't say, "And how can we stop it?" although the thought crossed my mind.

"Apparently Stephanie had some problems after she moved out to Phoenix; I don't know what they were, Pris didn't say, but she mentioned them in a phone call a couple of months ago. Maybe it was financial, or maybe Stephanie was homesick. I didn't get the impression that it was anything serious; if I had, I'd have called her. At any rate, Peter has several clients in Phoenix, so when he went out there Prissy asked him to check on

Stephanie. Of course, the result was not what Prissy had in mind. Now he sees Stephanie as often as he can, which is much too often, according to Prissy."

"How long ago was it that they started dating?" I held back a yawn.

"You mean, is there hope it will burn out soon?"

I grinned. "Okay, that, too."

"I think only about a month or so." His head nodded. "She hasn't been gone all that long."

"Since August," I said, letting out the yawn. "So tell me what's happening with Austin Edge. Anything good on that front?"

"I'm not sure that good is even a possibility, regardless of what we do." He started explaining, and I closed my eyes and dozed off.

It was the pounding on the door that woke me. Matt jumped and I almost landed on the floor.

"What in the world—" I said, trying to figure out where I was and what was happening.

Luckily Matt was quicker. He pulled open the door while I was still getting to my feet.

"Uncle Matt," Stephanie said breathlessly. "Where's Christopher? He's not in his bed and—" She stopped when she spotted me.

"What?" I said.

"Christopher is gone!"

"He's asleep in there." I pointed to our bedroom.

"Oh, God." She ripped back the folding doors and saw Christopher. "Oh, my baby." With that she moved to the side of the bed and knelt down to take hold of Christopher's hand.

Matt and I tiptoed in beside her in time to see Christopher mumble in his sleep, then shudder slightly and open his eyes. When he saw all of us, he said, "Hi, Mommy."

"Hello, sweetheart. Are you okay?"

"I'm restin'." He closed his eyes and fell back into sleep. Poor little guy was exhausted.

Stephanie paused a moment longer, touching his hand and watching his rhythmic breathing. When she stood up, we all moved into the living room.

"I'm sorry," I said softly. "I should have left you a note. I didn't think—" I shook my head to clear away the fuzz. "I guess I didn't think at all."

Matt closed the sliding door behind us.

"I thought—I was sure—" She was breathing hard, her skin flushed. "I guess I just panicked when he was gone and I couldn't find you."

I put an arm around her. "You're shaking. Come and sit down."

"It's just the cold." She tried to laugh it off as we moved toward the sofa. "I overreacted. Mom says I do that; I'm sorry, I didn't mean to be that way."

"How about if we make you something hot to drink?" I asked.

"Oh, no, thanks. It's late."

Matt sat down on the chair. "Are your mom and dad home yet?"

She shook her head. "No, not yet. Just Jeremy's there, and he's sound asleep."

"Then you don't need to get back right way; I will make coffee," I said, standing up. The only lucid thought I had was to keep Stephanie as long as possible, although I wasn't sure why that was important. Maybe I wanted her to feel protected with us around, the same way Christopher seemed to feel safe. Or on some level I may have wanted her to talk so we could discover what was really going on.

Matt is one of the best listeners I know, and if Steph wouldn't talk to him, she wouldn't open up to anyone.

I started to reach for the coffeepot, but Stephanie stood up. "Don't make any for me. I'm exhausted, and I'm sure you are, too." She started toward the bedroom. "I'll just get Christopher—"

"I'll carry him for you," Matt said, rising.

"Steph, why don't you leave him?" I asked. I gave Matt a quick look. "He's sound asleep, and we don't mind."

"But he's in your bed."

"It doesn't matter; there's plenty of room." Again I shot a glance at Matt, and this time he got the message.

"It's fine with us," he said. "Maybe Christopher will sleep better without all the activity you've got over there."

Stephanie hesitated. She glanced toward the bedroom and bit her lip while seeming to consider. Finally she nodded her head, speaking slowly. "Okay. I think maybe you're right. If you're sure."

"We're sure," I said with finality.

"Just let me kiss him good night."

Matt slid back the door enough for her to get through, while I found an extra blanket to wrap around her shoulders.

When she came back out she said to me, "I really am sorry, Jolie, for barging in here like I did."

"It was my fault." I held out the blanket. "You'll want this."

"No, thanks, I'll just run." She went to the front door. "Call me if he wakes up and needs me. Good night," she said over her shoulder as she hurried out, closing the door behind her. She was gone and only a chill from outside remained.

I looked at Matt. His expression told me he was as worried as I was. "Tomorrow," he said, "I'm talking to Prissy. And then I'll see what I can do with Steph. I don't like this." He slid his arms around my shoulders, pulling me toward him. "I feel like I've gotten you involved in something, and it worries me."

"It's not your fault; I'm the one who wanted to come to Austin for the party. That is why we're here."

"Oh, that's right, the Christmas party."

"And now you have all the problems at Austin Edge."

Matt rested his head on my shoulder and groaned before he looked up. "I will be so glad when this week is over and we can go home."

"And we'll live happily ever after?"

"At the very least."

❋ CHAPTER 21 ❋

HANDS TOUCHING my face woke me.

I opened my eyes to find Christopher patting my cheek as if I were a family pet.

"What are you doing, little bug?"

His voice came back a whisper. "Checkin' on you, Aunt Dolie. Are you sleepin'?"

"I was." The room was dark, so while I couldn't see Matt clearly, I could detect his unmoving form. "Come here. You don't want to wake your uncle Matt; he's very tired." Christopher curled up close to me and I said softly, "You're supposed to be sleeping, too."

"I am."

Christopher wriggled in my arms and I kissed his ear. The feel of his baby-fine hair and the soft skin brought back the days when Jeremy was that little. There is what I like to think of as a universal motherhood reaction to young, whether they are babies, puppies, kittens, or most any other warm-blooded creatures; at that moment I was overwhelmed with it, and with the feeling that Christopher needed protection.

"Get some rest, little bug. I love you."

He closed his eyes and let out a satisfied sigh. "Night, Aunt Dolie."

I held him like that for a long time, while my mind worried over all the little oddities that had me concerned about Christopher and his mother. When I finally realized that worry wasn't going to help, I crept out of the bed and began getting ready for the day. I had a plan.

It is not physically possible to close a car door without making noise, but I did my level best in the dark of that cold morning. In my hand I had two microcassette tapes that I'd taken from my own recorder. One was blank while the other had ramblings on a mystery I was plotting, and both were being sacrificed for the cause.

Skirting the dead leaves, I crossed the patio, punched in the alarm code, then used the key to let myself into Prissy's house. Once in the warmth of the kitchen, I slid off my coat and waited to see if I could hear any noises from above. There was nothing except the soothing hum of the central heat.

With great care to avoid bumping into the furniture, I headed for the stairs. A night-light on the upstairs landing helped me see the way as I tiptoed carefully up each step. I silently blessed Prissy's contractor for making the flooring so solid there wasn't even the tiniest creak or groan. On the landing I left my shoes and moved in my stockings toward the office. At the door I paused again, but still there were no noises.

Not waiting for my luck to change, I went straight to the desk and ducked underneath it, removing the tapes from inside the recorders and replacing them with my own. It hardly took a minute. Then I was up and out the door, but this time I did hear sounds and they seemed to be coming from Stephanie's room. I moved closer to her door and pressed my ear to the wood; there weren't specific noises that I could identify, just a rustling as if someone might be walking the carpet inside the sitting room.

I started to go in, actually had my hand on the knob, but I discovered that the door was locked from the inside. The soft rattle I'd made with the knob silenced all sounds from the room.

"Steph?" I whispered. "Are you okay?"

The door opened and in the dimness, with her long hair flowing over her white flannel nightgown, she looked like Lady Macbeth.

Her face appeared pale. "Is Christopher—"

"He's fine. Sound asleep," I assured her quietly. "I just came in to get something and I heard you moving around. Are you okay?"

She nodded. "Of course. Just restless." She took in my clothes. "Where are you going so early?"

"The agency. I want to be home by noon. Two at the latest. I'm tired of missing all the fun."

Her voice sounded rueful. "Has there been a lot of that? I seem to have more fun away from the house."

"I'd love to come in and talk."

More than anything I wanted to make things better for her and for Christopher, whatever that took, but until she chose to tell me what was going on, there was nothing I could do.

"It's too early, and besides, things are fine." The determination in the rigid set of her mouth made it obvious she wasn't going to let me close enough to help just yet.

I forced myself to smile. "Then when I get home we'll start having fun." I added a wink. She looked dreadful. "Get some rest; I'll see you in a couple of hours."

She nodded, and as I turned to go I heard her close and lock the door.

The tiny tapes were like hot coals in my coat pocket, and my fingers hovered, never quite touching them. As I crossed the empty lobby the beautifully blended voices of a chorale were singing "Silent Night," and Ted Polovy was unlocking the second elevator.

When he turned and saw me, he saluted and said, "Getting a jump on the day, huh?"

"Something like that." I veered around him, head down, plowing forward like a bull. I was on a mission.

"You ever worry about going up there?" he asked, moving just enough to block my path. "To Rose Sterling?"

I stopped. "No, why would I?"

"One copywriter died up there. Someone killed her, and the cops don't know who did it yet."

A feather of cold whispered across my shoulders and down the neck of my coat. "That's an ugly thought. And I wish you hadn't brought it up."

"Spooked you, huh?"

"Maybe. Would you like to go up there with me and check the place out, just in case?"

He grinned and rubbed his fingers across his short hair, scratching just above his ear. "I figure you'll be okay."

"Thanks."

He continued to touch his bristle of hair as his face grew serious. "You know, I still feel bad about Desi dying. Kind of responsible. Damn, feels bad, you know? Like I should've done something—"

"They say if someone wants to kill you, they will. Even the president is vulnerable, and you weren't here to protect Desi."

"I'm here to protect everyone."

"That's a pretty big job. Seems impossible to me."

"That's what the boss keeps sayin', but for me, I just don't like it. And I mostly don't like that it was Desi." He seemed almost wistful. "So many lousy people in this world and it had to happen to her. It doesn't seem fair; should'a happened to someone else—not someone of her kind."

"I guess it happens to any kind."

He brought his hand down and looked at me, sad-eyed. "But it shouldn't." He shrugged. "Maybe I'm just being fanatical, and what do I know? I'm just the security guy."

"A nice security guy," I said. "And you see a lot."

"Just doing my job."

I smiled, and finally said, "And I think it's time for me to start doing mine."

"You have a nice day, now, hear?"

I nodded and waved as I moved away.

By this time Brenda Lee was Rocking Around the Christmas Tree, but when the elevator doors closed, they shut out all sounds except the whir of the machinery. I pulled my coat tighter around me and jammed my hands into my coat pockets; my fingers touched the two tapes nestled in the bottom. There didn't seem to be much holiday cheer anywhere this season.

When the elevator doors opened I found myself enveloped in the silence of the seventh floor. I felt nervous about entering the empty offices, and that was Ted Polovy's fault.

Inside the door the scent of the Christmas tree calmed me. What is more inviting than the smell of pine and the jangle of holiday ornaments?

Almost in passing I stopped in my cubicle to toss my coat and purse on my chair before hurrying on to Nola's office; I seemed to remember that Nola carried a microcassette recorder to client conferences.

Hers was perhaps the prettiest office in the suite, with a beautiful wooden desk with Queen Anne legs. On top of the desk was a green Acer computer—that was Nola's style. Near the door two client chairs flanked a small wooden table that held one of the holiday floral arrangements left over from the party. Brass accessories glowed in the gray dawn light, adding a warmth and richness conspicuously absent elsewhere.

I glanced around but didn't see a recorder out in the open, so I tiptoed to the desk and slid open the top drawers. I felt like a party guest poking through the host's medicine cabinet. When I didn't find what I was looking for, I closed the drawers and started out of her office. On the way out I happened to spot a large leather sample case tucked back behind a tufted chair. It seemed the natural place to keep a small recorder, and I justified looking inside by telling myself that if Nola had been there, she wouldn't have minded.

When I lifted the flaps I found several bright blue folders leaning enough so that I couldn't see the bottom of the case. I lifted two out. The labels read PRECIS COMPUTING and MIND GAMES UN-LIMITED.

If they were clients, I'd never heard of them. In retrospect it seems rude, but there was no premeditation involved when I opened the top file and discovered a marketing proposal for Precis Computing. The budget was almost a million dollars. The odd thing about the proposal was the letterhead. Rose Sterling used a dusty rose paper with silver gray script at the top. Proposal covers were gray with raised silver lettering. They were striking enough to be recognizable even at a distance. The paper I was looking at was a textured gray-blue with a sweeping logo in navy. Millennium Advertising. The address at the bottom on Far West Boulevard seemed vaguely familiar, but I couldn't place it.

I flipped two more pages and discovered some advertising copy for Precis, again on Millennium letterhead. Desi Baker's initials were at the top as the copywriter.

The proposal brought up a number of interesting questions, such as: Who was Millennium Advertising? Were they a competitor and had Nola just happened to get a copy of the proposal? Why had Desi been writing for them? Had she been moonlighting and Nola discovered the transgression? Or were Desi and Nola both involved with Millennium? Perhaps jumping ship to join them?

If Nola was in a better mood today, I decided I'd ask her.

With real purpose I looked under the files, didn't find a recorder, checked in the side pockets of the case and again came up empty, then put everything back and slid the case to its original position.

I decided on a quick visual search of the other offices. I stressed the *visual* to myself, meaning that I was only going to look without touching a thing. I did just that in Ralph's office, slowing only to take in the weird arrangement of the plastic cartoon characters on top of his computer. They were in a V formation, all facing down one character—a beleaguered Dilbert.

I looked around the desktop, credenza, and file cabinets. No recorder.

If I waited until the staff arrived to ask for a recorder, it would be too late to listen to the tapes, so I did a quick search of Fred, the art director's, office. I came up empty and checked Amber's desk, where I found a drawer practically filled with nail polish. The space not used for cosmetics contained a vast assortment of promotional pens from what looked like every radio station, printing company, and specialty firm in the area. It didn't yield a cassette recorder.

The offices of the royal family, as Donna Katherine called them, were almost as intimidating to me now as they'd been when I worked full-time at Rose Sterling. I merely glanced around Audry's office from the doorway, and did the same at Chester's.

In Michael's I caught myself drifting forward, pulled in by the scent of his aftershave. I had come into this office too many times in the past, supposedly to drop off something I had written, but sometimes, tucked between the pages of a proposal, I would have a card for Michael. Or a note. It had been dangerous, leaving written proof, but in retrospect the danger was part of the attraction.

One time in particular I remembered I slid the papers across his desk, and Michael had looked up, smiled, and while we casually discussed a client campaign, he had been stroking my hand with his fingertips. It gave me a shivery feeling just to think about it.

Then I remembered that Audry had come swooping down into the office. I had heard the step outside the door just in time to pull my hand away and fall back into the client chair. As if I had been sitting there the entire time, as my mother would say, keeping my hands to myself.

Looking at Michael's desk, his space, I felt remorse, along with the recognition of thrill at the danger I had faced.

Maybe all of us have that little bit of excitement junkie within us, just enough so that when he have no exhilarating highs in our own lives we read books or go to movies to experience it vicariously. The daring have always captured us, from Amelia Earhart to Buzz Aldrin. And sometimes we are the daring—for good or for evil.

I stepped into the hallway, then turned to look toward the offices one more time. From that spot I saw not only Michael's office, but Chester's as well. The similarities caught me. Neither Michael nor Chester had a computer, a file cabinet, or any stacks of files sitting around cluttering the tidy surfaces of their office furniture. They did have some newspapers and magazines, mostly the same ones, such as *Austin Business Journal, Advertising Age, Broadcast Weekly, Newsweek,* and the *Wall Street Journal.* They also had lovely seating arrangements for their clients, and large executive chairs for themselves.

In looking around something else struck me—except for the tree by the front door, Christmas was absent from the suite of offices. In years past there had been decorations everywhere. The agency decorated the open areas, and the rest of us had added special touches to our own offices. A garland of plastic ivy hung with real candy canes had circled my cubicle, and I'd put red bows and silver tree balls in a pothos that was my permanent companion at Rose Sterling. That was another thing that was missing—plants.

I could understand how the party had created some problems; after all, most of the furniture had been shifted elsewhere, so decorations would have been just that much more to move—but plants?

As I stood there wondering, the lights in the building across the street came on, reminding me that the rest of the staff would be arriving soon. I shifted my brain to business mode and scanned Chester's office, then Michael's one last time. Neither had a microcassette recorder sitting around.

Next I poked my head into Donna Katherine's office, and literally stopped short to take in the transformation. It was as if she had gotten everyone's Christmas spirit and tried to cram it in too small a space. A two-foot-tall angel with a creamy satin gown and glittery gold wings was hung so that it hovered in midair in the center of the office. A wreath of hard candies, complete with a small pair of red scissors for snipping off the little goodies, graced the cloth of her temporary wall. A flocked artificial tree was attached to the top of her computer. It was surrounded by a red felt skirt that had small packages affixed. Three poinsettias were grouped near the door with a small train and village circling them.

On the temporary wall above her computer was a sign that said, I ONLY HAVE TWO SPEEDS AND IF YOU DON T LIKE THIS ONE, THE OTHER ONE WILL REALLY DRIVE YOU CRAZY. She had tacked some fake holly and a puffy red Santa to it.

I didn't think she'd have a recorder, I couldn't come up with any reason why she would have, but I looked around anyway. Her files were locked, as was her desk, which I suppose made sense for a financial person, and there wasn't anything in sight that wasn't for decorative purposes.

Without much real hope I moved down the hall and popped into the conference room. It was amazing—there, right on top of the credenza, along with a metal insulated coffeepot and some nondairy creamer, sat not one, but two recorders. As the old saying goes, whatever you are hunting, you'll find it in the last place you look.

I snatched up the recorder closest to hand and hurried back to my own office to listen to the tapes.

✦ CHAPTER 22 ✦

PRISSY'S WAS the first voice I heard, convincing a woman to serve on the Friends of the Library board. The woman was apparently new to the community and Prissy made her feel welcome, as if the post were a special privilege; for all I knew, it was. I stayed with the conversation until the end, expecting something major to be said. There was nothing.

Next I heard Stephanie calling the Children's Museum checking on their hours. I ran the tape forward, listening to the high-pitched garble of voices, and after a short tone I slowed the machine and heard a male voice say, "Hello?"

"Hi. It's Ed."

"Hey, Ed, how're you doing?"

"Fine. I wanted to find out what you thought of the office space you found. The one over on Spicewood."

"Right, the one I viewed on Saturday. I thought it was great. Good location, nice view, and the management group seems anxious to get it leased. They want too much for it, of course, but that's Austin for you."

I finally realized it was Ross who had taken the call. He is somewhat of a specter to me; while I've been around him, I never really talk to him, or more important, listen to him talk. He always seems the peripheral person—the floater loosely attached to Prissy.

He has always seemed nice enough, but his energy had always appeared to be expended outside the house. As if his career was more important than his family, or maybe he worked long hours to support the lifestyle they had chosen.

I'd never noticed any particular bond between Ross and Stephanie, and now it left their relationship open to questions. At some point I had even wondered if Ross was the source of Stephanie's problems.

"If you want to take a look at it," Ross was saying. "I'm going back there at noon today. . . ."

It didn't tell me anything new about the man.

Next Ross spoke with a woman I presumed was his secretary. They went over airline and rental-car information for a trip in early January.

I kept trying to figure out when these calls had taken place, but there was nothing to pinpoint the dates. At least a few days earlier.

Another short tone and I heard a male voice say, "Hello?"

Stephanie cut in quickly, "Peter, thank God! I'm about to lose my mind! I tried talking to her, just like you suggested, but it didn't do any good. My mother is living in some dreamworld—"

"Whoa! Slow down, take a deep breath." I recognized the mellifluous tones of Peter Javitz.

"I can't slow down; I can't even think." But she did take a loud breath.

"Good," Peter said. "Now, you tried to talk to your mother, and what happened?"

"I told you, nothing. She won't even listen to me. She's like a Stepford wife! She just keeps saying that I have to stop acting like a little girl—like it's my fault."

"You know that's not true. Nothing that happened was your fault. You do know that, don't you?"

A pause before she said, "Sometimes I blame myself."

"That's crazy, Stephanie. All that expensive therapy and you're going to start beating yourself up again?"

"I know, I'm just so confused. And I know it could have been a whole lot worse. Maybe that's what scares me."

I realized I had clenched my fists as I listened to Stephanie continue her outpouring of half sentences. I was imagining some very ugly scenarios.

"And since she won't listen, she doesn't know the whole truth. She doesn't want to know. Oh, God, Peter, you can't imagine how I'm feeling. And my own mother, but then in a way, I guess I can't blame her. I mean, she's such a loyal person, but she doesn't have any idea what could happen."

"*Nothing* is going to happen. He's not drinking or taking drugs, and didn't the therapist say that was the cause?" Cause of what? I wanted to know. "If you see him even touch a glass of wine, or if you see any sign that he's using cocaine again, you run straight over here and stay with me until he's safely in jail."

"I can't do that. The whole story would come out and I can't handle having everyone know. Especially not Jolie and Uncle Matt." A shuddery sigh. "I hate feeling vulnerable like this."

When I had met Stephanie, shortly after her eighteenth birthday, I had marveled at how pragmatic she was and how smoothly she handled problems. Two years later, even after she'd had Christopher, I still believed Stephanie was far more competent at that age than I'd been. Since then I'd been certain Christopher hadn't suffered because of her single status; now I wasn't sure.

Peter began using a lighter tone. "We're always vulnerable, though, aren't we? Lesson in life number four twenty-two." As if he were trying to tease her out of her fears. I was beginning to dislike the man more than before.

"I know, I know. It's just, you know me, I hate pretending nothing happened. I hate being nice."

"My little firebrand." What an ass he was. "You did act; you got the situation handled, and now you live with the aftermath, just like we all do."

It didn't sound like he was taking her fears much more seriously than Prissy, but I was. I had seen Stephanie last night on the verge of hysteria when she couldn't find Christopher. Whatever had happened in the past, real or imagined, it had scared the hell out of her.

A scenario was edging into my consciousness, one that repulsed me and heightened my worry. I rubbed my forehead as Peter's voice went on.

"Let's talk about it at dinner tonight. I'll see if I can help you forget your troubles."

"I can't go, Peter, I just can't. I can't leave Christopher. Why don't you come here and I'll fix us dinner?"

"That won't work. After dinner I have to attend a party at the university; they're honoring a friend of mine and I'm making a speech about him." He dropped his voice and said softly, "I want you at my side. I want your strength and your beauty with me, just like I always do. What do you say?" When she remained silent he added, "Let your aunt and uncle baby-sit, then you won't have to worry about Christopher. Nothing is going to happen, and getting away will help you put things in perspective."

Stephanie took her time responding. Finally she said, "Okay, I guess. What time?"

"I'll pick you up at seven-thirty."

Which effectively cut off my chances of hearing what I wanted to. Damn. If anyone asked me for an opinion of Peter Javitz, they would certainly get a biased one.

Another short tone came from the tape and Jeremy was on the phone talking to Matt. Something about a Christmas present. I hit the fast-forward button quickly just in case it was my present they were talking about. After that Prissy had a hurried conversation about a New Year's Eve party that she and Ross were going to drop by. While she was getting directions I moved on, and when I stopped the tape a female I couldn't identify was speaking.

"There just isn't anything available on that day. If you'd like, I can put you on a wait list for standby."

"No, not during the holidays." I recognized Todd's voice. "Look, while I'd rather leave on Thursday, if you can't get us anything, I'll take Friday. We can fly into Dulles, National, or BWI, it doesn't really matter."

Todd just now booking his return trip? That would mean he

was staying in Austin several days after Christmas, and if he was the reason for Stephanie's fears, this wouldn't be good news.

But what if he wasn't the source? What if someone else in the house was causing her fear? There was only one other man, and I shivered at the ugliness of the thought.

"Would you hold a moment?" the woman, apparently a travel agent, asked. "I'd like to check something."

The soothing effect of the instrumental Christmas carol that followed was disrupted by Todd's muttering. "Sometimes, Todd-boy, you act like you aren't bright. You knew better than to put off making these reservations. I mean, right in the middle of the holidays and you just blew it off. I hate it that Dad was right, but sometimes you don't—"

The music and the muttering both stopped as the woman came back on the line. "I think I have something. It's not a direct flight, and you're going to have a three-hour layover in Atlanta, but it's at five-fifty in the evening on Friday."

Friday, one week from today; that seemed awfully far off.

"Layovers aren't important," Todd responded. "Just book it."

"One more thing, because of the holidays and the late date, the cost is going to be substantially higher, but I can get both of you on and seated together."

"Great. That's good."

A flight for two? Was that why Todd was always chasing out of the house in such a hurry? A new girlfriend in Austin? An old girlfriend? I wondered what Prissy thought of that. Not that I was *sure* Prissy had been attempting to get Stephanie and Todd together, but I suspected it despite the apparent mismatch. Stephanie preferred her men more mature, and seemed to need someone solid to lean on, although had anyone asked me, Peter Javitz wasn't that person.

The agent was rattling off flight numbers and times, so I hit the fast forward, and when I heard a new timbre of voice I slowed the tape again.

"How about if you meet me at the Hyatt? I always seem to get lost up in Round Rock." I recognized our friend Trey Atwood's voice immediately, but then I hear it all the time when I call his wife, Diane.

It was Matt who responded. "I don't mind, but I'll have to beat you at tennis tomorrow."

"In this weather, have you lost your mind? They say it might snow. Just get me a map for Christmas—"

I had been in the room during that conversation, so I skimmed on, still listening carefully, despite the fact that I had little hope left that I could identify the person who had attached the recorders. Prissy was the obvious choice, since it was her house and she was a whiz at computers and such. Ross was number two on my list, but I couldn't quite work out why he'd do it. Prissy might be checking up on Stephanie, especially because of her involvement with Peter. But Ross?

Stephanie might also be responsible, although she wasn't into electronics and didn't seem to have any reason to be spying on her family. Or did she? Was the victim fighting back? Damn. And who was the aggressor?

The tape ended, and after muttering at least one or two words that didn't reflect the true spirit of the season, I put the second microcassette in the recorder.

The first voice I heard was Jeremy talking to a young woman I assumed to be Alicia. There are some things a mother shouldn't hear, and I felt strongly that this was one of them. I moved past it to the next call, which was merely a series of computer-generated sounds. I suspected it was a modem connecting to the Internet. I heard that same sound five more times before a human voice was discernible. It was Matt speaking crisply and using succinct language that let me know he was talking serious *bidness* as it's known in the South.

". . . assume the majority of the stockholders are unavailable during the holidays, and I feel that leaves us in a precarious position. We can't in good conscience get a stay, while the board could . . ."

It was not something I wanted or needed to know. The finger that was on the fast forward button was getting sore, but I pushed it again, only to be rewarded with more computer sounds and then the end of the tape.

I scowled at the tape, willing it to speak. And not only did I want it talking, I wanted it saying what I needed to hear.

When the agency phone rang, I almost jumped.

"Rose Sterling."

"Good morning," Matt said, in his sexy just-awake voice.

A wave of guilt swept through me; while he'd been innocently sleeping, I'd been listening in on his phone conversations. It seemed to me that if I was to have any scruples at all, I was going to have to get a cat and name it that.

"Good morning," I said. "Did you just get up?"

"About twenty minutes ago. Are you all right?" he asked.

"Of course. Why wouldn't I be?"

I could hear the smile. "You sound like you've been up to something. Eh, 'Lucy'?"

"Not me."

"You got up awfully early." The smile was gone when he added, "Did you have trouble sleeping?"

It brought home to me how lucky I am to have Matt. He is a wonderful man, kind, intelligent, and even handsome, but his best attribute is that he loves me steadfastly, regardless of my mood, or his, and despite any untoward circumstances. Standing in the middle of Rose Sterling, where my past tugged at me like a demanding child, it was good to remember that.

"Thanks for asking," I said. "Actually, Christopher woke me up, and then I couldn't seem to drift off again. Where is he?"

"Believe it or not, he's still asleep." I could hear the concern. "I wish I knew what's going on. Before I leave I'm going to talk to Prissy; maybe there's a simple explanation for all of this, but I can't think of what it could be."

"Me neither. And I guess I should tell you that I took matters into my own hands. I did something. . . ." I paused. Taking the tapes had seemed righteous and moral, practically heroic, at the time I'd done it, but now I wasn't sure.

"So what did you do?" he asked.

"Well, I took the tapes out of those voice-activated recorders and brought them to the office."

"Oh, good. Instead of having some anonymous person tapping our phone lines, it's my wife who's doing it."

"I just thought I could figure out who put the recorders there, except now that I've listened to the tapes, it seems everyone in the house has been on the phone. Or one of the phones and they didn't say a damn thing important."

"You calling us boring?"

"Neil Simon didn't write our dialogue," I said. I added seriously, "And no one seemed to be cautious of what they were saying, either."

"Why should they be?" Matt asked. "Whoever hooked up the recorders didn't plan on anyone else listening to the tapes."

I knew that, or I would have if I'd thought it through. "Well, hell. So I learned nothing, and wasted time listening to boring conversations. Although there was a call of Stephanie's with Peter Javitz that concerns me. Not their relationship, either, but Stephanie sounded really scared. Something bad happened to her, Matt, and during the call she told Peter that Prissy wouldn't listen to her. She was really upset."

Matt paused before he spoke. "I'm not much for jumping into the middle of someone else's business—"

"I know, but I think she needs help. Moral support if nothing else. It sounded—" I fought down my suspicions. I had no proof of what I was thinking, and no reason to malign anyone, yet. "It sounded serious."

"Okay, I'll try to find out what's going on. If there's some way we can help, I'm for it, but . . ." I could almost hear his frown. "But if Stephanie and Prissy shut me out, we'll have to accept that as their decision."

I let out a relieved breath. If Matt was going to get involved, I was sure everything would be all right.

"But don't forget the recorded phone calls," I said. "Those are our business since someone tapped our conversations."

"Which my wife listened to."

"In my favor, you should know that I fast-forwarded through a call of Jeremy's and several others."

"The boring ones or the personal ones?"

"Cute, Matt. So here's the deal. I replaced these tapes with some others, so the machines aren't empty. Unfortunately, anyone who listens to them is going to know the tapes have been switched."

"As long as they don't know that it was you who switched them." I was silent for so long that he added, "Obviously they will know. How is that?"

"One of the tapes has my voice—I was plotting a short story. Of course, anyone could have taken it out of my car."

"I may have an extra tape in my briefcase, and if I do, I'll replace that one."

"Thank you." I let out a sigh. Then I remembered. "Oh, shit!"

"What?"

"We're being taped! And I can't tell you which recorder it is."

"Great. Look, I'll go in and pull both tapes. Damn." Matt swears only under extreme circumstances.

"I'm really sorry—"

"It's not that," he said. "It's just everything. This was supposed to be a vacation, and you're working every day, and I'm involved in Austin Edge. We were supposed to have some time together."

"I know." I hadn't intended to sound quite so wistful.

"Next month," he said. "I don't care where we go as long as it's just the two of us. Together."

There was a delicious flutter in my stomach region; from Matt's voice it was apparent that was going to be some wonderful vacation. "I'm ready," I said, my voice a croak.

"Good. Maybe we'll try a beach in Mexico? Someplace warm."

"Sultry," I purred.

"I'll tell the travel agent you said so."

I let out a long sigh. Too little of life was like this. "Okay. And I'll dream about it while I look out the window at the cold."

"Ah, yes. The cold." Damn. I'd pulled us back to reality. "And now," he went on, "I'll go get those tapes. And talk to Prissy."

"And handle the problems at Austin Edge."

He swore softly again. "I may be late tonight, but it won't be by choice."

"I know. Just hold the thought of that vacation."

"I will. I love you."

"I love you, too."

I sighed, knowing there was a sappy smile on my face. I wanted to bask in the glow of that, but before I could even get the receiver back on its hook, the other line rang.

❖ CHAPTER 23 ❖

J OLIE, HI; it's me, Prissy."

"Prissy," I said. "How are you?"

"Fine. Listen, I've been in my office—"

My stomach tightened. I simply wasn't cut out to be a spy among family. "Prissy, I'm really sorry. . . ."

"For what? I don't mind looking up these articles. It's actually been fun." In my fear, I hadn't noticed the excitement that underscored her words. "But, Jolie, you won't believe what I've found out."

"Articles?"

"The ones you gave me last night on mistletoe. Someone doctored them. The copies you have are not the same as the original articles that were published!"

My brain was making slow manual shifts. "Are you sure?"

"Absolutely! Most were originally a warning to parents to keep it away from their children and pets. And listen to this. 'Both children and adults have died from eating the berries, although it is rare.' The toxicity level is low for a poison."

"Interesting. I would assume that meant she had to ingest a lot of it."

"That's what I think. But wait, there's something else I have to tell you. When I compared the articles, you know, the copies you gave me to the originals, the look was almost identical. Font, type size, column width, and all, copied almost perfectly."

I had to think about it. "So how did that happen? I don't get it—oh." I got it.

212

"Someone," Prissy was saying, "rewrote the articles and laid them out on a computer. It wouldn't be hard to do. I could do it in three different software programs I have. Then you print it out, and make a copy so the difference in paper doesn't show. Voilà! A magazine article, a newspaper article, and an excerpt from a book all look genuine."

And it would certainly be easy to do at an advertising agency. We had two graphic design programs that would make it a snap. We also had dozens of different fonts, so the letters would match either magazine or newspaper type. And once those were photocopied, they could be given to Desi as reason to eat or drink mistletoe. A plant that would kill her.

The skin between my shoulder blades prickled into goose bumps. "Pris, could you fax the articles you found over to me?"

"Sure. What's your number?"

I gave it to her, and after she had written it down and repeated it, she asked, "Do you want me to talk to the police?"

It was tempting. "No, that's okay. Just fax the things to me, and I'll handle it. Oh, and, Prissy, thank you."

"Actually, it was fun. Let me know if there's anything else I can do to help. I'm going by the library later, if you need more research."

I promised I would and hung up. Rather than stand hunched over the fax machine, waiting, I first found Sergeant Bohles's card in my purse and carried it with me while I made myself a cup of tea.

A number of people at the agency were capable of dummying the articles on mistletoe, but another question I hadn't spent much time thinking about was, who had the motive to kill Desi?

Who indeed?

My first thought was Audry, if it was true that Desi and Michael were lovers. The jilted wife had reason for anger, especially if she thought that Michael was going to leave her again. I wondered if Audry would kill to keep her husband. It didn't seem likely; it supposed a level of passion that I'd never seen in Audry except toward her work.

213

There were also a lot of ifs. If Michael and Desi really had been lovers. If Audry had known about it.

Something else occurred to me; the note shoved under the bathroom door had said, *I* still *love you,* as if the affair between Michael and Desi had ended, but Michael wanted it to continue. That brought up another scenario. Suppose Desi had walked away from Michael for whatever reason, and Michael decided that if he couldn't have her, then no one could. It was all too common a motive for murder.

I shook my head. I could imagine Michael loving Desi; I could even see him loving her passionately, but I couldn't accept him trying to possess her. Michael simply wasn't a possessive man.

The microwave dinged and I took out my cup and put the tea bag in it. The word *possessive* was reverberating around in my mind. Donna Katherine adored Chester, might even be considered a little possessive of him. What if she felt that Desi was replacing her in Chester's affections? After all, it was Desi who had given the speech about Chester during the party.

I thought about that one for a while, then discarded it as unlikely.

So what about Fred or Ralph? Or even Amber?

Would they? Could they? Did they?

It set up a chant in my head, like a riddle with no ending and one I couldn't solve. Time to get moving.

I went into the copy room. Three sheets of paper plus a fax transmittal page were on top of a pile of recently received faxes. Prissy had done great work; she'd found the original book page, the newspaper and magazine articles. All said more or less the same. Mistletoe was a poison, and all parts of the plant were toxic, although the berries were the most dangerous. It caused symptoms such as vomiting, diarrhea, and slowed pulse. The book mentioned digitalislike symptoms, and listed drugs that could cause the same types of problems when taken in large doses. Crystodigin, Lanoxin, Digitoxin, and last, Purodigin, which could only be administered through an IV.

I handwrote my own cover sheet to Bohles explaining what he

was getting and faxed everything over to the police station. He could call me if he had questions, or he could fax or E-mail me. Ah, the wonders of modern technology.

Somehow I put my brain into work gear and plowed head. I had done what I could for Desi Baker; now I would finish her job.

When the rest of the staff began arriving I didn't even look up. I did, however, stop when Chester came in and began to rub my shoulders and tell me what a wonderful person, and writer, I was.

"Thank you," I said.

"Oh, and look, your tea is cold. I'll get Donna Katherine to make you a fresh cup."

"No, no," I said. While Donna Katherine may pamper Chester, she wouldn't appreciate serving me. Besides, I didn't want to break the flow of work. "I'll get some when I finish this ad."

He patted my shoulders. "I won't disturb you then," he said as he tiptoed toward the door.

I was nose-down in my keyboard sometime later when Sergeant Bohles called. "You sent all these articles?"

"Yes. Those are the originals. My sister-in-law pulled them off the Internet somehow."

"What do they tell you?"

I tried not to sound as if he was disrupting me, but frankly, he was. "That mistletoe is a poison, just like I knew before." I stopped. "Is that what you wanted me to say?"

"So how did the articles get changed?"

I saved the piece of copy I was working on and turned my attention to the conversation. "Graphic design and layout," I said. I went on to tell him what could be done with a computer and a little skill.

"So a graphic artist could have done it."

"Well, yes." Funny, until then I'd pretty much ignored Fred, but the man was obviously a whiz at graphic design. So was Ralph Richardson. For that matter, so was Prissy, and my son, Jeremy. There was no telling how many people had the means and

215

method to re-create the articles. Motive was another matter. "Actually, a lot of people—"

"Mrs. Wyatt, can I get back to you? I have another call I have to take."

"No need. Unless you have something else you want to ask me."

"Not a thing. Unless you want to tell me why you walked back to that handicap stall." He paused and I could almost hear his smirk. When I didn't respond he said, "Didn't think so. Thanks for your help."

Desi Baker smiled out at me from her photo on the wall. Maybe she was thanking me for doing what little I could to see that her work was finished and her killer caught. Or maybe she was in a place where it no longer mattered who had murdered her.

"Jolie?"

It was Michael, standing inside the doorway, close enough to let me know he wasn't just saying hello in passing.

"Good morning," I said.

Michael was in his casual Friday attire. Khaki slacks that fit beautifully on his long legs, loafers with print socks in colors that matched his collarless print shirt. Michael always looked like a male model, perhaps because his dark eyes held enough intensity to remove him from the everyday, and his smile was the earthly equivalent of a solar flare.

"How are you this morning?" he asked.

"I'm fine."

He glanced at the stack of files on the edge of my desk, and at the computer screen, which held an ad for a car dealer.

"You have turned out an incredible amount of work this week. I'm not sure what we would have done if you hadn't been willing to help. The one thing most of us aren't able to do is write copy."

He was right about that. Chester, Audry, Michael, and even Nola seemed incapable of that task. Chester had once said that even classified ads were beyond him, much less anything that required creativity. It was an amazing statement considering that they were all in advertising.

"Oh, you'd have figured out something," I said. "You always do."

"Perhaps, but you've still been wonderful." Michael glanced again at the desk, saw my empty teacup, and said, "Can I have Amber bring you some fresh tea?"

The simple question caught me off guard. "What? I'm sorry, what did you say?"

"Would you like some fresh tea? I could have Amber make it for you."

I stared at him. The tilt of his head, the inflection of his voice along with the offer itself, were echoes of an earlier conversation.

That's when I saw the truth of it all. Michael was a younger, more handsome version of Chester Sterling. Chester had lost the good looks of his youth by the time I'd met him, while Michael could have replaced David, if Michelangelo had known him. It was those differences that had kept me from seeing that underneath their physical attributes both men were the same.

Both were kind, charming, and easygoing, but neither one was very productive. It had been Rose Sterling, Audry's mother, who had built the agency from its inception. I now realized that after her death, Chester had let the business function as best it could until Audry came along. She was the one who took the reins, because someone had to, and she was the one who got it growing again.

Audry Sterling-Sherabian had married her father.

"You've done so much," Michael was saying. "Worked so hard . . ."

"I've enjoyed it." I assessed Michael Sherabian in a way I should have done years ago.

He twitched his shoulders. "I understand you're almost finished with your work here."

"Another hour or so and I'll be done."

His dark eyes melted with sadness. "And then you'll be leaving again."

"Yes."

It should have mattered that my absence would affect Michael, but now that I could clearly see him, I also realized some truths about my feelings for him. Our relationship hadn't been about Michael, it had been about my need. My father had been dying, Jeremy had been growing up and pulling away as little boys do, and there had been a horrible hole in my life. I had needed someone to love, and someone to love me in return, so I had created a Prince Charming. He was my own perfect man, but he was a mirage that I had clothed in Michael Sherabian's body.

As I looked at Michael I felt an incredible sadness mottled with guilt. I had never loved him. Not really. Probably because I had never really known him. I had never gotten beyond the exterior to find out what was inside. I had to wonder if anybody ever had.

I stood up because it was time for closure. "Michael, I owe you an apology. I'm sorry that I hurt your marriage—" I fumbled. Knowing the truth and offering it to him were two different things. I swallowed and said with painful honesty, "I'm sorry for everything."

He nodded slowly, looking terribly vulnerable and alone. I think he understood, and it had to hurt like hell. "It's been wonderful seeing you again, Jolie, whatever the circumstances. Your husband is a lucky man."

"Thank you. Audry's pretty lucky, too."

His shrug said it all. He knew that Audry didn't think that, and he suspected she was right.

In that moment I came closer to truly caring about him than I ever had, but it was love mixed with pity, not a combination that Michael would welcome.

"Well," he said, stepping back awkwardly. "I guess I'd better let you finish. Did you want that tea?"

I started to say no, but it occurred to me that Michael would like to feel useful. "I'd love some. Some mint tea would be nice." I handed him my empty cup.

He took it with a brief smile. "I'll send Amber right back with it."

Useful in his own way. "Thanks."

I sat down at the computer, feeling lighter than I had in months. I still wasn't proud of what I'd done, and I'd always regret the hurt I'd caused, but at least all those feelings didn't have to cloud my future.

For a moment I was tempted to call Matt and tell him what I'd discovered, but besides the fact that I didn't know where to reach him, I didn't think this was something he needed to hear. He could just benefit from my discovery.

In the picture on the wall, Desi's smile seemed to reflect my own. She looked so fresh and young, so unburdened, which was much the way I felt now. It made me think she hadn't been having an affair with Michael. Instead, I hoped she'd been a friend to him; that would explain Michael's grief.

And somehow I had the feeling she'd seen the real man more quickly than the rest of us. Certainly more quickly than I had.

Another thought struck me—I wondered if that had been the cause of her death.

"I'm sorry," I said softly to her beaming photo. Sorry she had died, sorry that my feeble efforts hadn't helped find her murderer, and sorry I hadn't known her.

I brought my eyes down to the computer screen and rested my fingers on the keyboard. My presence at Rose Sterling Advertising had become a mass of sorrys, and it was time to get to work so I could put them behind me.

"Girl, you take good care, you hear me, now?" Donna Katherine said as she gave me a hug.

"I hear, and I will." We were standing in her office, her Christmas wonderland glittering around us. It even smelled like the holidays. "It was great seeing you."

"It was, and if you get tired of that good-lookin' husband

of yours, you just send him out this way. I'll put him to good use."

I didn't like that thought, but then Matt wouldn't much like it either. "Got it. You take it easy, too."

She twitched her hips and flipped a shoulder before she said meaningfully, "I always do."

This time I laughed. "Seriously, it was good seeing you again."

"You, too, and I'll be putting your paycheck in the mail before you hit retirement age. Oh, yeah, and, Jolie, you be sure and send us a card when your book comes out. I want to read it."

"I'll arrange a signing in Austin and see that you're all invited."

"Good, girl. Now, did you get a chance to say good-bye to Chester?"

"He's gone and Amber didn't know when he'd be back. Everyone's gone." I wasn't sure if I was sad about that or relieved. Chester's party, which now seemed aeons ago, was supposed to have been my triumphant return, a glorious tribute to my brilliance for writing and publishing a book. Amazing how life twists in its own way. Instead I had found Desi Baker dead, and ended up a copywriter, just what I'd been before I'd left.

As my dad used to say, the more things change the more they stay the same.

Donna Katherine's phone rang and she made a face. "Well, guess that's the bell calling me back to the salt mines. 'Bye again, Jolie."

Before she picked up the phone I waved and started for the front door. When I heard the swish of the ornaments on the Christmas tree I stopped. I didn't want any more drawn-out goodbyes. I didn't want to see Audry and feel the guilt again, or the pity for Michael. I didn't want to wonder if Ralph or Fred were murderers, which was a thought that continued to haunt me. It would even have been hard to face Chester, now that I understood him better.

I couldn't remain motionless in the hallway forever, though. With a forced smile on my face, I sucked in a breath and stepped around the corner, moving quickly, as if the momentum would push me out the door without any conversation. Nola was at the front desk, glancing through her messages.

"Hey," she said.

I slowed. "Hey, yourself." Those were the first words we'd exchanged since she'd stormed out. I nudged her elbow, causing the strap of her purse to slip off her shoulder. When she pulled it back up again I smiled. "Got ya."

She returned the smile. "You just now leaving for lunch?"

"No. Just leaving."

"You're not getting much of a send-off. How about if we have some hot chocolate first?"

Outside the window the sky was a dismal gray and tiny ice crystals had formed intricate patterns along the metal strips. The streets below were so hazy the sodden pedestrians had become shadows against the slick sidewalks.

"It looks pretty bad out there. . . . You think it will get any better if I wait?"

She shook her head. "Not a chance. But I'll tell you a shortcut to get where you're going."

Another of those old jokes we shared. Nola had come from radio sales, outside sales she'd always called it, where time was money and you had to know the fastest route to anyplace in the city. She'd also bragged she knew where all the best public rest rooms were, and where to find the quietest and cleanest pay phones.

Not that she needed pay phones anymore. The antenna of a cellular stuck out of her purse.

When I brought my eyes up to Nola's face she was watching me. Something was up; it mattered to her that we talked.

There was nothing to rush back to Prissy's for. Matt was no doubt at Austin Edge, fighting the good fight for the investors. Jeremy was wrapping Christmas presents at Alicia's. Christopher would be taking a nap.

Nola was waiting, still watching me.

"Sure," I said. "I'd love some hot chocolate, but you're buying. And flying."

221

"We're flying," she said, taking my elbow and ushering me out the door. "I don't want to stay here, and neither do you. There's a new little coffee bar we can get to by cutting through the parking garage."

"How come nobody told me about that sooner?"

"You don't ask, you don't get." She sounded grim as she added, "Especially around here."

❧ CHAPTER 24 ❧

As NOLA and I hurried across the lobby, Ted Polovy jerked his head toward the outside. "Be careful out there, it's getting slick."

"We're just going to the coffee bar, Mom," Nola replied with a grin.

Then we wrapped our coats tighter around us and hurried through the parking garage. Its half-empty state was a testament to the fact that people were leaving early, either because of the bad weather or for the holiday.

At the coffee bar Nola selected a small table that looked out on Sixth Street. I had expected charm and warmth, but the place was almost pure white with cheap plastic chairs and flimsy white metal tables. The most inviting element was the aroma. I imagined it as a mixture of every submarine sandwich that had passed through there with garlic, vinegar, and Italian sausage vying for the most attention. I sniffed a couple of times, trying to talk myself into something to eat, although I knew better. Too many meals mean too many pounds.

"There must be a million calories in this thing," I said, warming my hands around the cardboard cup of hot chocolate topped with a small mountain of whipped cream.

"Consider it an emergency measure," Nola said. "Without it we could freeze to death."

Outside the window I was grateful to see that there was none of the real ice the weatherman had threatened, but the frigid snap to the air suggested it was coming.

"So what's up?" I asked, huddling close to the table.

Nola made a quick face. "No pleasantries? 'Nice hair'? 'I like your coat'? 'How are the kids?' None of those things?"

"Your kids are fine or we wouldn't be here; I love the coat, probably because it's almost identical to mine, and your hair looks a bit windblown. As, I'll bet, mine is."

"You're a hard woman, Jolene Berenski."

"Wyatt," I corrected. "Jolene Wyatt. Matt says it has a nice ring to it."

Nola sat back in the chair. "When you start bragging on your husband, it's time to get down to facts."

"I wasn't bragging—"

She ignored that. "You know the other morning when I was in your office?"

"And trashed the place?"

"And cleaned it up," she added. Then she stopped, her expression going from playful to serious. "Damn, Jolie, this is really hard for me. It's all hard."

I blew on my hot chocolate, my eyes still on her. For the first time she seemed like an older woman to me, as if the sedentary culture of middle age gripped her so hard she couldn't do any of her customary quick movements. She didn't raise an eyebrow, fidget with her ring, or twitch her shoulders. She merely sat.

"Nola, what is it? You look so, so unhappy."

Another sigh, and a slow nod. "I am." Her eyes narrowed as she focused on mine. "Would you say I am a loyal person?"

"Of course."

"A good person?"

"Yes. You're one of the best people I know. You're kind, you're generous, you care about other people's feelings—"

"You're prejudiced."

"I probably am," I responded. "But for good reason. So what's going on? What was going on the other morning when you were looking for something in my office?"

The sigh she let out this time was almost a shudder. "I needed some copy. Remember I told you I was pitching a big new account?"

"Right. And you said that Audry was talking about cutting your commissions again."

"Yeah, she is, and when she told me that, it was the last straw. You can't believe what it's been like around there. I can't make a long-distance call without writing it down and justifying it. Hell, I was going home to phone my out-of-town clients because it was just easier to pay for it than put up with the nonsense, but James put his foot down. He said no matter what kind of trouble Rose Sterling was in, it wasn't our place to subsidize them. Especially because he just started his own insurance agency last year, and we're still not seeing a profit. I'm supporting the family and his business."

Which could certainly put a strain on anyone, especially a woman who took her responsibilities as seriously as Nola.

"I'm sorry," I said.

"Not your fault."

"No, but I'm sorry it's happening to you. It's got to be difficult."

She nodded. "Not that anyone at Rose Sterling seems to care. Hell, Jolie, I don't think they've even noticed. Certainly not the Ice Queen."

"But what about Chester? Have you tried to talk to him?"

She took her time formulating a response, and when she spoke the words came out slowly. "I know you think a lot of Chester, and I agree with you he's a very fine man, but, Jolie, I don't know if he's much of a force at the agency right now. Used to be that he'd do something if you asked; he really cared about us, but he's just a figurehead now. Audry has the say-so. Only Audry."

Her words saddened rather than surprised me; they merely confirmed my own conclusions. "I can appreciate that," I said, nodding. I sipped some chocolate before I asked, "So what are you doing about it?" I already suspected the answer to my question, and even had some proof at the office, but she needed to talk.

With just a touch of defensiveness she said, "I'm starting my own agency. I pitched that account for myself."

"Under the name Millennium Advertising."

"You found the copy." She rolled her eyes, her movements showing some of her old energy. "So what do you think? Am I crazy? Am I a terrible person?"

"Well, you're not crazy. You're a very good salesperson, and I assume you can handle a business. Austin's growing again; you should do very well."

"But was it wrong to pitch the account before I quit?"

Which was the heart of the matter; or perhaps more honestly, the conscience of it. I allowed myself to think about it. Nola was on straight commission, meaning that if her accounts didn't do business in a given month, she didn't make any money. As far as I could tell, her time was her own. I only had one quibble. "You used Desi to write the copy."

"But not on Rose Sterling time! She did it on her lunch hours, or after five, or at home. Believe me, this was a self-preservation move, not a way to hurt Rose Sterling." But we both knew Audry wouldn't see it that way.

Nola caught her breath and went on again. "And I paid Desi for the time she put in. Now, maybe it wasn't what I'd pay a regular freelance writer, but we had a bonus deal worked out. If I got the account, she got the difference plus some additional. Jolie, I wasn't out to hurt anybody, but I have to take care of myself and my family. You know how that is. Of all people, you should understand."

Nola had been my confidante through more than one crisis in my own life when I had been a single mom, trying to raise Jeremy and in general hold things together. She'd had her problems, too, both personally and financially. More than once we'd brown-bagged it together, pretending we were bringing food from home in an effort to lose weight rather than to save money. And we'd shopped at the Junior League Thrift Shop when we couldn't afford new clothes any other way. I'd cried on her shoulder over men, money, Jeremy, and my career. I'd trusted her with secrets and she'd honored me the same way. If we had to give each other advice, we knew the order of priorities: family came first, then friends, then business. It was a credo that worked, at least for us.

"I do understand," I said. "In fact, if you need help with copywriting when Millennium takes off, I might suggest someone. She lives out of town, but her fees are reasonable, and hey, she's just a fax away."

"Are you serious?"

"Sure."

Nola smiled, flipping her coat back. "I can't tell you how much better I feel. I thought about becoming a Catholic, just so I could go to confession." She sat forward in the chair, then leaned back, letting out relieved breaths. "You know, I'm going to hold you to that promise of writing copy for me."

"I'd love to. When will you know about the account?"

"January third, and I swear to you, I'm turning in my resignation the minute I know. I've already written the letter."

"I've got my fingers crossed." I held them out to show her that I really did.

And still something niggled at the back of my mind. Could Desi have written the copy, and then used her knowledge of Millennium Advertising to blackmail Nola? Not that Nola would have responded by killing her; Nola simply wasn't that kind of person. But maybe James had done it to protect Nola—

"You don't look happy about something," she said.

"I keep thinking about Desi's death. And just about Desi, I guess, too."

"What about her?"

"I don't know." Nola watched me patiently until I phrased the question. "You said she was ambitious. Is that right?"

"Yes. Which is why she was so hot about working with Millennium. She figured she could move ahead in a new agency a lot faster than she could at Rose Sterling. She could get around me a lot easier when she wanted something than she could Audry, too." There was some anger in her voice.

"But were you worried about her? You know, did you think she'd push too hard? Maybe try to get your clients?"

The response was succinct. "I didn't say I was going to hire her. I said that's what she wanted."

"Oh."

"I hadn't decided, okay? But it was doubtful. She wasn't honorable. At least I didn't trust her to be." She drank hot chocolate, taking in big gulps as if it were time to go.

"Hold it. Amber says that Desi was straight arrow—absolutely perfect in the honor department. So what am I missing here?"

Nola put down her drink, sat back, and frowned. "Are you serious?"

"One hundred percent. Amber swears that Desi was a straight shooter. And wait a minute, so does Ted Polovy. You know, the security guard in the building."

"My, my, isn't that interesting."

"And Fred thinks she was wonderful, too. Honest, demure . . ."

"Yes, but Fred still thinks it's 1970. He's disappointed because he went to Town Lake last weekend and couldn't find the love-in he thought they were holding."

I laughed. "Well, he did sound a little out of touch. Okay, so he's always that way, but it was most noticeable when he was talking about Desi. Like maybe she wasn't quite real."

We both sipped chocolate, and finally Nola shook her head. "You'll have to figure out your own truth about it, Jolie. I think Desi was honorable when it suited her."

"Wasn't it Camus who said that every man has a moral code of his own likes and dislikes?"

"The man was ahead of his time—it sure is true these days." She stuffed her napkin in the now-empty cardboard cup and tossed it toward the trash can. When it went in she said, "Two points."

"So what about Desi and men? How was she with them? Half the agency seems to have been in love with her. Male half."

"She said something to me once about her ex-husband. I got the impression he was abusive, and it changed something in her."

Nola shook her head with the frustration of not being able to find the words. "Men were like cats or something. She liked them, sort of charmed them, but she just wasn't having any, you know? As if she could control her destiny more easily if she didn't get involved with men."

"Interesting." Not being the athletic type like Nola, I got up and put my cup in the trash. When I was seated at the table again I said, "So you don't think she was sleeping with Michael?"

Nola looked at me for a long moment. "Jolie, I only know for sure of two women who've slept with Michael Sherabian." She raised an eyebrow. "I'm looking at one of them."

I refused to flinch. "And who was the other?"

"His wife."

"Oh." Long pause, while I tried to tough it out.

It was Nola who broke the silence. "Well, kiddo, now we know all of each other's guilty sins."

"Not all," I said. "Let's not mention any more, on the off chance that one of us may have forgotten."

"Good thinking." She looked at her watch. "Guess I'd better run. I can't believe tomorrow is Christmas Eve. Lord, and today's the day my mom is flying in."

"Do you have to pick her up?"

"No. James's new office is closer, so he's going to get her, but I don't envy him. I told her that two days before Christmas was going to be impossible; I'll bet the airport looks like rush hour on the freeway. And it's Friday on top of it. Always a bad day for travel."

Something about Friday and travel hit me unexpectedly. Today was Friday. "What time is it?" I asked.

"A little after three. Why?"

Todd was flying out at 5:50 P.M. on Friday. With tickets for two people. I had assumed it was Friday of next week, but what if I was wrong? What if he was leaving today? That second ticket needn't be for a girlfriend—

Things fell into place with a tiny click.

"I've got to run." I meant that literally, jumping up and running for the parking lot.

It had begun to drizzle and I slid my way along the slick highway with hundreds of other cars, our headlights beaming yellow and barely penetrating the dark and cold afternoon. All the muttered curses, all the promises to God, didn't speed up the traffic as I crawled through the nasty weather at thirty miles an hour.

Just let me get there in time, I prayed.

Between swipes of the windshield wipers, I tried to calm myself. Other people were at the house. Prissy was there, maybe Stephanie. Surely they would stop Todd. Wouldn't they?

The lights in front of me glowed brighter red, and cars slid to a halt. Another car lurched into my lane, and I stepped on the brakes fighting the wheel as the Intrepid slid to the right. I stopped just inches from the car ahead of me.

"Asshole," I snapped.

I put my attention back on the road, and when the exit appeared out of the haze in front of me, instead of relaxing, my constricted muscles remained tight.

The residential streets were easier to traverse. Very few cars were out, and the lights from the big houses in Prissy's neighborhood gave off warmth and hope that everything was as it should be.

"Just let Christopher be there," I prayed silently.

In the wide driveway was a car I didn't recognize and I pulled in beside it, parking too close. My feet crunched on the ice as I made my way around that other vehicle. It had a child's car seat in the back, and that frightened me into hurrying, so that I lost my balance and had to grab the door handle to remain upright.

Maybe the car belonged to a friend of Stephanie's, I told myself, planting my feet more firmly. Someone her age who also had a little one. Surely that was it. Except it seemed very bad weather for a visit.

With quick, careful steps I made my way toward the back of

the house. At the corner I turned onto the patio and stopped, stunned.

Christopher was sitting alone, three steps up on the outdoor staircase. He wasn't wearing a coat and his tiny body was wracked with shivers. Tear tracks had dried on his face.

"Oh, my God! Christopher, you'll freeze to death out here." I ran up the steps, pulling open my own coat so I could envelop him in it.

Just as I reached him I heard another voice behind me. "Stop right there. Don't you go near him."

❧ CHAPTER 25 ❧

It sounded like the voice of God—demanding and commanding—but I didn't hesitate. I threw open my coat and reached for Christopher. The material caught on something behind me and I fell to the tile on one knee.

Even as I yelped in pain, I thought it was an accident. I jerked at my coat, and hopped up the step to get hold of Christopher. "What in the hell—?"

"I told you not to do that." It was Todd.

Somewhere my brain was registering his words, but they made no sense, as if the real meaning were hidden in code.

"Are you crazy?" I demanded. "He'll die of exposure."

"That boy has been coddled too much by women, and I won't have any more."

"He's a baby. You don't leave a baby out in this weather." I pulled Christopher to me. His hands were purple with the cold, and his body shook. I wrapped him up with me in my coat as fury coursed through me. "I don't know what your problem is, Todd, but this is criminal—"

I heard a crack on the tile; it sounded like a baseball bat. I jerked around, falling to a sitting position.

"Todd—what in the—"

He was holding a set of nunchaku. Two thick, short wooden sticks attached on one end by a short length of chain. They are a martial arts weapon, cruel and lethal. He flipped them expertly, coming up a step so that I could feel the rush of air as one spun within inches of my face.

He didn't stop even when I flinched backward.

"Todd, cut it out."

The nunchaku landed in his hand effortlessly, as if responding to my command.

"Christopher is being punished," he said. His voice held resignation, as if this was unpleasant but necessary. "I have the right to do that—I'm his father."

I wasn't a bit surprised. But I was furious. "Todd, you may have some rights where Christopher is concerned—"

"I have *every* right. I am his father." He slapped the nunchaku again, and the contained ferocity of the act shook me out of my anger. It was replaced with a gut-level fear.

Christopher was like a little animal, burrowing against me.

I heard the quiver in my voice, and hoped it was from the cold as I said, "Todd, I know sometimes children can be difficult—"

"He is not difficult, he is spoiled rotten! He does exactly what he pleases no matter what I tell him. That is unacceptable. When I left Phoenix, I left Christopher on the condition that Stephanie would raise him right. Well, she hasn't. I should have known she didn't have it in her."

He didn't mention what else I suspected—that he'd been abusive to both Stephanie and Christopher, and it had all been blamed on drugs. Maybe drugs were in part at fault, but I was beginning to realize that Todd, just Todd, was to blame.

And Prissy never knew the truth, wouldn't hear it. Didn't want to know what her best friend's son was really like. God help them all.

I took a breath. "I'm sure it's been difficult. But now that Christopher's punishment is over, I'll take him inside."

"No! It's not done. You go inside and mind your own business."

A tiny whimper came from Christopher as he pressed himself even tighter against me.

"Christopher is a baby, and this could—" I stopped. I didn't want to frighten Christopher any more than he already was. With great effort I brought my voice under control. "He has to get inside. Certainly you understand about exposure." The gray skies were sending down sleet. I had to get Christopher out of the weather.

I started to stand and the nunchaku whipped around, smacked against the wall, and flew toward me. I cringed, yanking Christopher with me. My back hit the hard step above and I let out an involuntary cry.

"All of you women are weak. You're ruining Christopher, turning him into a wimp. He has to be tough. Strong, like a man. Don't you, Christopher?" When there was no response Todd leaned closer so that I could smell his breath. "Don't you? Answer me!"

The little voice responded. "Yes, sir."

"And who am I?"

Christopher's lip quivered, but he said firmly, "My fodder."

Now I was the one who was shaking.

Sleet stung us. My jaws barely moved as I forced myself to say calmly, "Todd, I didn't mean to countermand your authority—"

"I wasn't going to press my duties with Christopher. I just wanted to see him," he said, tilting his head with some sick version of pride. "After all, he is my son. But then I saw what was happening to him. How he didn't behave. Coming into my room twice after he'd been told not to! You knew better, didn't you, Christopher? Didn't you?"

"Yes."

"You speak up when I talk to you!"

"Yes, sir."

"Getting away with being a spoiled brat. That's what you are, aren't you? You're a very bad boy, aren't you?"

"Yes, sir."

"No!" The word shot out of me. "He's not bad." The nunchaku flew again, but I went on. "Christopher may have *done* something bad—we've all done some bad things—but he's not a bad boy. He's a good boy. A very good boy."

Todd flipped one of the sticks upward and caught it deftly, so that the two pieces of wood lay in his right hand. Deceptively peaceful. He stood up straight, like a drill sergeant. "That's reverse psychology. Pop psychology. Weak bullshit."

"No. It's fact. As his father, you know Christopher is good, or you wouldn't bother with him." I pulled the coat tighter; it barely closed around Christopher. He was still cold, but the shaking had lessened.

When Todd didn't respond I glanced toward the house. The lights were on, but apparently no one else was there. Todd noticed my look and said, "Stephanie went with Peter, and then Prissy got a phone call from Brackenridge Hospital. She was told Ross was in an accident. I volunteered to keep Christopher so she could go."

The world was spinning too fast. "Is Ross——?"

"He's fine. Probably at his office." Todd glanced at his watch. "It should take Prissy another ten minutes or so to get to Brack, and I'll be gone by then."

Relief made me weak. Christopher almost slid out of my arms; I pulled him closer. "You're going away now," I said.

It was misplaced hope on my part.

"*We* are leaving. Christopher and I. Aren't we, son?"

I could feel Christopher tip his head forward slowly in a terrified nod. His words were a whispered, "Yes, sir."

Friday. I had been right, it was today.

Todd reached out toward us. "Christopher, we're just going to leave your Christmas presents, we don't have time to fool with them now. I want you to stand up and go wait for me at the car."

"No!" I jerked away, the cry like a wound.

The nunchaku flew again. Todd leaned closer and said, "I am not an unkind person, but you are forcing me to do things I'd rather not. You're being unreasonable. Let go of my son."

"Todd, you can't go. It will kill Prissy and Ross——" He jerked Christopher out of my arms, ripping him away with brute strength. "No," I cried. "You can't do this, it's kidnapping——"

With one hand he set Christopher on the ground, and held

me at bay with the nunchaku. His eyes still glaring, he said, "Christopher, go. Now."

"Please, Todd, no." I hurt to my soul. "Please, don't—"

"Move, Christopher."

Christopher said quietly, "Good-bye, Aunt Dolie. I love you." He started off.

"You can't!" I jumped up and Todd shoved me back. I slipped on the icy steps and my head smacked the tile. Pain jolted through me and the sky spun. "You can't—"

Todd's face wasn't in focus as he said, "You made me do that; you just remember it was your fault." He started away.

I got to my knees, and my stomach lurched. "No—"

"Wish everyone a happy holiday from me." There was no sarcasm in the words, the last Todd said to me as he hurried toward his car.

My head went forward, until I could feel the freezing railing pressing against my forehead.

In the hazy background a car door opened, and Todd's barked command was lost in the slamming of it. Then a second car door opened and closed.

I gulped in air, and saw that my tears had frozen on the step. A car engine started.

No! He'd have to kill me to get away with Christopher.

This time I tripped on my own coat, then slipped on the slick patio. It didn't matter; I half ran, half slid, falling more than once. The only pain was in my heart. I had to get Christopher back.

The lights of Todd's car raked over me as he swung around on the circular drive and I could see Christopher watching me—straining at the car seat. I could almost hear his cry.

Then Todd reached back and tried to hit Christopher. He missed by inches.

"Son of a bitch," I said, yanking open my car door and jumping in. My eyes were trained on Todd's car as I started the engine, backed around the circle, then swung out into the street. The sleet and rain had formed an icy sheet on the asphalt and suddenly my car broke loose; I was gliding sideways across the street.

With stiff fingers I whirled the cold steering wheel, and like a ballet maneuver, the car began to turn again. It slowly straightened.

I frantically looked for Todd. At the end of the block I spotted taillights. God, I hoped they were his.

My knees were shaking, and I forced myself to step down on the gas pedal. The wheels spun and the car didn't move. With another curse I tried again, this time more carefully until the Intrepid started forward. Todd had grown up in the East; he had the advantage of knowing how to maneuver on ice and snow. I had the advantage of a heavier car, and one other thing: I had absolutely nothing to lose.

Todd turned right. I switched on my headlights and started to pray. He was still a block away from me, adding distance with every second that passed. At the corner I braked lightly, looking to my left. A decorated Christmas tree lit the yard beside me. I noticed it as I arced around the corner, the wheels finding nothing solid to cling to. Thank God the street was empty.

My heart almost broke as I realized that Todd was even farther away, and if he got to the freeway, there was no way I could catch him. In the crush at the airport it would even be more difficult to track him down.

In desperation I searched for some way to catch him. I had an idea, and no way of knowing if it would work until I tried it. The windshield was fogging, making visibility even worse in the twilight.

With great care I flipped on the defroster, then turned the steering wheel. The car slid until it hit the curb with a jolt, then the right front tire jumped up and stayed firm on the grass. Perfect. That was the way I was going to drive until I was closer.

It actually worked. I came to a driveway, but I held the car steady. We slid across the concrete and back up the other side. We missed a telephone pole by inches. A mailbox loomed up, and rather than jerk the wheel, I brushed it, the front fender grating against the metal box before it hit the ground.

It shouldn't have been that close to the street anyway.

The important thing was that I was gaining on Todd. I could see him, still on the road, driving at a speed that probably galled him.

I was less than forty feet back.

What I needed now was a plan.

❧ CHAPTER 26 ❧

W<small>E WERE</small> still in a residential area; only two cars had passed me on the icy road, but I didn't want to risk endangering someone else. Unless I had to. I was desperate and it showed in my thinking.

By now Todd had seen me. He tried to drive faster, but even he had his limitations; the car couldn't pull away. I stepped on the gas, bouncing as the tires went up and over a planter edged in brick. I jerked my foot off the accelerator and the car slowed.

"Damn it."

Again I pressed on the gas pedal until I was just a few feet behind Todd. I could see him clearly now, hunched over the wheel like Cruella DeVille. I could see Christopher, too. He was sitting ramrod-straight in his car seat. I hoped he was buckled in.

With a prayer and a hope I pressed hard on the accelerator. The Intrepid bucked forward, began to slide, and just kissed Todd's back bumper.

I honked the horn, waving for Todd to stop. He stared forward, his posture grim and determined. It was clear he was going straight to the airport and nothing was going to deter him.

Out of the gloom and mist rose a stop sign; Todd had to be weighing his options. If he didn't slow down, he had a better chance of reaching the highway without interference from me.

I looked down the cross street as best I could, but by now I was a good thirty feet back, my vision blocked by houses. When I looked forward again I realized Todd's car had picked up speed; he was going to run the stop, which meant I would have to as well. I flicked on my emergency flashers and started honking my horn, then I increased the pressure on the gas pedal. My right foot was shaking. The needle on the speedometer rose slowly, from fifteen to twenty to twenty-five. Out of the corner of my eye I caught the glare of headlights, coming from my left. They didn't have a stop.

"Don't do this to me!" I laid into the horn, letting it blare a warning.

It might have been my adrenaline pushing the car until we were doing almost thirty. Thirty-five. Todd was beyond the intersection, Christopher was safe on the other side. I continued to honk the horn, I flashed the lights, then closed my eyes and prayed as we went straight through the cross street.

In seconds I was right behind Todd. He was waving me back, but I kept coming. I gestured for him to move over and let me by. Miraculously, he eased to the right. I could see him talking, swearing, as I began to pull around him. My idea would work only if Christopher was strapped in the back on the other side of the car. He was. I drew even with Todd's car, keeping a good ten feet between us. He kept twisting his head to watch me. I waited until I was half a length in front of him, then with stiff movements I swung the steering wheel right. As if in slow motion the Intrepid lurched toward Todd's car. I saw his look of fury, then fear, as the Intrepid rammed into his door.

Metal crunched. Both cars rocked and bobbed. Together they picked up speed, slamming across the icy asphalt until Todd's front wheel jumped the curb. Tenaciously the Intrepid hung on. With one more nudge of the gas pedal I had Todd's car pinned between mine and a telephone pole.

With careless hurry I swung open my door and jumped out of the car. When my feet hit the ice they went out from under me and I grabbed for the door handle, just missing as I went down. The asphalt was hard and slick. I heard an engine behind me, and suddenly I was blinded by more headlights from a car rounding the corner. In a purely reflexive move, I let go of the car door and slid under the frame.

The other vehicle stopped just inches from my half-open door.

"Are you all right? Is anybody hurt?" Only the man's Reeboks and his jean legs were visible.

"I'm fine." As I reached out to grab the frame, his hand clutched at mine instead. He pulled me out and helped me stand.

"There's a baby in the other car," I said, already feeling my way toward the back fender, hanging on to the Intrepid for balance. "My nephew. Please. We have to—"

"Should I call the police?"

"Yes." It was like a miracle. "Yes. Call the police."

He started in the other direction, but I hardly noticed. I was on someone's lawn now so that I could move quickly. Through the rear passenger window I could see Christopher, hear him crying, "Aunt Dolie, we need help."

"I'll get you, little bug. Don't cry." I grabbed the door handle and jerked, but Todd had it locked. Son of a bitch.

I tried the front door; it was also locked.

Todd was screaming at me. "Look what you've done! You smashed my door and I'm trapped. I think my arm is broken."

Frantically I looked around. Not five feet away a bush was covered with a tarp—held down with bricks.

"Get me out of here," Todd yelled. "Now. Do you hear me? Christopher, shut the fuck up! Now, I want out now."

I picked up the brick and planted myself solidly next to the front passenger window. "Christopher, close your eyes and look the other way. Hurry!"

Todd realized what I was about to do. "You could kill me! You can't just—"

I reared back and flung the brick into the passenger window. It bounced off harmlessly.

Todd became even more abusive. "Damn it, you stupid bitch, you can't—"

I grabbed the brick again, only this time I imagined Todd's face where I aimed it. With my adrenaline pumping I smashed the brick into the glass. Millions of glittering shapes scattered around me, a few still clinging to the safety sealant as the glass shattered; it was almost beautiful.

"Aunt Dolie!"

I unlocked the back door and threw it open. Christopher was strapped in his car seat, his coat lying on the seat beside him; a knit cap poked out of the pocket. I unhooked the strap on the car seat and jerked the restraining bar over his head.

"What about me? Why aren't you helping me?" Todd was flailing, trying to get at us, fumbling to undo his seat belt at the same time.

"He can help." I gestured toward our good Samaritan's car, only to see that he was driving off. "Quick, look at me," I said to Christopher, ramming his cap down on his head.

"You sent him to call the police, didn't you?" Todd screamed. He had his hand on the seat belt, but so far hadn't been able to unhook it. "You're going to pay for this! You're going to jail for kidnapping. Christopher is my son, and you can't take him. You rammed my car on purpose; I'll get you for assault."

"You've got the charges right, but the person wrong."

It wasn't much for a last insult, but the best I could do. With one arm around Christopher's body and one around his head to shield him, I said, "Come on, little bug." As if he could help. With one mighty heave I brought him out and for the first time he was safe, clinging to my neck, almost choking me. "It's okay, baby, you're fine now. Come on." I set Christopher on the ground and reached back into the car for his coat.

That was a mistake.

Todd grabbed my hand and bent it backward at the wrist. I felt the pain to my marrow. "No!" I tried to jerk away, but he increased the pressure and I waited for the bones to snap.

"Not so tough now, are you, bitch?" Todd snarled, almost smiling as he held fast to my wrist. "Now you're going to get me out of here, and then you're going to drive me to the airport."

Any second my wrist was going to break. "Please, no more—" I gasped, and lowered my head as if I could escape the pain. Christopher was clutching at my coat; he'd started to cry.

242

"Let go!" I begged. My head went down and I saw the nunchaku on the floor behind the passenger seat.

Any port in a storm, any weapon in a pinch.

Ignoring the pain I took hold of one end of the nunchaku with my free hand and flipped them upward.

I knew instantly there wasn't enough power, but the weapon itself had force. The other stick jerked at the end of the chain, hitting the dome light, blacking it out.

This time it was Todd who gasped and flinched. I swung the weapon again, accidently hitting the back of the seat, so that the other stick dropped harmlessly. Todd released my wrist just as I whipped the nunchaku in a third, more powerful, swing. It hit the rearview mirror, then bounced back, catching Todd on the side of the head.

"Goddamn it!" he yelled.

"Watch your language, asshole!" I jerked backward, out of the car, before I realized the jacket was still inside. This time I stayed low until I could snatch it out.

It took more precious time, but I had to get Christopher warm. His face was pale as I struggled to zip up his jacket. In the reflected streetlight we edged around the two cars while I pulled up his hood to cover his ears.

Hand over hand we moved along the back of Todd's car, my frozen fingers barely able to grasp the frigid metal. When we reached the other corner, I realized the Intrepid was five feet away across slick asphalt. It sat in the street like a cold hulk. "Hang on." I slid my feet slowly, taking careful little steps until we could reach the bumper; Christopher was clinging to my hand and my coat. The door creaked ominously as I pulled it open. Todd was still yelling at us, mixing his threats with curses and pleas. I ignored him.

"Get in the backseat. Hurry, Christopher." His teeth were chattering as he scrambled in.

"Thank you, Aunt Dolie," he said, his voice very little.

"Oh, Christopher." I kissed him quickly, trying to secure the seat belt with frozen fingers that refused to cooperate. "I'm sorry

Todd got you, but you were very brave, sweetie. Very brave." Finally the lock clicked into place. I tugged at it once for security as I added, "You are good and brave."

"I'm cold, too, Aunt Dolie."

"Here." I took off my coat and wrapped it around him, then slammed the door.

I jumped in the front seat and started the car. "Hang on. And stay brave just a little longer."

With the gearshift in reverse, I gave the car some gas. Tires spun and the two cars remained locked together as if in some battle to the death.

"Are we stuck, Aunt Dolie? Todd will come and get us!"

"No, he won't, because we're not stuck. See?" I opened the door and rocked the car, which did no good at all. "The road is just a little slick, but watch what happens." Once again I tried the gas pedal, only this time I used all the control I had. "Gently, gently, see, we're moving."

It was wishful thinking. The wheels spun, smoke lifted from the front of the car, and neither vehicle shifted more than an inch or two.

Todd's mocking laugh caught my attention. He appeared to have the seat belt undone and was crawling toward the passenger door. Dear God, he was coming.

✴ CHAPTER 27 ✴

THIS TIME I prayed. Maybe I didn't deserve to be safe, but Christopher did. "Hang on, now, Christopher," I said. "We're leaving." With one last prayer I touched the accelerator. The car slid back a few inches. In my joy I quit pressing on the gas and the car plunged forward. Again it hit Todd's car, knocking him off balance. A string of expletives mauled the air.

"Okay, here we go." I closed my eyes and tried again. Slowly and with great care we eased backward. Todd was out of his car now. He had to stop because another pair of headlights was coming toward us.

I couldn't think about those things; I let the Intrepid slide to a stop, then I put it in drive.

I closed my eyes, gave it just the tiniest amount of gas, and without a roar, or even speed, we crept away.

I carried Christopher toward the lobby of the high-rise building that housed Rose Sterling Advertising. The place was beginning to feel like a second home and I was looking forward to seeing Ted Polovy, hoping for a little reinforcement.

Once over the threshold I realized there was a woman at the security desk. "Where's Ted?" I asked her, looking behind me, as if Todd might appear.

"Not here."

"But, I thought—" I guess I'd thought he worked twenty-four hours a day.

"Gone for the night," she said. The fluorescent lights in the lobby made her skin appear a brownish yellow, and her voice held no curiosity at all.

"Oh." I hadn't realized until that instant how much I'd counted on having someone here; someone who carried a gun, and would use it in our defense. Someone who would believe what I had to say without background information. Now we were on our own. But then, we had been all along.

"You want to sign in?" she asked.

"Sure." It was all I could get out without giving away how I was feeling.

I shifted Christopher to the desk and wrote my name. My nose was wet, but that was from the cold, just the cold, I told myself, sniffing hard. In the bottom of my coat pocket I found a linty tissue and blew my nose, before adding the name Rose Sterling to the next line of the sign-in book. The guard leaned toward Christopher and said, "Are you going to do some work?"

He shook his head. "No." By now he was warmer, but his face remained pale and pinched with a bright red nose. That could have been the cold, too. "My Aunt Dolie worts harder."

"Works," I corrected.

The woman nodded. "And, honey, we all do." She reached behind her and came up with a candy cane, which she handed to Christopher. "Here, have you been a good boy?"

Christopher blanched. His eyes fixed first on her, then on me. "I don't know. Aunt Dolie—?"

"Yes, you have. You've been a very good boy. You *are* a very good boy."

The woman picked up on the seriousness of my tone, and while she probably didn't understand it, she dropped her teasing manner. "A little bird told me that you are a good boy. Here." She handed over the candy. "Merry Christmas."

Christopher took it with the solemnity of someone accepting a Nobel Prize. "Thank you."

I tried to smile a thank-you as well, but I doubt I succeeded. She acknowledged my nod and then pointed to the elevator. For once it was waiting, its doors open. I hurried us in that direction.

"Where we going, Aunt Dolie?"

"To my office, it's up on the seventh floor." I was clinging to Christopher, holding him to calm myself, hoping it was all going to be okay. The agency was the only safe place I could think of for the two of us to wait. "You want to push the button?" I stepped closer to the panel so he could press the seven. And the nine and eleven. The doors closed and we started our ascent.

My insides were shaking, just like my outsides had been earlier. At one point during the drive on Mopac my legs had quivered so violently I'd wondered if we'd make it. I had turned up the radio and started singing loudly. "Jingle Bells." I think we sang it seven times on the trip.

And all along I had wondered where Todd was. I knew he'd gotten help; another car had stopped as we drove off. I was fairly sure he wasn't hurt badly, but beyond that, there was a chance that his car was drivable, and he was capable of doing the driving. It was that thought that had frightened me most and followed us like a specter.

He could have come after us, and I didn't dare go to the police station because I couldn't ask for help without getting Child Protective Services involved. Their mission is to safeguard the child in any situation, and when things are unclear, as they certainly would be in our case, Christopher would be whisked away and it might take hours, even days, to get him back.

"When are we gonna see my mommy?" Christopher asked. His staunch efforts to remain brave were becoming harder to maintain.

I hugged him tighter. "In a little while. She's at a party right now, and I don't want to take you back to your grandma's until we know that your mommy's home. And I want your grandma and grandpa to be there."

"Can Todd find us?" he asked, sliding one arm under my heavy coat collar to hang on a little better. I kissed his cheek.

"No, sweetie, he can't. Todd doesn't know where I work." Or did he? Someone could have told him. And if he knew the name of the agency, he could look it up in the phone book to get a location. He could be here now, he could have arrived ahead of us—

My heart started hammering.

I took a deep breath to calm myself. Todd was behind us. It didn't matter what magic he worked, he couldn't be in this building or in these offices. It simply wasn't physically possible. "We're safe here," I said to Christopher. "We'll have something warm to drink, and then in a little bit we'll go home, when we know everyone is there."

"And Todd is in jail. Or dead."

Even three-year-olds know about dead these days.

I held on to his hands, warming them. "Everything will be okay. The police will take Todd and he will never come to hurt you again. Never." Only I couldn't be sure that Todd would never come back. In our world there are no such assurances.

The elevator stopped and I attempted to smile. "Here we go." I set Christopher down and ushered him out.

While Christopher was walking on his own, I noticed that he was so close his feet kept brushing mine. I reached down and took his hand.

It was only a little after five, but the place was locked, the lights dim. I used the key I'd forgotten to return to let us in.

Once inside, I stopped and listened. There were only the creaks of cold window glass on a blustery night. "See the Christmas tree? Isn't that beautiful?"

"Who are the presents for?"

There were only three, and I'd hardly noticed them before. "I think those are for the people who own this company. Or maybe they're just empty boxes, you know, wrapped up for decoration." I urged him down the hall. "Let me show you my office, okay? We have lots of fun things."

We went cubicle to cubicle, checking each one for signs of a stranger. I knew Todd wasn't there, knew he couldn't be, but I had to peek behind the desks and peer around the plants.

"Look at the toys," Christopher said, pointing to the top of Ralph's computer. "Are those your toys, Aunt Dolie?"

"No, those belong to a friend, but I know he'd like you to play with them."

I scooped up all the little plastic figures, handed a dalmatian to Christopher, and we moved on. It was Donna Katherine's office that Christopher liked best. "It's Christmas!" All the decorations seemed to bring a little color back to his cheeks, or maybe it was just the glow from the lights around the waving Santa and the tiny ceramic village. "This is my friend Donna Katherine's office. Pretty, isn't it?"

"Is she a elf?"

I thought of Donna Katherine's tall thin body. "No, not an elf. Just a lady who likes Christmas."

"Aunt Dolie, look!" He pointed to the tiny rail cars. "There's a elf on the train. I like elves."

"Come on," I said, swooping him up into my arms and heading for the break room. "How about something nice and warm to drink?"

"Okay. Hot chocolate? I like hot chocolate. And whit cream, too."

I had been thinking more of chamomile tea, but that was out and hot chocolate in.

Once I had it fixed, with some tea for myself, and we were seated at the tiny table, it was time for me to do something. All the way in the car I had focused on getting here—getting Christopher in a place that was safe and warm, with something hot to drink. Our physical safety had been my only thought, but now there had to be a next right step. Unfortunately, my mind was still too revved up with fear for me to think.

"This is good, Aunt Dolie." Half a cup was already gone; I hoped it was helping.

"I'm sorry there wasn't any whipped cream," I said.

Christopher leaned closer and patted my hand. "It's okay." He looked around. "How do you work, Aunt Dolie?"

"I write commercials. Like you see on TV."

"I see TV."

"I know."

"Once there was a dragon on TV. A big one. With green eyes." He sat up on his knees and I grabbed his arm to keep him steady. "If I was a dragon, you know what I could do?"

"Be careful. What could you do?"

"When I see Todd, I could fire him!" He breathed what he imagined to be hot air toward me. A low growl accompanied it. "And then I'd fire him again. And again."

"Honey, you won't see Todd anymore."

"But if I do," Christopher said, climbing down from the chair, "you know what I could do? I could punch him, and kick him, and sock him hard!" He reared back and did a karate kick, then two quick chops with his little hands. "See, Aunt Dolie, I could get him."

"Yes, you could." Was I helping him get past the fear or increasing the likelihood of nightmares? "And you were already incredibly brave. Incredibly.

"Now let's go make some phone calls." I took his cup and mine, then marched toward Donna Katherine's office. On the off chance that someone came in, I would be able to hear them, and she had all the Christmas paraphernalia for Christopher to look at. "Follow along, do what I do. Hup, two, three, four."

"Are we bein' soldiers, Aunt Dolie?"

"Nope, we're just marching."

"I could be a marching elf." He strutted beside me, lifting his knees as high as they would go. "Up two, three, four. Up two, three, four . . ."

While Christopher played with the miniature train, I got busy calling numbers, trying my best to track down some reinforcements. Prissy was not home, nor was I successful with my calls to Brackenridge Hospital to see if she was still there. The icy front had caused a rash of accidents which overloaded the emergency room capacity, and on top of that, Brackenridge was designated to care for the indigent and homeless who were streaming in suffering from cold and exposure. The woman on the switchboard had been sympathetic but unable to help. The nurse on the floor had no sympathy left.

"I think I saw the woman you described, but I have no idea where she went. I don't think her husband was here—wait! You can't go down there, sir, and I've told you that twice. Look, I'll be right with you!" I'm sure she didn't intend to sound so vicious. "You might try the other hospitals," she said to me.

I barely got my thank-you out before she hung up.

Christopher stood up and said, "Can I go look at the tree?"

My first reaction was to say no. I didn't want him out of my sight, not even for a moment, but common sense reminded me of the futility of that.

"Sure, you can see the tree."

I followed him to the front office, double-checked the front door to make sure it was locked, and then used the phone at Amber's desk.

I tried Ross's office first only to get a recording that referred me to his home, and an additional number, which I wrote down and called immediately. It belonged to his assistant, but she was out Christmas shopping, according to her teenage daughter, who wasn't sure when her mother would be home. Dead end. I hung up and tried Austin Edge hoping to reach Matt. There I got a jolly holiday greeting, with no other numbers mentioned. Next I attempted to remember Ross's cellular number, which was another exercise in futility. It wasn't listed in the phone book either, and Southwestern Bell doesn't have cell phone numbers. I was straight out of luck and feeling bereft.

I dialed Nola's number. "Hey, kiddo, what are you doing?" she said.

"I'm having a bad day, Nola. A very bad day."

"You want to tell me about it?"

I desperately wanted to tell someone. I needed sympathy and if someone didn't get home soon, I was going to need help. "Hold on a second." I put the line on hold and turned to

Christopher, who was walking around the tree touching all the bulbs he could reach. "I'll be in the room with all the Christmas things, okay? Then I'll be right back."

He nodded, and I raced into Donna Katherine's office, pulled out the chair, and picked up the phone at the same time. "Nola?"

"I'm here."

"The most horrible thing happened." And then I told her. In detail, letting the anger come up again, along with the fear. When my words caught in my throat, I put her on hold, ostensibly to listen for Christopher, who was singing "Jingle Bells."

"Look, I don't like you two being there alone," she said when I came back on the line. "I'm coming down there."

"Absolutely not! Not in this weather—it's horrible out there. Are you crazy?"

"No, but you shouldn't be by yourself." She paused. "Look, you can come here. We'll have dinner, it's safe, it's—"

"And it's south," I said. "Way in the other direction from Prissy's house. Thanks, Nola, but with the roads icy, I think we're better off where we are. Somebody is bound to get home soon." Christopher came into the office and leaned against me, resting his head on my lap. "Look, I'd better go. Just hold a good thought for us, okay? And say hi to your mom for me."

"I will, but I may show up there."

"Please don't. We'll be fine."

When I had hung up Christopher said, "Aunt Dolie, I have a microwave."

"A what?"

"In my head. You know, like my mommy gets. A microwave."

A migraine.

As mothers have done for decades, I rested my palm against his forehead, but there was no fever.

"I'll get you something for it, and then you'll feel better."

"Yes, please."

He was running out of energy and bravery—it was long overdue.

"There's a first aid kit with all kinds of wonderful things to make you well," I said, trying to sound cheerful, "and it's right in the break room. Will you walk with me?"

He nodded, but didn't speak. A very bad sign.

Unfortunately, it wasn't in the break room. Probably because the police had confiscated the damn thing. Instead of swearing, I smiled, a heroic effort. "Not to worry, it's someplace in this building."

Surely that was true.

Christopher sniffled. "Aunt Dolie, my head hurts too bad."

"I know, sweetie." I picked him up and held him tightly as he started to cry. I made no effort to stanch the tears or to shush him. If anybody deserved a good cry, it was Christopher. No child should have to suffer what he'd been through, both physically and emotionally. His body heaved with the sobs.

"I want my mommy."

"I know, baby, I know." I rocked him back and forth, fighting my own tears, humming a lullaby that I had sung to Jeremy when he was that age.

✤ CHAPTER 28 ✦

EVENTUALLY CHRISTOPHER hiccuped to a stop. I rocked him a little longer, then said, "Here," reaching for a paper towel. "Here, blow." He did. "Good boy. Maybe a cool cloth will help your head."

"Yes, please."

And maybe the release of his tears would help, too.

I wet several paper towels, folded them up, then carried Christopher back to Donna Katherine's office. "How about if I make you a pallet with my coat?" I asked, folding the heavy wool. "I'll bet you didn't get your nap today, did you?"

"No."

"Here, come and lie down, and I'll put this on your head."

He stretched out, his eyelids already drooping.

I bent over and kissed his forehead, then gently placed the wet towels on it. "How is that? A little better?"

"Yes."

Seeing Christopher like this and knowing what he had endured was almost overwhelming. Children should be protected from abuse, from all abuse. Christopher was too little to protect himself; it wasn't fair that adults were allowed to brutalize our babies. And there should be a very special hell for people like Todd, hell with a one-way door so that adults who prey on children never get out. Ever.

My own head throbbed as I bent down to tuck Christopher in to his makeshift bed. As the shock wore off, the parts of my body that had made contact with ice, cement, or asphalt were needing the relief aspirin could give. It was on the agenda, although first I picked up the phone, hit the redial, and waited for Prissy's number to ring. It did, but again the answering machine came on. The first time that had happened, I'd left a message saying I had Christopher with me, we were fine, and I'd call back later. I'd been careful not to leave a number in case Todd had returned to the house. This time I just hung up.

"Is my mommy still gone?"

"Yes, she is. But don't worry, she'll be home soon. Just rest."

"Don't go away, Aunt Dolie. Please?"

"I'm not leaving. I promise."

"Okay." He closed his eyes, then said, "Can you turn down the light?"

"I'll see what I can do."

"And when I finish resting, may we go home?"

"Yes we may."

I found the switch that turned off the short row of fluorescents over where Christopher was sleeping, then I sat beside him on the floor, rubbing his back until he fell asleep.

Once he was deep in slumber, I got up, my knee joints creaking and every muscle complaining. I wanted to stretch out on the floor along with Christopher and sleep away this nightmare, but our prolonged absence would cause a panic for Stephanie and Prissy. Probably for Matt and Ross, too. Jeremy might even worry.

I started through the offices on a quest for a pain reliever, and while my movements were weary, my search was more thorough than it had been earlier when all I'd needed was a recorder. Not that the recorder had done me any good.

Or had it? Maybe the tape would prove premeditation on Todd's part. Premeditated kidnapping? I pressed my palm to my forehead. I needed help. I needed aspirin.

The one thing I was almost positive of was that Stephanie had installed the little recorders. None of the conversations on the tapes were prior to her arrival. Was she using them to get some kind of evidence against Todd? She wouldn't need it now because I would be a witness to his abuse, and I would be happy to testify in any court we could get him in.

By now I was rifling Nola's office, but she had nothing medicinal in her desk. That was a sure sign she'd already been cleaning it out in anticipation of leaving.

Ralph's cubicle was next and it contained new packs of chewing gum and Gummi Life Savers, neither of which could cure a headache. Fred, our graphic artist, didn't have a desk, just a drafting table, and the cabinets he used for paper and tools didn't harbor anything edible.

I inspected the copy room with extra care, since that would be the next logical place to put a first aid kit, but it wasn't there. After that I moved into Audry's office, and noticed how I stayed as far away as possible from the windows. I'd also turned on very few lights, as if someone could see me from the street seven stories below. It wasn't possible, at least I was sure I couldn't be recognized, but even convinced of that, I couldn't make myself get closer to the glass.

Audry's office didn't appear to contain anything personal. No chewed-on pencils, no little sticky notes with scribbled messages, not a nail file or vitamin. Finally, in the very back of a credenza drawer I found a small makeup bag with a hairbrush, a lipstick, a lip pencil, and some Tampax, but no aspirin.

Michael's side drawer held a brand-new bottle of antacids, the giant economy size, still full. Unfortunately there was nothing for pain. I went next door and discovered that Chester had one small prescription bottle in his desk. Lanoxin. I noticed it was dated yesterday. Another new bottle.

Several thoughts struck me at once. First, that during their search the police had taken far more than just Desi's trail mix. They must have confiscated all the medicines, drinks, and foods that were in open containers. Sergeant Bohles and his crew had probably needed trucks to carry all the huge bottles of aspirin, ibuprofen, acetaminophen—the whole gamut of pain relievers—as well as sinus pills and allergy medicines. And antacids; after all, in ad agencies people thrive on pressure and die of heart attacks in their early sixties.

Heart attacks?

Heart attack. Digitalis. Lanoxin.

They'd all been mentioned in the articles on mistletoe! Unfortunately, I couldn't remember exactly what had been said. I actually reached for the phone to call Prissy before I realized she wouldn't answer. Then I remembered: The faxes she'd sent me were still here at Rose Sterling. I had inadvertently left them in Desi's desk.

The wind howled outside the glass walls, and the lights flickered.

Within seconds the power came back on, but the momentary blackout jolted me enough that I went to check on Christopher. He was sleeping soundly, and after pulling the corner of my coat a little higher on his shoulders, I hurried to my old office.

I remembered folding the faxes and sticking them in a drawer.

Without hesitation I pulled open the center drawer and reached for them. Now they were lying open and facedown.

Someone had read these faxes and left them unfolded.

I felt a moment of heartsickness; someone had gone snooping in my desk. Then I took a breath and put it in perspective. I had left the agency permanently. This was no longer my desk, and any of the Rose Sterling staff might have had a legitimate excuse to look through the drawers. They could have read the material, as could Sergeant Bohles or one of his people. Whoever it was hadn't taken the faxes, and might not have even known what they were.

Only the person who murdered Desi Baker would understand their significance. The odds were seven to one in my favor it wasn't the killer who had found them.

In light of everything else that had happened, I didn't have the energy to worry about it.

Instead, I scanned the papers in my hand, homing in directly on the technical information on the chemicals. Lanoxin was mentioned along with Digitoxin, Crystodigin, and several others. " . . . slowed the heart and were especially dangerous when taken by a person who was already low in calcium or potassium. This could include persons who were dieting and exercising heavily." That might well describe Desi Baker.

"This family of drugs can act almost instantly, depending on the amount of food in the stomach, dosage, and susceptibility of the person ingesting it." It was basically like digitalis, the same drug used by Agatha Christie in *Appointment with Death*. The first reaction to a drug overdose of Lanoxin would be increased heart rate, which Desi would have assumed was a normal reaction to waiting to give her speech about Chester. By the time she'd left the dais she'd have been sick to her stomach, then she'd experience vomiting and diarrhea. Then death.

Was Chester capable of giving Desi Lanoxin? I sank into the chair, feeling as if someone had sucked the marrow from my bones. I couldn't believe such a thing. Wouldn't.

Damn.

I folded the articles carefully, my brain whirring as fast as a locust's wings. The Lanoxin had been in an unlocked drawer that was accessible to anyone in the agency. So why all the articles on mistletoe? Could Desi have ingested both, increasing the symptoms and hurrying death?

Perhaps she had been drinking mistletoe tea for several days with only slight effects, then at the party as a last-ditch effort the murderer slipped some Lanoxin into her food. The high level of the chemical would make death almost instantaneous, and without a very clever medical examiner, it might have passed for accidental. All the murderer had to do was remove the mistletoe articles from Desi's office.

And Nola had searched Desi's office.

But that had been on Tuesday. Who had been there Monday morning? And what was the motive? Men or money? The faltering fortunes of Rose Sterling Advertising . . . and who had access to Chester's pills . . .

I rubbed my throbbing forehead. Better to think of aspirin first, and the only places I hadn't checked were Amber's desk and Donna Katherine's; I moved to the front office. When I flicked the light switch, I discovered a pile of torn wrapping paper against the far wall and a scattering of Styrofoam peanuts on the gray carpet. Apparently the unopened presents had been too much for Christopher to resist.

With an involuntary groan, a response to bruises, not Christopher's actions, I bent down to clean up. It appeared the packages had been nothing more than decorative empty boxes, but to make sure, I ran my hand through two of them; I found only a few more of the lightweight Styrofoam peanuts. The third box was also empty, but I spotted one small item on the floor, almost hidden by the scattered peanuts. It was a computer disk with a fresh, bright blue label.

There was no writing on it, and I put it on the desk with the faxes. Just in case. After that I scooped the remains of the presents into Amber's wastebasket.

I was on the far side of the tree making one last inspection of the rug when I heard the key in the front door. I looked toward Donna Katherine's office where Christopher slept. The outer door began to open. If I ran toward the other office I would give away Christopher's presence and put him in danger. I had to stay here and hide.

I was completely behind the tree before I realized how foolish I was being; only office personnel had keys. It couldn't be Todd at the door. But even knowing that, I didn't leave the safety of my concealed spot. Instead I waited, tense and alert. The door opened with a whoosh of air, and then I heard soft footfalls on the carpet that stopped at the front desk. After that there was only silence, a listening silence.

I wanted to step out and see, but I couldn't. The tension from the dangers we'd already faced clung to me and held me rigid. Even as I chided myself for being foolish, the overhead lights went out, leaving a thick blackness.

Power failure? Ice buildups somewhere?

I noticed a ray of light from under the front door and a haze of color from the direction of Donna Katherine's office. Very clearly, whoever had come into the office had turned off the lights and was now standing in the dark. Waiting. Just as I waited.

My throat tightened. Who was this intruder? What did they want?

My biggest fear was for Christopher. I would endure anything before I would put him through another minute of pain. And still I didn't move.

A jumble of thoughts struck me as I crouched in the darkness. I could confront this person, whoever it was, and somehow get him or her out of the suite. But even if I accomplished that, how would I alert the guard to Christopher's presence? He couldn't be left here alone.

I didn't have much bravery or adrenaline left.

With a resolve that came only from my love for Christopher, I stood up and, in doing so, brushed the tree, setting off a rattle of ornaments. A flashlight beam arced across the room and caught me in its light.

❧ CHAPTER 29 ❦

THERE WAS one heart-stopping moment of light blindness, then a voice in the dark said, "Jolie?"

I blinked several times, but still couldn't see. "Who is it?"

"Oh, damn. Darn."

"Ralph?" I said. "Is that you?"

"Yes, sorry." He shifted the flashlight until it cast a shadowy upward beam on his face so he looked like a monster. "But what in the world are you doing here in the dark?" he asked.

"I wasn't in the dark until you turned out the light," I said. I sounded testy. "And what are you doing here? And why the light?"

"It's a long story."

In the blackness with only a flashlight illuminating the space between us, I began to see possibilities. Frightening possibilities.

Had Ralph been in love with Desi? Or perhaps just enamored of her in a schoolboy way that never touched on reality. Had he heard the rumor of her affair with Michael, true or not, and reacted with murder?

I didn't believe it.

"Ralph—"

Another key sounded in the door. Ralph jumped, flicking off the light and hitting the side of the desk in a way that sounded painful. "Damn! Quick!"

Even in the dark he found me; his hands grabbed at my shoulder and he pushed me farther back behind the tree.

261

"Wait, what—"

"Be quiet! Nothing. Trust me."

Then the door was open and a switch was flicked, but instead of turning on the overheard, it merely lit the tree where we were hiding. Even with the glow of the tiny colored lights we remained invisible.

It had all happened too quickly for me to think. Who was the good guy here, and who the bad? How should I have responded? I never got to choose, I merely reacted, tucked silently at the rear of the tree.

The new arrival paused near the door, then shut it firmly and made a movement toward the desk. Then silence. Too much silence.

It stretched on and on, and in that time I flashed to the faxes and the computer disk sitting on Amber's desk. There was the Lanoxin, too. Solid evidence of the person who'd killed Desi Baker, and now I was pretty sure I knew who that person was. At that moment it did me no good.

With a tiny shift I could see the desk through the fir branches and tree decorations; it was merely a shape on the edge of the darkness. I shifted again and Ralph's grip became harder. His expression was fierce. I twitched my arm to get some relief and he scowled at me.

I mouthed, "Let go," ready to scream if necessary.

He eased his grasp only a fraction.

What in the hell was going on?

I heard a shuffle of paper, but I still couldn't see anything.

What was this new person doing? Reading messages? Picking up mail?

Then I heard the words, "Son of a bitch!" The thick accent told me it was Donna Katherine.

She moved and I could see her red hair as she whirled around and started for her office.

I couldn't hold back any longer—she would find Christopher, and I couldn't let any more happen to him. I shoved at Ralph and in the same moment called out, "Wait! Donna Katherine, stop!"

She jerked around so quickly her heavy purse hit the wall. "Damn!"

Donna Katherine had every right to be here checking her messages, regardless of the time of day.

"Hi," I said, exhaling mightily and stepping even farther away from the tree. Ralph remained in his hiding place, and despite my conclusions, I still didn't understand all that was going on. "What are you doing here?" I asked.

"I might ask you the same thing." Her usual flippancy had been replaced by an intensity that could have been the result of my sudden appearance.

"Well, it's kind of a long story."

She waited, staring at me. "You've been following me, haven't you?"

"What? No, not at all." That made no sense. "Following you? Why? And how would I get here ahead of you?"

"By going the wrong way on a one-way street."

"I didn't do that. I—" I rubbed my forehead again, hoping to ease the knot of pain, or at least give me time to think. "It's been a very long day."

She stared at me, her jaw stiff with distaste. "You've got some faults, Jolie, but stupid isn't one of them." She waved my faxes and the computer disk in the air, her gold bracelets jangling. "How'd you figure it out?"

I remembered Donna Katherine wrapping packages as the police did their search of the building; right under their noses she had hidden the computer disk. And the hell of it was, I wasn't sure what was on it—I only suspected.

I nodded toward the things she was holding. "That's the proof."

"Oh, you think so?" With that she gripped the disk in both hands and did a quick jerk that cracked it in half. One more hard twist and the metal labeling popped off. A fragile, thin gray circle, the disk itself, was revealed.

Ralph leaped out from behind the tree. "No!"

Donna Katherine cocked her head. "Well, well, look who's

joining the party! Mild-mannered Ralph." She didn't slow her movements, she simply crumpled the disk.

"Damn!" He lunged toward her, but I was in the way. It gave Donna Katherine time to tear the disk with her teeth, and by the time Ralph reached her, there were two rents all the way through it. Donna Katherine stepped smoothly back out of his grasp, but handed over the shattered remains of the computer disk.

With a sweet smile at me she said, "I don't know what got over me just now, I can't believe I did such a thing. I can't think why I would."

"Maybe they can save some of the information," Ralph said, staring with disbelief at the broken pieces in his hands.

"Now, darlin', that's just not possible; you know that. But don't be upset. Why, it's almost Christmas, and now we can all go home. Or wherever."

"I have copies of two invoices from Desi's files," Ralph began. "And copies of the articles on mistletoe you gave her. Jolie, you found those, didn't you? And now the police have them. Donna Katherine, they'll prove you doctored the information and got Desi to—"

Donna Katherine cut him off with a wave of her hand. "You know, when you work with computers as much as we have, you figure out folks can create anything they want with the right software. Even false evidence. Like those invoices you were talking about and the articles. I'm not sure why you think they're so important, but I'll bet Miss Desi made them. Can't prove otherwise."

"They're real," Ralph said. "And the money. The police will find the money you embezzled."

In all my years at Rose Sterling, Donna Katherine had always worked alone. Then Desi Baker came along. She had obviously found discrepancies in the financial records and had kept invoices as evidence of it.

"Ralph," I said, "how much did you say Rose Sterling charged the clients at those fairs?"

"The bank deposits show a thousand dollars per client, but the invoice I found in Desi's desk was double that."

So Desi had discovered the embezzlement, and then what? Had Donna Katherine placated the younger woman, getting her transferred into copywriting? No, that wouldn't have been enough. Had Donna Katherine promised to make restitution? Yes, that must have been how it worked, only Donna Katherine had no intention of giving the money back, and so Desi had to die.

I'd never thought of Donna Katherine as clever. I'd believed she was hardworking and a little ditzy, but I'd been wrong. She was a very resourceful woman, and it showed in the way she'd covered herself.

When I'd come around looking for a bathroom, it was Donna Katherine who'd sent me, Michael's ex-lover, downstairs to find the body. That little bit of quick thinking implicated me.

No doubt Donna Katherine had also sent Desi down to that bathroom, or maybe she'd taken her there, promising to bring help.

I looked at Donna Katherine, wondering how she could live with herself. "You really are a piece of work."

The many fabrications were coming to mind, like the comment about Michael wailing in the bathroom, and the convenient rumor that Desi and Michael were lovers. That had thrown suspicion on both Michael and Audry, when in truth, neither one had a motive to kill Desi.

And there was the note slipped under the bathroom door.

"You wrote the note, too," I said. "The one signed M."

Donna Katherine merely raised one eyebrow.

It was Ralph who put it all in perspective. "Right from the start you've lied and stolen, and then you did murder to cover it all up. I don't understand how anyone could do that, especially not steal from Chester." He stopped and shook his head as if sickened. "And then to kill Desi . . ."

Donna Katherine chose to ignore the last part. "I did not hurt

Chester," she said firmly. "I love Chester Sterling—he is the kindest, gentlest, most wonderful man in the world, and I would never hurt him. Never."

"You embezzled a hell of a lot of his money—"

"If, and let me repeat, *if* I took money, which I did not, it would have been *for* Chester. It would be his retirement fund to protect him from his bloodsucking daughter."

"With a little left over for you?"

"You know, Ralph," she said, "I think you've missed some things."

"Oh?"

"Do you have any idea how many hours I have spent here at Rose Sterling? Do you? I have put in at least ten hours of overtime every week of my career. Get out your calculator and figure it out—that's over four thousand hours of overtime. Overtime!" She was on very solid ground here, her analytical mind spitting out the figures she had obviously brooded over as she carried out her personal plan for vindication. "At least Chester used to give me some kind of bonus at the end of the year, but not Missy Tight Pockets. No, sir. She'd just tell me to go home if I mentioned how many hours I was putting in; she didn't have any idea how long it took to do my work."

"And so you embezzled. And then to cover it up, you killed." Ralph hit the word hard.

Donna Katherine glared. "Let me repeat one more time for your feeble brain that I did not do any of those things. But if I had taken money, it would have been my money. Do you understand? Money owed to me. You start figuring out how much money I was due, plus interest, plus all those vacations and sick days I never took."

Just as Matt had told me, when people are stealing money, they don't dare take a minute off; they can't because someone else would discover the thefts.

But surely Donna Katherine had to know she'd be caught eventually. One good audit would have done it, and once the police suspected her of Desi's murder, there were a hundred ways they could prove that the embezzlement was her motive. Bank accounts, purchases above and beyond her income, invoices that didn't match—all manner of evidence would convict her. It didn't seem very smart for a woman like Donna Katherine.

Ralph leaned against the front desk. "Come on, Donna Katherine, just between us, you stole the money, didn't you? And when Desi found out, you promised to pay it all back—she was just naive enough to believe you'd do that. Except you changed your mind and killed her to make sure she wouldn't talk."

There was something odd about the way he stood, with his hip thrust out and his right leg forward. I couldn't understand why he was in such an awkward stance until I spotted the bulge in the front pocket of his corduroy pants. It was rectangular and small. Ralph had the voice-activated recorder in his pocket.

Donna Katherine realized it the same time I did.

With a laugh she reached into her big black leather purse. Very expensive black leather purse, I noticed. "You can take the tape recorder out of your pants, Clark Kent." She brought her hand out of her purse; it was holding a small revolver. "And I need you to give it to me. Then I can leave this place and never come back."

"You have a ticket to Rio?" he asked.

"Darlin', let's just say that where I'm going, you can't find me. And neither can anybody else." She glanced at her watch. "Now, hurry it up, Ralph. Jolie's got to tie you up, and then I'm out of here. I wouldn't have come back at all, except I wanted that stupid disk. I'll be taking the pieces with me, just in case."

"What about the hard drive on your computer? I'll bet there's evidence there."

"Darnedest thing," she said. "My hard drive crashed today. There's not a solitary thing on it. Nothing."

I had to look away so she wouldn't see my expression. Prissy had said even information that had been erased could be retrieved from a hard drive. No telling what the police would find on Donna Katherine's computer, perhaps even the fake stories on mistletoe.

"Okay, Ralph," Donna Katherine said, growing visibly impatient. "Hand over the tape recorder. Now."

"The police usually find fugitives from justice," he said, not moving. "They'll catch up to you somewhere, you wait."

"That's not your concern; just give me the recorder. If you don't, I'll shoot you; I mean it!"

Stone-still and smiling, he said, "I think I'll just keep it for myself."

"Ralph!" I snapped. "Give her that damn thing." The man was even upsetting me, and I didn't have the extra tension of a gun in my hand.

"Relax, Jolie," he said. "This may be the last time you ever see Donna Katherine as a free woman. The police will find her—"

"No, they won't," she snarled. "Give me the recorder."

"You have a phony ID?" he asked. I was hardly breathing. "Fake passport?" he went on. "Swiss bank account?"

She pulled back the hammer of the gun. "I'm fixin' to shoot your sorry ass if you don't do exactly like I tell you. First, give me the recorder!"

He didn't budge.

I stuck out my hand. "Ralph, stop acting stupid!" I had no intention of dying so he could play hero. Besides, Christopher was in the other room. "Hand over the tape recorder."

"Listen to the lady," Donna Katherine said.

I was afraid to take my eyes off her, afraid I wouldn't see her squint, or stiffen her arm, or do any one of the things that would come right before pulling the trigger.

Out of the corner of my eye I saw Ralph slide his hand in his pocket and bring out the recorder. I started to relax, then realized he was moving awkwardly again. Oh, God . . .

Donna Katherine stiffened.

Ralph lifted the recorder and, with a flick of his wrist, threw it at her.

I hit the floor just as the hammer came down.

The bullet whined over my head, and a Christmas ornament shattered. Ralph leaped the distance to Donna Katherine,

268

knocked the gun from her hand, spun her around, and flattened her against the wall. His military training stood him in good stead.

As he pulled out handcuffs he said, "Jolie, we need the police. Sergeant Bohles. Call nine-one-one."

Once I could stand, I ran over to the two of them, my breathing ragged. I didn't know who I was angriest at, Donna Katherine for killing Desi, or Ralph for endangering all of us. "Listen to me," I whispered savagely, "Both of you, keep it down! There's a baby asleep in Donna Katherine's office, and he doesn't need to hear any of this!"

The two of them turned to stare at me as if I'd lost my mind.

Then I ran to call the police.

✽ CHAPTER 30 ✽

CHRISTMAS MORNING started with the little voice once again outside my door. "Aunt Dolie! I need you!" Only this time Christopher was so thoroughly bundled up against the cold only his eyes were visible. Even his nose was hidden in a scarf. Jeremy was right behind him, saying they needed us because Prissy wouldn't let them touch the presents until we arrived.

"Puts everything in perspective, doesn't it?" Matt said with a grin once we had shooed the boys out and were getting dressed.

"Now we're just needed to give out presents." I pulled on a sweater. "I like that better."

We arrived at the big house within five minutes to find Prissy in the kitchen.

"Merry Christmas," I said, giving her a hug.

"Merry Christmas." She bent down to pull sweet rolls out of the oven. The coffee was already brewed. "Want some tea?"

"I'd love some. You know, I've never told you this," I said, "but you set a standard the rest of us can never live up to. You're too perfect."

She laughed. "It's only because I'm too insecure to just kick back and let myself go. If I had your self-confidence, it would be different."

"My self-confidence?" I had started toward the cupboard for a cup, but I stopped and turned to look at her. "I think we need to talk."

"Oh, your tea is already made." She smiled. "But I nuked it this morning."

"There's hope for you yet."

Then Stephanie was in the kitchen pouring coffee, and Christopher arrived, demanding that we hurry. "It's getting too late!"

We all moved into the great room as Jeremy, who was standing near the tree, announced, "I'll play Santa Claus."

"And I'll help!" Christopher added, tripping over a huge present that Matt had brought down from the apartment. "That's a big one," he said, righting himself.

"It's something special for Jeremy," Matt said, winking at me.

It was a duster, just like the one Jeremy had borrowed from Matt. This one differed slightly in that, against my feeble protests, Matt had stuffed the pockets with money. Big money. Not enough to buy the new pickup Jeremy had been openly hinting for, but enough for a decent used one. He would have to get an after-school job to support it and make the insurance payments, which I thought was a good idea.

"Cool! I love big presents." Jeremy grabbed the box and put it beside the couch. "This will be my pile," he said, turning to Christopher and holding out a square present. "Here, Christopher, put this one over there. It's for you."

"For me? Oh, thank you."

As the two boys divvied up the packages, making stacks all around the room, Ross started a fire in the fireplace and Prissy handed out napkins. Stephanie came to sit beside me.

"Merry Christmas," she said.

"Same to you."

"And thank you again." Her dark eyes seemed much older and much wiser, but she also looked peaceful.

"You'd have done the same if it was Jeremy," I said.

I had spent so much of the last two days at the police station and courthouse I'd decided if I ever got back to Purple Sage, I'd never leave again. I'd given a statement that would be used against Donna Katherine, who was in custody and being indicted on murder charges. Formal charges also had been filed against Todd, including kidnapping, assault, and endangerment of a child.

271

There were others, but I'd lost track. Unfortunately Todd had flown out by the time the police began their search, and now he was believed to be someplace on the East Coast. They did know that he'd arrived at Baltimore Airport, so they were tracking him from there.

It had not been easy telling the story to the police. Especially for Stephanie, because, as I had suspected, there was a great deal more to tell, and much of it was unpleasant.

Todd and Stephanie had dated during her second year in college; when she'd discovered she was pregnant, Todd had waved good-bye and headed East. However, all the oohing and aahing he heard from his mother and his "aunt" Prissy about the adorable Christopher started him wondering if he'd made the right choice. It was his mother's death that spurred him into action, searching for what he then considered his rightful family, Stephanie and Christopher.

Todd had arrived in Phoenix shortly after Stephanie, and had settled into the apartment next door just as if he belonged. While Stephanie had been wary, Todd had set out to woo both her and the son he didn't know. Those first few weeks had been wonderful, and Stephanie had even told her mother the truth about Christopher's parentage. It was shortly after that when the not-so-subtle shifts in Todd's behavior started. Todd became the abuser. Primarily it was emotional abuse and most was directed at Stephanie. It was then she realized he was doing drugs and began pulling away, but Todd refused to budge. He began to *discipline* Christopher, just as his own father had disciplined him. Peter Javitz entered the picture, convincing Todd, in a very civilized way, to move on.

And while I still didn't like the relationship between Pete and Stephanie, I couldn't help but think more kindly toward him.

All the problems might have ended there had Todd not called Prissy and played on her sympathies to get an invitation for Christmas. She didn't know the full extent of what had gone on in Phoenix, and had only slight doubts about the plan.

Even when Stephanie arrived and tried to tell her mother the truth, she hadn't wanted to listen. After all, Todd was her best friend's son, and Prissy had a hard time separating her feelings for the two.

During the last two days there had been many tears and recriminations. Thank God the worst was in the past, and while we did have to live with the past, and in some cases make restitution, there were better times ahead.

"Have you decided if you're going back to Phoenix?" I asked Steph as she accepted a package from Christopher.

"Yes, I am."

"Oh." That wasn't what I'd expected to hear.

Then she smiled. "And Mom is going with me. We'll pack up everything and get us moved back here probably by next week."

"That's wonderful! And Matt and I will take care of Christopher while you're gone." I glanced over at Matt, who had turned his head when he heard his name.

"I don't know if you want Christopher for a whole week," Stephanie said. "He can be a lot of work."

"Obviously," Matt said, leaning forward to better see Stephanie, "you don't remember what you were like at that age. He is easy compared to you. We'll take him."

Christopher was just walking in front of me and I grabbed him. "Did you hear, little bug? You're coming to my house!"

"Goody."

"And you're going to stay for a whole week!" I scooped him onto my lap, but he wriggled down.

"Aunt Dolie, please. I'm givin' presents."

"Well, pardon me."

He held up a six-by-three-inch box with red wrapping paper and a green ribbon. "It's for you. And you're s'posed to open it right away."

"I am, huh?" I shook the heavy little box, then looked at the tag. It was from Jeremy and Matt, both of whom were grinning at me. "Okay," I said, ripping open the paper. The box came from a print shop. "What in the world?" I pulled off the lid and discovered business cards. My business cards with a pale ivory card stock and black script that said: *Jolie Wyatt. Author.* "I don't believe it! These are wonderful, thank you." I leaned around Steph to hug Matt.

"What do they say?" Ross asked.

I picked my way around the presents to hand him one. "My card." Then I gave Jeremy a hug. "Thank you."

"You're welcome. Merry Christmas, Author."

I tried to thread my way back through the maze of packages, but stopped midway. "This is unbelievable. Would you look at all these presents."

"Look at mine, Aunt Dolie!" The mountain beside Christopher was taller than he was. Every one of us had gone overboard and we knew it, but after the past week, we'd indulged. Next week he started therapy.

"You sure got a lot of packages," I said.

Christopher's face grew serious. "Does this mean I'm a good boy?"

"It doesn't matter whether you got a lot of presents or not, you're still a very good boy," I said.

"Very, very good," Prissy added.

"And what about me?" Jeremy demanded. "Am I good, too?"

"You're perfect," I said.

He grinned. "That's nice to hear; of course, I had to pry it out of you."

Christopher waved his arms at the packages. "It's time for presents!" He hopped toward a large box but tripped on Jeremy's feet, knocking him off balance. The two of them began to fall. Jeremy reached out to save them and hit the Christmas tree. It teetered, the stand tipped, and the tree began to list crazily. With a tinkling of ornaments it started over and came to rest against the far wall, its lights twinkling merrily.

There was a stunned silence. Slowly we all turned our eyes to Prissy.

She was staring at the tree, blinking in disbelief. Her mouth opened.

A giggle came out. It rolled into full-fledged laughter. After a moment she took a breath and said, "Not perfect; just wonderful."